THE PUPPET MAKER

JENNY O'BRIEN

Storm
PUBLISHING

Ebook ISBN: 978-1-80508-025-1
Paperback ISBN: 978-1-80508-026-8

Cover design: Henry Steadman
Cover images: Shutterstock

Published by Storm Publishing.
For further information, visit:
www.stormpublishing.co

For Alan

*Can't put the puppet bowing
That just now dangled still.*

–Emily Dickenson

diversion from his monotonous task. An arm, a leg, a torso. A body.

There was no consideration for neatness; Mammy would have been horrified by the quality of his stitches – but Mammy wasn't here. She'd flown away and taken most of his happy memories with her.

PROLOGUE

Ladybird, ladybird fly away home,
Your house is on fire and your children are gone.
All except one, and his name is Dan,
And he hid under the baking pan.

The rhyme burrowed through his mind, following the trail of ancient tracks and tunnels forged by countless repetitions, all on the knee of his mam, her golden web of finely spun hair tickling his cheek as she sang ditty after ditty in her breathy, slightly off-key voice.

Mammy had sewn too, he remembered, licking the end of the string before twisting it between grubby fingers and aiming at the large eye of the sailor's needle. She'd knit and sew in the evenings, while they grouped together in their cosy home, the perfect little family. As a memory it was one of his favourites, but then he didn't have that many to compare it to.

With the needle threaded, he pulled together the slippery skin and started again, in out, in out, in out, stuffing back the odd bit of rag and wool as he went, the rhyme filling his mind, a

ONE

'We won't be long. Just need to get some bread and milk,' Penny said, picking up a basket and starting to move to the door.

'Twolley.'

'Okay, sweetheart. Twolley it is.' She swapped the basket for a shopping trolley and lifted her daughter into the child seat. Today wasn't the day to deny her anything or indeed to correct her speech.

'Want Wabbit.'

'Oh, yes. We mustn't forget Wabbit.'

Penny dropped the faded pink toy into her lap. Wabbit was over two now and starting to show his age along with his insides, her gaze drawn to the loose stitching, which revealed a wisp of white stuffing. He could really do with a wash and a stitch or two, but no amount of cajoling worked. If she didn't have her cuddly friend with her, she wouldn't eat or sleep, and Penny was too tired to argue the point.

She watched a moment, ignoring the chill wind whistling through the car park, the threat of rain only a whisper away. She watched her daughter even though she could map her features from memory. Every line and curve. Every tint, shade and tone.

Her baby-soft skin and pink cheeks under a pair of mesmerising periwinkle blue eyes. The way her fine blonde hair sprang from her head in a mass of curls. The shape of her plump body under her coat and scarf. All the joy in her life in this wondrous warm, snuggly bundle, which was the biggest surprise of all.

Penny had never wanted kids. When she'd first discovered the set of parallel blue lines, she'd thought her world had ended, and in a way it had. Her grandparents had disowned her. She was thrown out of the house with the clothes on her back and the few euros she'd saved up from her summer job at the café down the road. Homeless at sixteen could have been a lot worse if it hadn't been for the women's shelter...

Pushing memories of those hopeless early days away, she lifted her head from where she'd been staring at her daughter and scanned the car park instead. If she didn't concentrate on what she was doing she'd be late back and that would be disastrous.

The car park was busy. Too busy for anyone to notice a lone woman pushing a trolley with a squeaky left wheel across the tarmac to the neon lit entrance, which was just the way she wanted it. There was safety in crowds. A place to merge with the landscape. A place to hide. A safe place away from him.

Her hands tightened on the trolley bar, the skin thinning over whitened knuckles, her fingers reddened from the cold. With a quick jerk, she scanned her immediate surroundings before hurrying into the store. There was no way he could have followed her, was there? She wished she could feel more certain. He'd followed her before. He'd shadowed her right across town and to McDonald's. It had all been completely innocent. A woman she'd got to know in the park asking them to her son's birthday party. A small gathering over burgers and milkshakes. She hadn't given it a second thought.

Penny fingered her cheekbone, remembering the ugly bruise, the pain, even though it had happened months ago. The injuries had faded but the memory remained, ripping a hole in her confidence and her self-belief. The slap and the punch that followed. The realisation that she'd escaped both her grandparents and the shelter only to find herself in an even worse predicament.

With her chin now tucked down into her scarf and her face turned away from the security camera, she made for the aisle up ahead, her arm stretching towards the top shelf.

Nappies. Milk. Strawberry yogurts along with spaghetti hoops. Broccoli. Apples. Sausages. Fish Fingers.

She ran the list through her mind as she reached for the items, the pile of food growing with all of her daughter's favourites and, for once, not bothering about the cost. It made a nice change. A mother out with her child doing what any normal parent would be doing.

A stroke of her baby-fine hair. A hug. A kiss to her wind-chilled cheek.

'Mammy.' Her face scrunched up, her perfect bow-shaped mouth opening.

'We'll be going in a sec, sweetie. I just need to get something for our tea.'

TWO

Dublin District Court was situated in East Essex Street, more famous for its location in the heart of bohemian Temple Bar, with its many bars and restaurants, than any legal associations. But, after a morning spent in a stuffy courtroom, where they'd witnessed a family ripped apart at the seams, all the two detectives wanted was to escape the area.

'Let's leave the car, Paddy. I could do with some fresh air. In fact, it's near enough time for lunch,' said Alana Mack, a detective in An Garda Síochána. She didn't wait for a reply as she cut across Parliament Street and towards City Hall.

Traffic was heavy along Dame Street, a broad artery, Trinity College at one end, and home to countless banks and financial institutions. Tempers appeared to be fraying left right and centre if the din of beeping horns was anything to go by, but it was hardly surprising considering Christmas was only a month away. The pavements were the same. Jam-packed with people both young and old going about their business. Blocking the footpath as they dawdled on their mobiles, their hands thick with bulky purchases.

'Excuse me. Need to get through. Thank you. If you could

move your shopper, please. Thanks. Oh, sorry.' Alana stopped briefly to apologise to the man who'd stepped backwards into her path, to the detriment of both his ankles and his shirt, the takeout cup now dangling from his fingers, empty.

'Fucking hell. Mind where you're going, you stupid cow,' he said, frantically swatting at his previously pristine white button-down, the material moulding to his skin in a rash of brown splodges from where he'd chucked his frothy coffee down his front.

'I don't think you meant that, did you, sir?' Paddy flashed his ID card. 'Now, apologise to the nice lady and be on your way.'

'Sorry, I'm sure.' He muttered something else under his breath, which Alana couldn't quite catch. No doubt another string of four-letter expletives to add to the list of eyebrow-lifting obscenities.

Alana felt her temper flair. After two years of working together, she should be used to Paddy's ways, but he was over-protective and, as a grown woman in addition to being his boss, she was heartily sick of his behaviour. They were heading for a showdown, but not in the middle of the street. No, she'd speak to him but in a time and place of her choosing.

The problem was that she liked the man, which had nothing to do with his appearance and everything to do with his person-ality. She shifted her gaze to take in his handsome features topped off with dark brown hair, a smattering of premature grey at his temples. Looks were immaterial. As a recently divorced woman, men were off the agenda, certainly for now, and even if she was looking for a relationship, it wouldn't be with someone on the team. No. Paddy was a good copper, one of the best she'd ever worked with. He was also a gentleman from the top of his head to the tips of his brown loafers. If there was a door to open, he'd be first to push it before stepping back and waiting for her to enter, just as if there was a load to carry, he'd always be there to take it, so she didn't have to. Alana didn't have a problem with his gallant behaviour, far from it. All she wanted was to occasionally open her own doors and carry her own shopping not to mention fight her own battles.

'There. The lights are turning red. If you'd like me to...?'

'No, Paddy, I wouldn't,' Alana said as she propelled her wheelchair forward and across the road safely to the other side, before swivelling in the direction of the deli they'd agreed on for lunch. She knew he meant well, but she didn't know how much more of his well-meaning behaviour she could take.

The deli was as crowded as the street, the smell of freshly ground coffee drawing customers into the shop like fish into a net. Alana eyed the salads, meats, and cheeses with interest, already planning her tea. She never left with only her lunch – there was no attraction in cooking for one. It was a ready-meal, or the deli and she knew which she preferred.

When it was finally their turn, much to his annoyance, she refused to let him pay.

'No, this is on me. What about nabbing the table by the window? It looks as if they're about to leave,' she said, more than happy for him to take the tray. Alana had learned many new skills since losing the use of her legs, but manoeuvring her chair while holding on to a tray wasn't one of them.

She waited while Paddy shifted a chair to make room for her at the table before wheeling into place and securing the brakes. There were some things she had to accept that she couldn't do. It made her more determined than ever to continue to do the things that she could.

The smart, New York-inspired deli was a welcome addition to the business district. Somewhere to grab a bite when they were in town on business and away from the coastal suburb of Clonabee, and the oppressive gaze of their boss, Detective Superintendent Ray Reilly – known as Ox Reilly behind his back, and on occasion to his face when the situation warranted.

Ox headed up the Clonabee branch of the National Bureau of Criminal Investigation, the NBCI, which had been set up over two years ago as a sop to the societal pressures exerted by local politicians and the media alike. Clonabee was a backwater with antiquated ideas and a less than glorious history with regards to diversity. Appointing a woman into a senior position was their way of pandering to the masses. It was Alana's job to ensure that they hadn't made a mistake. Never a day passed when she didn't regret her move from the Serious Crime Review team – the SCRT – at Dublin South Central. Her life might have been very different if she'd decided to stay put, but she couldn't change the past, no matter how much she wanted to. At the time, the move to managing her own team had been a welcome shift, an opportunity to adjust her work-life bAlanace. Little did she know that within six weeks of the transition, her marriage would be history along with the use of her legs.

Alana stared out of the misted window, her hands cradling her cup of tea, the warmth leaching into her fingers, her mind taking her down a blind alley of remorse and recriminations while her attention focused on the homeless man outside, his arm rammed into the bin right up to his armpit.

The disparity between the Christmassy scene unfolding behind him in a stream of picture-worthy images and having just witnessed those two beautiful children being taken into care was both harsh and shocking. Yes, the case was now closed and the children's safety assured, but that didn't stop Alana from thinking about whether there was something more they could have done to keep the family together. It wasn't anybody's fault that their mother had died or that their father was unable to grasp the rudiments of childcare even with all the support on offer. Removing children from a parent was always the last resort. She'd be lying if she said she didn't have doubts as to whether they'd done the right thing despite report after report detailing his many failings.

With a shake of her head, she dispelled the thought but not before making a promise to check in with the children's social worker as to their welfare and how the visitation rights were going.

Promise made, she concentrated on the tramp. His uncovered head in the frosty air. His thin jacket with holes at the elbows, the telling glass bottle sticking out of one of his pockets. Threadbare trousers held up with string. Grubby trainers without laces.

'God. The world really is a very cruel place,' she finally said, losing her appetite when seconds before she'd been hungry enough to order a slice of cheesecake to follow her bacon and brie sandwich.

'That it is, Alana, that it is,' Paddy said, watching the homeless man as he lifted a bulging bag above his head with a raging battle cry before tucking it inside his jacket and continuing his search. 'Likes a bit of pop too,' he continued, taking a large bite of his wrap, which appeared to be stuffed with what amounted to all of her five-a-day in one sitting.

Alana pushed her untouched sandwich away and started on the slice of cheesecake. It was a long time since she'd felt anything but dismay at the level of poverty and destitution that they came across during their working day. It was all very well being on the front line trying to make a difference, but the work they were doing barely made a mark on the streets. They certainly couldn't keep up with the demand for their services or meet their targets. She rested her fork across the empty plate and reached again for her cup. Reilly had scheduled a catch-up meeting in her calendar for this afternoon. Alana knew what it was about, she always knew what it was about. The same old dig at her arrest rates in relation to her staff budget. There wasn't a thing she could do to increase the former or indeed to reduce the latter.

With her drink finished and Paddy's plate empty, Alana

donned her woolly hat and rearranged her ponytail. Instead of leaving her sandwich, she popped it in a spare serviette and placed it on her lap next to her bag of deli items.

'Always the shortest hour in the day.' Paddy strolled to the door and, stepping back, gestured for her to precede him. 'What's on the agenda for this afters then, apart from that missing man?'

'Thanks for reminding me, not,' Alana said, pulling a face at the case that had been baffling them for the last week. The disappearance of recently retired Aidan Crossey, who'd seemingly vanished without a trace. 'With a little bit of luck, media interest in the case will have dropped off a cliff.'

'I wouldn't bet on it. It has all the makings of the perfect "locked room" mystery apart from...'

'The fact that he disappeared from his house,' Alana parried, her voice dripping in sarcasm.

Aidan Crossey lived a quiet life since his retirement and, if his neighbours were to be believed, did the same thing each week without fail. The evening of his disappearance was no different. Crossey had been observed turning in for the night at his usual time of ten fifteen by the woman living opposite. It had been bin night, or at least that had been Irene Smith's excuse for noticing the time so exactly. Alana hadn't been in on the interview, but that hadn't stopped her from forming ideas as to the woman's interest in the bachelor. It wasn't something that she could prove with any degree of certainty. Noting when someone closed their bedroom curtains and switched off the light wasn't a crime, and neither was a call to the Guards when his bottle of semi-creamed milk wasn't retrieved from the doorstep in a timely manner the following morning. There was being observant and then there was stalking. By the time the Guards had turned up in their squad cars, the milk carton had blown and any trace of what could have happened was hampered by a sustained media offensive on the lackadaisical attitude to what could have been a man dead in his bed. With reporters hounding them from one side and the chief from the other, they were fast losing any sense of proportion. The man had been there one night and gone in the morning, leaving no clues as to what had happened. There'd been no sign of a break-in and nothing missing from the property, which included a seventy-five-inch television in the lounge and top-of-the-range MacBook on the coffee table. There'd also been no activity on his bank account. There was also no body to autopsy, which had to be viewed as a bonus.

'Sorry. I guess I'll carry on combing through the files to see what gives.'

'As I will his background,' she replied, slipping on her gloves and following him out the door.

The vagrant had moved to the doorway opposite, an old tin plate strategically positioned in front of his feet. There was a dog too, a small brown terrier type.

'Here.' She handed the man the sandwich along with a tenner as she wheeled past.

'Thank you, missus. God rest your soul.'

'You know you shouldn't give them...'

'Can it, Paddy, and it's not a "them". It's a "him". The money is for the dog, if you must know. If he chooses to drink it instead. Well, there's a special kind of hell for animal and child abusers. I don't think he's the type.'

'How do you know what type he is?' Paddy said, struggling to keep up with her now she'd crossed the road and was clear of the traffic. The streets were empty away from the busy thoroughfare, the cafés and pubs dotted around quiet and, in some cases, closed until the evening trade hit. Even the smell was different. No hint of freshly ground coffee among the aromas oozing out of doorways onto the pavement. Instead, the stench of stale beer and the occasional whiff of stale piss dominated.

Alana paused, waiting for him to catch up, a little smile dragged up out of nowhere despite her thoughts.

'Because of his wagging tail if you must know. Dogs only wag their tails when they're happy. Even an "animal ambivalent" like me knows that.'

'Down, girl, or you'll make holes in my only decent pair of trousers.' The doc scratched the terrier on the top of her head before standing to his feet, the creak of his knees a staccato of sound in the sudden quiet. 'You've been lucky to find such an accommodating butcher I must say,' he said, his attention on the freezer bag bulging with something moist and red.

'Butcher my arse. I found it down the bottom of one of them bins along Dame Street.'

Alfred watched his friend, Tooley O'Toole, retrieve a pocketknife from his trousers and select one of the blades, his mind puzzling over his find. The bins along that stretch were emptied last thing on a Monday and a Thursday, the reason they always targeted them on Tuesday and Friday afternoons. Any later in the week was risking contamination by rats and flies. No matter how hungry he was, there were limits to what he was able to eat; the smell of maggot-infested rotting meat was one that he'd take to his grave.

'Hold on a second, Tooley. How full did you say the bin was?'

'Full.' He waved the knife in the air, obviously impatient to show off his spoils.

'As in fuller than you'd normally expect on a Friday?'

'What's that got to do with anything?'

'I don't know. Hopefully nothing, but let's be on the safe side, eh, my friend,' he said, dropping his cracked glasses onto the end of his nose. With his free hand, he selected a pencil from his inside jacket pocket and used it to inspect what he could see of the contents, gently shifting an interested Terpsi-chore away with the side of his leg.

The bag was one of those thin, clear plastic ones with tie handles and a white label intended to detail the date and the contents – in this case left blank – but it was clear to an expert like Alfred what was concealed within. He wouldn't be eating tonight.

'Ah.'

'Ah. What?' Tooley was getting impatient and somewhat annoyed.

Alfred placed his hand on his friend's shoulder and the other on the handle of the bag, lifting it well out of Terpsichore's interested nose. 'Now don't go off on one, Tools, but we need to take a trip down to the police station and hand this in. Believe me when I say I'd like nothing more than a nice bit of fresh meat instead of the dregs we have to put up with, but not when I might be eating one of my friends. Enemies I'm not so bothered about,' he added, managing a brief chuckle to try and dispel the sudden tension in their makeshift bedsit.

All colour drained from Tooley's face.

THREE

The small seaside town of Clonabee was slotted between Blackrock and Booterstown. A thorn of a place. A concrete jungle hemmed in by its shiny neighbours and therefore the ideal place to site an offshoot of the Dublin crime team. The criminals were far from happy with the initiative, and it must be said neither were the gardai. Instead of a quick restorative walk along the seafront during their break, they were stuck with a high-rise, overpopulated suburban area on a parr with Ballymun and Tallaght, and a scrap of wasteland the developers optimistically termed *prime, beach-fronted real estate*.

Back at the station, Alana took the lift up to her office on the second floor on the pretext of dropping off her coat. She could have easily left it in the squad room, but she wanted two minutes to herself before meeting with the boss. With her shopping on her desk, and a mental note filed in the 'I must remember to take it home before I leave for the day, unlike the last time' box, she picked up her mobile and took a few minutes to delete the new messages from Colm, her ex-husband. Since their separation and subsequent divorce, he'd taken to contacting her two to three times a day. She was thinking about the possibility of taking out an injunction if it continued, when the device rang in her hand. She checked the screen to see who it was before answering.

'Afternoon, ma'am. It's Mary from the front desk. I need you to come down. We have a situation here that I'm unable to deal with.'

The reception area was in chaos, or maybe it just seemed that way because of the cacophony of noise coming from the very small, very angry child in the middle of the floor, clutching what appeared to be a moth-eaten rabbit. There also seemed to be an inordinate amount of shopping bags, the name of the local supermarket embellished on the side.

'What's going on, Mary?' Alana continued to watch the girl, her hair partially hidden under a woolly hat, a large pink pompom hanging by a thread.

'You'd best speak to Garda Slattery, ma'am,' she shouted, tilting her head in the direction of the tall, anxious-looking policeman standing off to one side. Alana couldn't blame him for not wanting to get any more involved than he had to. The scream was deafening. 'He's the one that brought her in.'

'Garda Slattery?' Alana wheeled herself across the room, positioning the chair in front of him before looking up. He was one of the recent additions to the station, from Templemore. Past his probation but still wet behind the ears. There'd been some gossip about him being the son of someone important. Billy Slattery, that was it. It was the first time she'd had any dealings with the guard apart from the occasional nod in the corridor and canteen. The hope was he wasn't as nervous as his bobbing Adam's apple indicated or, indeed, anything like his newspaper mogul of a father. She offered a small smile of encouragement when what she really wanted to do was stick her fingers in her ears at the deafening decibel-shattering scream.

'Sorry about the noise, ma'am, but I didn't know where else to take her,' he said, having to raise his voice to be heard.

'That's fine but why's she here in the first place?' Alana cast around for a parent or guardian hidden among the staff who'd come out of the offices to see what all the fuss was. 'Surely there's a relative?'

'That's the thing. They're nowhere to be found.'

Alana restrained herself from shaking her head at probably the worst report she'd ever received from a guard, her gaze on one of the station secretaries trying and failing to comfort the girl.

'Okay, start at the beginning, if you wouldn't mind.'

He lowered his shoulders in what might have been relief. It could also have been frustration. Alana didn't know or care which. The clock was ticking on her meeting with an already disgruntled superintendent. She'd better have a very good reason for being late.

'I was called to the supermarket at 13.05. One of the customers reported an unaccompanied child screaming in one of the trolleys. They put it out over the system. When no one came forward they phoned us.' He spread his hands. 'Here we are.'

'Indeed. And the shopping?'

He blushed right up to his hairline. 'I didn't know what to do so I bought it.' He continued only when Alana didn't respond. She didn't quite know how to. It smacked of either stupidity or ingenuity. Only time and more information would decide which. 'It was probably foolish but it's all kiddies' stuff. You know. Sausages and beans and things. There's even a bag of nappies.' He shrugged. 'I thought it might come in useful.'

'I'm not sure how we're going to claim nappies back on expenses, but I'll see what I can do.'

'Mother of God, you've brought me to a madhouse, so you have, doc. What's that bleedin' noise?'

Alana turned to glance behind her only to try and blink away the scene, but the images kept coming. The two tramps arguing in the doorway. The girl's pitiful wail that had lowered to a heart-wrenching chord of despair. The superintendent striding down the corridor, Paddy bringing up the rear.

'What on earth is going on, Detective Mack?' Ox Reilly said, raising his voice to a shout, which was loud enough to flood the space with the remaining of the office staff. It had the additional effect on the child, who shut up so quickly that Alana hurried to her side, her wheelchair making short work of the distance.

'That's what I'm trying to find out, sir,' she said, barely registering his look of disapproval. 'If we can delay our meeting.' It wasn't a question. 'I'll be with you as soon as I can.' With that she stretched her hand out to the girl, while at the same time indicating with the flick of her eye that Paddy should deal with the two unkempt gentlemen cluttering up reception.

'Hello there. My name is Alana. I do like your rabbit. What's his name?'

The girl, no more than a toddler at a guess, hugged the soft toy even closer. She didn't make a sound apart from the occasional hiccup, a remnant from her outburst. Alana had limited experience of dealing with children, which was putting it optimistically. Kids were a group of the population she tended to avoid, apart from her best friend's offspring, whom she hadn't seen for a few weeks now. She couldn't say exactly how long it had been – certainly long enough to feel guilty at the thought.

'Slattery, is there anything sweet in that lot?' she said after a moment, one eye still on the child, the other on Paddy and where he was ushering the two men into one of the interview rooms. 'You know. The kind of thing I can offer her as an enticement. Chocolate, biscuits, sweeties.'

'There's a packet of Haribo's,' he said, rummaging through one of the bags.

'Perfect. Thank you. Haribo's are my all-time favourite.' She dropped her voice to a conspiratorial whisper as she started to pull the bag apart. 'Especially the red hearts and fried eggs,' she continued, making it up as she went along. In truth, Alana had a difficult relationship with sweets, prompted by a mouthful of fillings due to a poor diet and insufficient funds for dental visits as a child, but the girl wasn't to know that.

She took her time in selecting the most colourful heart and, holding it up between her thumb and forefinger, inspected it, a small smile breaking at the sight of the child's riveted gaze. 'I don't know though. I don't want to spoil my lunch, but I can't put it back in the bag either. Would anyone like it? What about you?' she asked the girl, the red heart now lying in the centre of her palm. 'It would be a shame to waste it.'

The girl shuffled towards her on her bottom, her tongue clenched between her teeth, her hand outstretched, obviously wanting the sweet but not wanting to come too close.

'Or what about your rabbit, if you don't want...?'

The sweet disappeared in her gloved hand and then her mouth before Alana could finish the sentence.

'Wabbit don't eat.'

'Oh yes. How silly of me. I'd forgotten and what a smashing name for him,' Alana said, hiding a smile at the girl's look of indignation that the pink toy could ever be a boy.

'Wabbit's a girl.'

'Silly me again. And what's your name, sweetheart? I need to know, if we're going to be friends.'

The bottom lip started to wobble but the tears held off for now. 'Casey.'

'Casey what, love?'

Casey shrugged, her lower lip continuing to tremble.

Alana leant forward to tuck a blonde curl back under the

girl's hat, her heart dropping in her chest at the answer. The hope was that Casey had been left behind by mistake, but there was something about the whole set up that reeked of a different scenario. Specifically, the length of time she'd been left and the trolley brimming with kiddie items. Alana had been shopping with her friend Kari, who had twins, on enough occasions to know that that's not how it worked.

'And do you know where your mummy and daddy are, Casey?' she said, watching as a fat tear formed in each eye before overflowing on to her face.

'Want Mammy.'

'I know you do, sweetheart, and we're going to help you find her. Why don't you climb up on my lap and finish these sweets while I have a chat to Garda Slattery. You're quite safe. I'll make sure of that,' she said, fastening the brakes before helping her up, her hand looping around the girl's waist to secure her in position. It was clear to see by the fists rubbing her eyes that the child was heading for a nap and Alana's lap seemed the obvious solution. God only knew what she was going to do about her meeting, she thought, relishing in the feel and smell of baby-soft skin only a whisper away. If things had turned out differently, she might even now be... Alana flung the happy image aside in favour of the harsh reality of an abandoned girl. It was long past the time to mourn the baby she'd lost.

'Slattery, I'd like you to head back to the supermarket and find out about their CCTV. With a bit of luck that's all it will take. In the meantime, I'll get one of the team to chase up any cameras along the road adjacent. If that doesn't throw up anything, we'll follow up with a call for dashcam footage.'

She ignored the 'yes, ma'am' in favour of wheeling towards the desk. 'Mary, if you can get the duty social worker to phone me, please. I have a funny feeling that we're going to be needing one before long. I'll be with the Super, if you need me.'

FOUR

'Al, wait up. There's something you need to see.'

Alana stopped and turned to face Paddy, who was looking decidedly rattled.

'What is it? You know I'm already late for my two o'clock meeting,' she said, her voice soft, her hand still cradling the child curled up in her lap.

'I'm sorry but the Super will have to wait. This is far more important.'

The interview room was small, made smaller by the two men lounging back on their chairs, paper cups cradled between their fingers and a nearly empty packet of milk chocolate digestives on the table between them – a packet that looked suspiciously like the one she'd dropped off at the squad room first thing that morning.

'This is Petey O'Toole, known as Tooley, and Alfred Gaunt, ma'am,' Paddy said, forging ahead with introductions. 'Gentlemen. Detective Alana Mack. If you can explain to her what you told me.'

Petey started to speak only to be interrupted by Alfred. 'It's all right, Tools, I'm happy to explain. Good afternoon, Detective. Firstly, apologies for taking up your time,' he said, nodding at Casey curled in her lap. 'However, we wouldn't be here if we didn't think it was necessary. In short, earlier on today my good friend Petey found a bag containing some meat, which he thought would do for our supper.' He paused a moment, seeming suddenly reluctant to continue, his attention drawn to Casey.

'It's all right, Mr Gaunt, she's asleep and will hopefully stay that way, if we make sure to keep our voices low. I take it the issue is with the meat?'

He nodded. 'It's by my feet but I'm not sure I should show you. It's still in its original bag, which may have some forensic significance.'

'I assume you have some medical knowledge, Mr Gaunt?' she said, trying to remember where she'd heard the name before, certainly not recently but there was something about his tone and mannerisms that had an eerie sense of familiarity. She rarely forgot a face but had always been hopeless with names.

'You could say that,' he said, obviously reluctant for her to pursue the matter, so she let it drop for now.

'Okay, we'll get to that in a moment. And the meat?'

'Human. Specifically, offal.'

Alana's eyes widened. She didn't know what she'd been expecting but not this. 'Offal as in liver and...?'

'Kidneys. Yes. Excuse me if you think I'm teaching you your job, but I suggest you ship this off to a forensic pathologist for urgent inspection. Dr Mulholland is a good man. He'll know the urgency.'

Alana made her way to the squad room, Paddy by her side, the packet of meat safely secured in a specimen bag, dangling from his fingers. Meat wasn't the correct term, but Alana didn't know what else to call it until she'd had some medical verification.

The squad room was situated on the first floor, a bright, airy space with five desks spread out across the room. There was space for at least another two but not the budget, something that she was at constant loggerheads over with the DS. Ox kept banging on about crime rates, which were on the rise, in contrast to the disappointing arrest rates. Alana's counterargument of falling detective numbers had so far fallen on deaf ears, but she was determined to battle on in spite of the, so far, brick wall of an outcome.

She was pleased to see that all three detectives were present. Detectives Lorrie Deery and Flynn O'Hare were the most junior members of the team but easily made up for their inexperience by a competitive streak, which was sometimes difficult to manage. Tatty Kearney was in her mid-thirties, but her maturity held her in good stead for her role as the station's family liaison officer. She was also Paddy's sister. It was Tatty that Alana turned to in the first instance, conscious that time was slipping through her fingers.

'Tatty, how are you with kids?'

'Er.'

Alana managed to maintain a straight face. Tatty had never given any indication that she was anything other than a party animal. There were certainly no signs of the blonde settling down since her divorce. In fact, the opposite could be said to be true. But Alana had been catapulted into the middle of a difficult situation: there was no way she could take Casey with her to the pathology suite. There was also a possibility that a parent or guardian would turn up at the station to claim the girl, a ready explanation on their lips. No, the girl needed to stay here, and Tatty was the obvious solution.

'As my poor old ma used to say, there's no time like the present, and my arms are killing me,' she said, aiming for a bit of sympathy as she passed the still sleeping girl into Tatty's reluctant hands. 'She could do with being woken to remove her coat, hat and gloves. It's boiling in here. She's also probably in need of a drink and a wee. Slattery didn't say if she was toilet trained, did he, Paddy?'

'Don't think so. Weren't there nappies in the trolley?'

'Nappies in the trolley?' Lorrie interrupted, playing with her earring, her short, spiky hair at war with her conservative black top and trousers. 'Just what have you two been up to during your lunch break?'

Alana ignored the cheeky insinuation. Instead she made her way to the front of the room, her tablet now on her lap so that she could make real time changes to the information on the whiteboard behind her.

'Listen up. We have a couple of ongoing situations that I need to brief you on,' she said, speaking rapidly. 'I know it's not what you want to hear with Aidan Crossey still missing but it can't be helped. Right. This poppet is Casey. We don't have a surname, but Casey can't be that common a forename, so that's a good place to start.' Alana inclined her head at Paddy before continuing, her meaning clear. 'She was found a little over an hour ago, at Clonabee supermarket with a trolley full of kiddie-related items. I've sent Garda Slattery to check the supermarket CCTV footage, and I'd like you to do the same for any along Poolbeg Way, Flynn. There must be some cameras along the route. If all else fails we can always put out an APB for the girl and, if it's not too late, something on the six o'clock news too.'

'I don't think that's a good idea,' Tatty interrupted, hushing the girl now she'd helped her off with her coat and offered her a drink from her water bottle.

'Why not?'

'This was in her pocket.' She passed a note to Paddy, who took a quick look and frowned before laying it on the desk for Alana to see, the tip of his fingernail holding it in place by the very edge.

The scrap of paper looked as if it had been torn from a diary. The words written in faint pencil. The letters rounded, almost childlike.

Please look after her. Her life and mine depend on you not trying to find me.

SIX

'You took your time in getting back.'

'Yeah. Sorry. Missed the bus.' Penny swallowed hard as she entered the kitchen, trying to remove the clog of tears at the back of her throat. She'd made a promise never to cry in front of him. With the shopping bag on the counter, she started to unload her meagre items, her fingers clumsy under Jasper's watchful gaze. The cat freaked her out almost as much as her brother did.

Hate was a strong word, too strong to apply to her confused feelings about Jasper. There was a time when she'd loved the ginger tom. His purring breath and warm cuddly body. But that was when he was a kitten. Now the sight of his piercing gaze following her, made her skin crawl. A shudder slipped between her shoulder blades, causing her jaw to clench and her teeth to grind together. Her brother had grown to love the cat, too, in as much as he could love anyone. So, Jasper remained.

'Pie and mash for tea,' she finally said, aware that her brother had followed her into the room, a watchful presence as she separated the shopping into piles... Milk, eggs and cheese for the fridge. Bread. Potatoes and beans to go with the steak and kidney pie. No food for Jasper. The bottom shelf of the larder cupboard was still full of his favourite brand.

'Don't care, do I?'

No, you wouldn't. You don't care about anything, including yourself.

She'd only told him about tea to fill the air with something other than the sound of her heart thumping in her chest, to still her nerves. To take attention away from what was missing from the situation. She needn't have bothered. It didn't take him long to notice.

'Where's the brat?'

'Gone,' she replied, the eggs in her hand as she pulled open the fridge. A bad idea to turn her back.

'What have you done with her? I gave you a taste of what I'd do the last time you disobeyed me, or are you thick as well as stupid?' he said, grabbing her arm and pushing her against the fridge door, the eggs cracked and bleeding on the floor between them. Her tea squashed and mangled under his feet as he pressed up against her, because there was no way she was eating steak and kidney pie.

The stench of his fetid breath, from the blackened tombstones that filled his mouth, a sharp reminder about how far he'd removed himself from the normalities of life. Brushing his teeth and his hair. Showering. Even changing his clothes into the fresh ones she left out for him. A reaffirmation that leaving her precious girl was the right thing to do, even if, at the time, it had felt like wrenching her heart out with a pickaxe. The world was an evil place, a lesson she'd learned as a teenager and the reason why she'd decided to remove her daughter from a situation that was only going to end one way: with either his or her death. All she could do was hope and pray that someone kind had taken her in, someone that would give her a future away from the canker that occupied this house, away from him. If she could have escaped too... but she'd tried that once and still had the scars to remind her that he'd never let her go. Now it was time to act, act like she'd never acted before while her heart snapped into a thousand irretrievable pieces.

She placed her hand on his shirt, trying not to recoil at the feel of his bones and their cursory covering of skin. She hadn't realised how thin he'd become. Emaciated. Clothes now hanging from his frame; but she couldn't think about that now. She couldn't allow sympathy to blur her actions or soften her resolve. If he sniffed out weakness, her life would be over, the growing madness no barrier to the ties that bound them together, stronger than steel.

'Come on now, Danny. It's best this way. A little girl among all this.' Penny waved her hand around the dismal kitchen, the air drenched with the smell of grease and decay. She didn't think he'd accept it, his next words proved her right.

'But where is she?'

'I left her in the supermarket over in Clonabee, far enough away so she wouldn't be able to find her way home.' Her heart splintered at the words, the uncertainties of what she'd done threatening to consume her.

'You know I'll be able to find her, don't you, Penny?' He lifted his hands to her face, his fingertips pressing into her skin, his gaze penetrating right down to her toes. 'I have friends all over the place, so don't lie to me.'

She wriggled out of his grasp, the scar on her back puckering at the effort, the sound of crushing eggshells filling the air. 'She's safe, that's all you need to worry about. Now, about your tea.' Penny turned to the sink to fetch a cloth, her expression falling away once her back was turned.

She only stayed because she knew he'd hunt her out and kill her if she left. That didn't mean that she wouldn't try again. Her pile of grubby fivers and tenners was growing into a sizeable amount. In a few weeks she'd run for her life, in the hope that this time he'd never find her.

SEVEN

'Come on, sweetie. We're going on an adventure but we have to be quiet, mind.'

'Dark.' The little girl sat up in bed, rubbing her eyes, no doubt wondering why her mummy had woken her up in the middle of the night instead of letting her sleep.

'I know but look, I have a torch to light the way.'

Penny showed her the torch before placing it deep in her pocket. She'd wrapped up warm. There wouldn't be a spare hand to carry anything and she didn't have a rucksack to sling on her back like most runaways. All she had were the clothes she stood up in, a small bag of food pilfered from the cupboard and a wodge of notes sewn into the lining of her coat.

'Here. Pop on your favourite jumper over your pyjamas and here are your shoes and coat.'

'Wabbit?'

'Oh, yes. We can't forget Wabbit, can we? Hold him tight under your arm.'

The house was old with creaking joists and windowpanes that rattled in their rotten frames. There was no money to fix anything, no choice other than to let the building crumble around them. The stairs were her biggest concern. Only yesterday she'd tried to memorise which ones creaked the most. He was a light sleeper, the slightest of noise caused by a mistake on her part and he'd be onto her like a hunter stalking... She blinked away the rest of the thought. It wasn't worth imagining what he'd do to them. She already knew.

One. Two. Three. Four. She counted the steps in her head, remembering to miss the fifth and the seventh.

The hall was long and narrow but, with the stairs negotiated, she felt entitled to let the air soak out of her mouth in relief as she stepped across to the kitchen past the ironing board and the rickety table to the back door beyond, whispering gentle encouragement as she went.

'Nearly there. You're doing grand.'

The back door had creaked until she'd sprayed the hinges with cooking oil the day before. With the door open, they slipped into the starlit night and started to run, Penny half dragging, half carrying the girl, tears of excitement mixing with a whole gamut of emotions she couldn't label apart from one. Fear.

They'd reached the gate. Only one more step to freedom. With her hand on the latch and her eyes on the future within her grasp, she paused, some sixth sense causing her to look over her shoulder and straight into the face of her brother.

EIGHT

Alana studied the words. There wasn't much to study. Two sentences written on a scrap of paper. Two sentences that turned a forgotten child into something far more sinister.

'Well, that puts a completely different spin on things, doesn't it?' she finally said, lifting her head.

'If it's genuine. I'll take it up to the Technical Bureau, to see if there's any forensics, shall I?'

'Good idea, Flynn. DNA and a handwriting expert for good measure. I know they're usually only involved in comparative analysis, but we could be lucky. We certainly won't get any acorns if we don't have a go at shaking the tree. Make sure to speak to Rogene Javier before coming straight back. She's good at bypassing the waiting list if it's urgent, and you can't get more urgent than an abandoned child.'

Alana remembered the wealth of forensics they'd already sent for processing from Crossey's house. An abandoned two-year-old had to take precedence over a man already missing a week, and she was enough of a control freak to want to ensure that the letter took priority. 'So, how many Caseys do we have to contend with then?' she asked, directing her gaze at Paddy, who had just come off the phone.

'Three in Dublin and eighteen in the rest of Ireland, aged between one and four years. The three here are all present and correct.'

'Which has to be seen as positive but annoying. Okay, let's hang fire on alerting the media until we have all the information in. I dread to think what they'll do with it. Instead, we'll concentrate our efforts on the CCTV to see what it throws up,' she said, watching as Flynn used the end of his biro to direct the paper into a fresh envelope.

'Sadly, Casey isn't all we have to contend with currently. A couple of down-on-their-luck gentlemen have just dropped off a package of possible *Silence of the Lamb* significance, which I'm about to take to Dr Mulholland for examination.'

Alana looked around the sea of blank faces, not in the least surprised at their confused expressions, but there was very little she could do to qualify what she meant in front of the child.

'Hold the fort while we're away and that includes coming up with a brilliant excuse for my absence if and when Ox gets in touch. We shouldn't be long, not least because we'll most likely be on bin duty later, if this does turn out to be a significant find. With a bit of luck, it's all a mistake and we'll be back before you know it,' she said, making for the door only to stop at the sound of running feet behind her.

'Me go too.'

'I'm afraid you can't, sweetheart,' Alana said, taking a moment she didn't have to hug the child, her hand reflexively brushing her mop of a fringe off her head.

Casey's face started to crumple, and Alana gave her arm a gentle squeeze. 'I promise I won't be long, and, in the meantime, you look after Wabbit for me.'

She headed to the door only to stop again, this time turning back to Tatty who was trying to console the child. 'Chase up that social worker, eh?'

Paddy offered to drive, and Alana let him even though she was perfectly able in her specially adapted car, which used hand controls instead of foot ones. Choosing her battles was all part and parcel of being wheelchair dependent, and the truth was it was far easier for Paddy to fold up her chair and stuff it in the boot of his Subaru Forrester, instead of having to dismantle it piece by piece.

In the old days, before her accident, her battles at work had mainly been as a result of her being a woman in a male-dominated profession. She sometimes looked back on those times through a mesh of wishful thinking before forcing herself to remember the reality, which had been far from rose-tinted. In some ways her life was better now. There was no fancy house or car; none of the trappings that went with being married to an esteemed psychiatrist. Instead, there was freedom to do what she wanted and when she wanted, the only downside being that everything took a little more thought and a lot more effort. Long gone were the days when she could jump in the car on the spur of the moment and just drive where the mood took her. Trips had to be prepared for now, and over-the-top planning wasn't in her nature. It was far easier to take a packed lunch than discover that the place she'd decided to stop off at, which looked to have good disability access, had nothing of the sort. Having to leave the toilet door open simply because there wasn't room enough for both her and her wheelchair was one of her all-time low points.

Clonabee General Hospital was situated at the other end of Poolbeg Way. A large, sprawling, mishmash of a place that the architects had designed with little thought for the aesthetics, or indeed car parking spaces, of which there were a limited number. They could have left the car, but Alana was keen to get back to the station as soon as possible, for no other reason than her lack of confidence in Tatty's ability to calm Casey.

They headed straight for the pathology suite, where they knew they'd be most likely to find Dr Rusty Mulholland, so-called because of his full head of carroty hair. A taciturn man, if ever there was one, but, allegedly, a pussycat since his marriage to Gaby, a former Welsh police officer. Over the course of the last two years, Alana and Rusty had forged a firm friendship, based on mutual respect and an appreciation for the difficulties each of them faced in their very different but equally stressful jobs.

She found him standing in the small reception, thumbing through his post when they arrived.

'Hello there. I was just heading to my office for a quick coffee, if you'd like to join me. I take it this isn't a social visit,' he said, his attention riveted on the bag that was still dangling from Paddy's fingers.

'A coffee would be brilliant, but we don't really have the time. I'm not sure where the day has disappeared to and it's a long way from being over...' Glancing at her watch she was shocked to see that it was an hour later than she expected.

'Probably to the same place mine has. Come this way.'

They followed him down a dimly lit corridor before taking the second door on the left. Alana knew from experience that the first led to the autopsy suite, a place she was all too familiar with.

Rusty's office was untidy, with files and books layering every surface.

'Plonk yourself over there, Pad,' he said, removing the mountain of journals from the chair opposite his desk. 'I'll be back in a jiff with your drinks and I'm not taking no for an answer. My kettle's broken, just like everything else in the place, so you won't even have to wait for it to boil,' he grumbled, grabbing a selection of mismatched mugs from the shelf behind the door.

The coffee was hot and wet, which was all Alana was expecting, but it was accompanied with a box of coconut creams, which she wasn't.

'Help yourself. A present from a satisfied customer,' Rusty said, causing Alana to pause, her hand hovering over the box, her mouth agape before closing it with a snap. The only kind of satisfied customers surely had to be dead ones, but each to their own. She wasn't of a mind to pass up on the chance of a biscuit, despite its possible dubious origins. The Irish speciality was one of her favourites, although she couldn't remember the last time she'd bothered to treat herself. Another item to add to the list of things she needed to change in her life.

'Now, how can I be of help? Something to do with the bag you're holding, Pad?' he guessed.

'You could say that. We had a couple of down and outs drop it off at the station just now. They found it in one of the bins along Dame Street.'

'You don't happen to know an Alfred Gaunt by the way?' Alana interrupted. 'Because as far as he's concerned the contents are of human origin.'

'Is that right?' Rusty's gaze homed in on the bag, with an interest that far outweighed the sight of the bloodstained plastic. 'I haven't heard of Dr Gaunt in years, not since he left the department. How did you find him?'

Alana detected a story in his answer, but she was too pressed for time to do more than mark it for later. 'Apart from the obvious fact that he's living rough, pretty good. Thin, of course, but then when do you ever come across any other kind of homeless person?'

'Very true.' Opening his top drawer, he removed a pair of blue disposable gloves, lacing his hands to arrange the rubber between his fingers before taking the bag and holding it up to the light. 'Do you have any objection if I remove it from the specimen bag and open the top?'

'Fire ahead now you're wearing gloves.'

The meat looked gross, dark red, shiny globules sticking to the side of the plastic. It also had that distinctive metallic smell that made Alana regret that biscuit. She wasn't a vegetarian, but by the same token she tended to eat the same sort of diet, which mainly consisted of fish, chicken, and the occasional takeaway to break the monotony. She couldn't ever remember eating liver and the thought of eating kidneys was enough to make her gag.

She watched him set the bag back into the clear plastic protective wrapping before laying it ceremoniously on his desk and inspecting it, keeping it well away from both his drink and laptop. After, he peeled off the gloves and washed his hands in the sink, all the while maintaining a tense silence. He only spoke when he was back behind his desk.

'I'm sad to say that Dr Gaunt is correct in his assertion about the specimen's origin. I take it you'd like me to dissect it before sending it off for DNA profiling?'

Alana ignored the last part, her mind caught up in the ramifications of his words. A murder investigation without a body was going to be tricky to manage. There certainly weren't going to be any suspects. It was the kind of case that the media loved. The gardai less so.

'How can you be so sure? You've barely looked at it,' she finally said, more in the hope of proving him wrong, though she knew Rusty didn't make mistakes or, she had never known him to yet. Meticulousness didn't make a person invincible, but he was also cautious, which did make mistakes less likely.

'I don't blame you one little bit for asking. Here, let me show you how easy it is to tell.' And with that he booted up his laptop and performed a quick search before turning the machine to face them. 'The key is in the kidneys. Human kidneys, as in the bag, have a smooth surface, whereas kidneys from sheep and pigs are what's called lobulated. I must tailor all this by telling you that there is a rare condition where lobulation can be found in the kidneys of adults, but I think we can discount that in this instance.'

'So, what? We're now looking for the rest of the body?'

'I'm afraid so. While life is sustainable on one kidney, the bag contains two. It also looks like there might be a liver and possibly the spleen. I won't be able to tell until I examine them properly and, of course, there are no guarantees that the items here are from the same individual,' he said, picking up his drink with one hand and selecting a biscuit with the other, all the time ignoring the bloody mass of tissue beside him.

'They might belong to Crossey,' Alana mused, unable to look away from the bag.

'They might. Easy enough to match from the DNA found in his house. I'll be sure to copy the Tech Bureau into any of my findings.'

Alana didn't comment on the SOCO officers' involvement. While Rusty wasn't personally involved with the investigation into Crossey's disappearance, because of the absence of a body, the whole of Ireland was briefed on almost a daily basis by the tabloids with thoughts and suppositions as to the man's where-abouts. If Alana didn't know any better, she'd think they had a snitch in the department.

NINE

As it was one of the major roads in and out of the city, they'd decided not to close off Dame Street, only the pavements on both sides of the road, but it was a complicated affair made more complex by the number of businesses that exited onto the street. Ox had reluctantly sanctioned additional gardai but not enough to shepherd all the workers on their way. Alana watched on, feeling useless, but there was little she could do until the Technical Bureau appeared on the scene to start on the bins.

Rogene Javier, Chief Technical Bureau Officer, was a formidable presence, and for all her no-nonsense personality, a very welcome addition to the SOCO team.

'I can think of lots I'd like better to be doing Friday teatime than rummaging around in the bottom of a refuse bin. Eating my chicken and pork adobo for one,' she said, her tone tinder dry as she plucked a paper suit off the top of the pile. 'How many of these tin cans are you expecting my team to sift through?' she continued, the emphasise on the *my* muffled as she adjusted the hood of the suit and stuffed her sharp black bob underneath.

'The ones along Dame Street for starters, but it all depends on what's found.'

'We'll be here half the night so,' she said, slipping blue covers over her shoes with an air of resignation that was clear to anyone watching.

Alana had already offered her services along with that of Paddy, much to his consternation, but she'd been turned down flat along with a: 'You stick to your job while I get on with mine.' Alana hadn't bothered to reply. Rog was an expert at always getting in the last word and Alana wasn't in the mood for challenging that.

It wasn't only Rogene's Friday evening that was suffering though, she remembered, as a sliver of guilt slid under her scarf, pooling in her stomach. It was all very well her working all the hours, but Paddy, Flynn, Lorrie and Tatty were as deserving of their downtime as the next person. In contrast, work was the one constant in her life and the only thing that made her get up in the morning when the temptation was to remain in bed. Working late and coming into the office early was her new normal, now that the need to rush home to prepare a meal had flown out of the window along with her marriage.

'Okay, then. We'll leave you to it and thank you again.' With that she corralled Paddy from where he was chatting to Garda Mallory, one of the guards sequestered to start on the CCTV cameras along the street.

'God, I could do with a drink,' Paddy said, towering beside her as she made her way up Church Lane past O'Neill's pub and the statue of Molly Malone to where they'd parked their car next to the post office.

'Well, it will have to wait. Think about your poor sister and the rest of them holding the fort,' she said, saying the words in a rush in order to conserve her breath at having had to negotiate Church Lane hill.

'The ideal would have been if the NBCI had taken over the

investigation.' He stopped beside his car and opened the door for her.

As a suggestion it was a good one. There was no question about their expertise and experience in dealing with challenging cases, and this one was nothing if not challenging, but Paddy hadn't taken into account the key element in all of this: Ox Reilly.

'Hah, you're having a laugh if you think the Super would ever give up on a case of such monumental importance to the bods over at the Bureau,' she said, sliding across into the passenger seat. 'This, as far as Ox is concerned, is his road to the top, never mind how many of us he squishes along the way. Mark my words, if he isn't planning his promotion to Assistant Commissioner as we speak.'

'At least it would get him off our back.'

'Again, charity isn't in his make-up.' She watched on as he deftly folded her chair in preparation for lifting it into the boot. She only spoke again when he'd settled behind the steering wheel. 'He'll be on our backs now from dawn till dusk until we catch the perp.'

'That's if we manage to catch him.'

'Could just as easily be a woman,' she said, pulling out her mobile and opening the screen before closing it again. 'No news from Rusty yet but another one from Ox. He wants to see me as soon as we get back.'

'Unlike him to work late.'

'As I said, this is his ticket to the big time,' she said, tutting at the traffic building at the top of Dawson Street. 'Pop your siren on or we'll be stuck here forever. Now, what do you make of the case?'

'It's a strange one and that's for sure. Organ trafficking is a thing but surely never in Ireland and certainly not when they dumped the organs after. What's that all about?'

'Search me! I was thinking more along the lines of any

possible religious significance or even a cult,' Alana responded, checking her phone again. 'But there's no sense in how they disposed of the liver and kidneys. Burning perhaps while they chant around the fire but...'

'I think you've been watching too many dubious movies, Alana, if you don't mind me saying.'

'Paddy, I don't watch those kinds of movies, as you very well know. *Sleepless in Seattle* is as violent as it gets.'

'If you say so,' he said on a laugh, pulling into the station car park and killing the engine.

'I do say so. *The Wicker Man* is far more your idea of fun than mine.' She reached down to unclip her seatbelt. 'Chivvy up the team, would you? I'll be right down after my meeting with the boss.'

Detective Superintendent Reilly inhabited a large office with panoramic views over the tiny stretch of Clonabee coastline which was given over to the fishing industry in its entirety. This would be the first time she'd met with him in his office this week, which was probably a record, one she was keen to smash. The less she saw of the man the better.

With the time now well past five, and his secretary's desk empty, she knocked and waited.

His 'enter' was curt.

There were no preliminaries. No 'hello'. No 'how are you?'. No 'It's good to see you. How can I be of help?'

'About time too. Any update on the body parts found? I would have expected a call at the very least.'

Alana took her time in replying, taking a moment to manoeuvre her chair into place, her fingers rearranging her trousers over her knees. Then she smiled.

'This is the first opportunity I've had, sir. What would you like to know?' She stared across the desk, enjoying the way the

angry rush of colour stole up his bullish neck and ruddy cheeks
to finally meet his bushy brown eyebrows head on. His nickname of Ox suited him. She certainly couldn't think of an alter-
native, apart from perhaps misogynist prick.

He leant across his desk, his bullish forearms in front of him
as Alana idly wondered what his blood pressure had risen to.

'Don't you come the little missy with me, young woman. I
asked you a question about what's going on in my department.
Be good enough to answer it.'

There was nothing Alana hated more than being referred to
as little missy, except perhaps young woman, but she'd pushed
her luck far enough for one day.

'As you already know, sir, two gentlemen brought in a bag of
what they at first assumed to be assorted offal.' She'd like to ask
him which one of the team had alerted him, but she was far too
clever for that. Possibly the same one that had been feeding the
media a running commentary of the Crossey case. She'd bide
her time and wait until she had some kind of proof. 'Luckily for
us, one of the men had some medical experience, which he used
before getting the frying pan out.'

Alana had thought about telling Ox the identity of Alfred
Gaunt, but decided to keep that piece of information from him
until she'd had the time to conduct a little research on the
doctor. She would have had to trust the DS not to divulge what
might turn out to be sensitive information. It wouldn't be the
first time that Reilly had dropped her in it just because he
could. It was all a game and one she was determined to win.

'And that appalling racket downstairs earlier?' he said,
eyeing her like a worm dangling on his hook. 'It's not what I
expect,' he went on, as if they were the centre of the universe
instead of some two-bit station that was very much in the
category of poor relation when compared to the NBCI or
even the SCRT. If she knew now what she'd known then
nothing would have made her swap her position on the team,

even the carrot of promotion, but there was no way back. Things had moved on across the service just as they'd moved on with her. Still, there was a sense of comfort in the familiarity of the station. They might be viewed by many as the poor relation when compared with the other high profile units but not with regards to capturing the criminals. Then they excelled.

'An abandoned child, sir. With a bit of luck, the parents will finally realise what they're missing and come to pick her up.'

'I wouldn't bank on it, Mack,' he said, a smirk breaking. 'Get out of my sight and start sorting this mess because I'm certainly not. If this level of performance continues, I'll have to see about rearranging the team.'

'Oh, about that, sir. I'll set up a Major Incident Room, and I will be in need of some assistance, in the form of extra staff and what have you.'

'You can take Slattery. He won't be missed.' He smiled, a rare occasion that set Alana's worry gene into hyperdrive. Why Slattery? What was up with him?

Alana heard the commotion before the steel doors of the lift had started to open, the screams an even more intense sound than before. Heartbreaking keening wails and moans. The squad room was in disarray with Flynn and Paddy standing back, while Tatty, Lorrie and some stranger with a head of frizzy grey hair tried to talk Casey down. It obviously wasn't working. Paddy joined her at the door.

'Who's that?' she asked under her breath.

'Eileen Griffin from Social Services. There's no news of Casey's parents, so she's planning on putting her with a foster family for the night.'

With that the room fell silent, a tense absence of noise as opposed to a comfortable break from the din, while they all

stared at the child writhing about on the floor, to see what she
was going to do next.

It wasn't so much a case of what she did as what she didn't
do. With a spasm, all her limbs extended, stretching out like a
starfish before the stillness came. No movement. No sound. A
complete reversal of the behaviour that'd had them all on
tenterhooks.

'My God, she's stopped breathing.' Alana hurried over to
her, completely helpless and, stuck in a wheelchair, unable to
do anything anyway. 'Quick, turn her on her side.'

'Nah. Leave her alone. She'll be fine in a moment. They
always are,' the social worker said. 'Never heard of a child dying
from holding their breath yet.'

Alana ignored her, her attention on Tatty as she rolled the
girl off her back, a gentle hand stroking her hair: doing precisely
what she would have done if it hadn't been for her blessed legs.
Alana had never felt as useless as at that precise moment,
suddenly rationalising everything she'd lost alongside the few
things that actually mattered – even though well-meaning
healthcare professions, family and friends told her differently.

'You're all right, Casey. Nothing bad is going to happen.'

The girl's eyes fluttered, her colour changing from blue to
milky white. Her eyes enormous in her deathly pale face.
Exhaustion and deep sadness mirrored in each muscle flicker
and breath. Casey needed to be fed before being tucked up
somewhere safe and secure until they could make proper
arrangements for her. In short, she needed someone to care.

The social worker must have read her mind with her next
words, but not in the way she'd been hoping.

'The family I was planning on taking her don't have the
room, but the Sisters of Mercy should be able to help. Frankly,
there are too many kids in similar positions for us to cater for.
Come on, Casey. I have a nice place for you to stay until we can
find your ma and da.'

'No.' It was more of a shout than a scream, but the intention was clear. The girl was going nowhere unless she was manually removed from the room, something which Eileen seemed prepared to do the way she bunched her bag over her arm and rolled up her sleeves.

'Enough of that, young lady. You're coming with me and that's that.'

'Mother of God, what's going on?' Rusty said from the door, the soft burr of his Cork accent a calming presence in the fraught room. Ignoring everyone, he strode across the room and, dropping onto one knee from his considerable height, placed himself in front of Casey. Eileen's hands dropped to her sides as she stepped back. That was the kind of commanding air he had. Alana was self-reliant as well as fiercely independent, but she let out a quiet sigh at the sight of him taking charge.

'Hello there. For a little person you sure can use those lungs. Is this the girl you were telling me about earlier, Alana?' he continued, plucking a small car from his pocket and placing it on the floor in front of Casey, his index finger starting to propel it back and forward. 'Sorry, my daughter isn't into dollies.'

'We're just trying to sort out some emergency accommodation.'

'Want Lana,' Casey said, suddenly standing and hurrying to her side, the car left abandoned by Rusty's feet, her small hands clutching at her leg – legs Alana hadn't been able to feel since her accident.

Reaching down, she lifted the girl up onto her lap, her arm wrapping around her, her mind buzzing.

She felt the eyes of the room turn in her direction, the weight of their stares only adding to her feelings of helplessness, because there was no way she'd be able to manage the girl even if she was allowed to. Excuses rolled in, tumbling one after the other and pushing aside any ideas she might have had of being able to cope. She didn't have a car seat for one thing, or a spare bed. None of the equipment needed to cater for the needs of a toddler.

Alana forcibly pushed the 'I can't' thoughts aside. She'd been let down too many times in her life by the people that were meant to love her the most, and she knew what it felt like to feel totally abandoned.

'I think that can be arranged, Eileen, don't you?' she found herself saying, the words almost popping out of their own accord. 'It would be a shame to bother the Sisters of Mercy at a time like this, and I do have my advanced police check, in addition to all these fine members of the gardai willing to vouch on my behalf.'

'What! No! This can't happen,' the woman gobbled, her chin wobbling along to the bulge of her eyes. 'You're not on my register for a start and... and... and.' She paused, her gaze swivelling from the chair and back to Alana, an angry flush storming her cheeks.

Alana was well aware of what she was inferring, as did the room, all apart from Casey, who'd settled on her lap, her thumb resolutely in her mouth, her tears starting to dry on her face. In a funny sort of a way Alana was interested to see what the woman was going to say next, but it didn't come to that.

'Oh, I think we can make an exception in this case, don't you? Mrs, er,' Rusty said, shifting to stand beside Alana in an expression of solidarity. 'I'm on the board of trustees of the Sisters of Mercy. If you like I can phone them. As Detective Mack says, it would be a shame to bother them and disturb Casey further, for that matter, poor little mite.'

'But what about equipment and what have you?' Eileen replied, clinging to her position even though the answer was right in front of her. 'Do you have a car seat for a start and what about experience with—?'

Rusty interrupted again, his hands shifting to his pockets,

an expression of intense boredom settling on his face and infiltrating his voice. 'You don't have to worry about that. I have a daughter around the same age and am more than happy to loan Detective Mack anything she needs.

'You're sure about this, Alana?' He turned back to her. 'Gabriella and I are more than happy to look after her until we find her mam.'

'I know that, Rusty, and thank you but it wouldn't be right now I've made a promise, though I'll gladly take you up on the offer of a loan of equipment and any advice that's on offer. There's also the small issue of tomorrow and what I'm going to do with her when I'm at work.'

'You know Gabriella will be more than happy to provide an impromptu child-sitting service, and Lara will love a bit of company.' He propped on the edge of the nearest desk, stretching his legs out ready for a chat and with no consideration for the lateness of the hour. 'Actually, it might be an idea to get a sample for DNA testing while I'm here. It will be easy enough to grab a swab stick from the Tech Bureau before I head off. We can at the very least add her to the system if no matches are found.'

'Thank you,' she repeated, her hand cradling the girl as she snuggled down to sleep, totally unaware of the chaos she was causing. Alana was annoyed that she hadn't thought of the issue of DNA before, but she did have a lot on her mind.

Eileen stormed off with a clear case of the hump and a promise to check in on Casey first thing in the morning. It was more of a threat and Alana couldn't blame her, all her confidence in her ability to look after the girl disappearing despite her good intentions and kind heart. Being responsible for a toddler was hard enough for anyone able-bodied but an inexperienced paraplegic brought with it a gamut of difficulties she couldn't begin to list. Her ground floor flat, while not purpose built, was chosen for its open spaces and wet room, but it was still only one-bedroomed, with patio doors to the smallest of gardens. Room for two chairs and little else. Certainly not somewhere suitable for a child to play in, even with the high wall surrounding the property.

Paddy yawned, suddenly reminding her of the time. It would be a good hour before she got home, but there was no reason for anyone else to stay on.

'I'm about to wrap it up for the evening and send this lot off to the nearest hostelry for a pint of their finest, Rusty,' she said, her meaning clear.

'In other words, what am I doing here when I should be in the middle of a traffic jam?' He jumped off the table with a bout of energy she envied from her useless hips right down to her useless toes. But, while she might have felt ready to drop with tiredness, Alana was the type of person never to admit it. 'I've had a proper look at the bag of goodies you dropped off and I can confirm that my initial thoughts are correct.'

'Ah,' Paddy said, joining the conversation for the first time. 'Dr Gaunt will be thrilled.'

'Once a doctor, always a doctor, Pad. I'm afraid there's more news and none of it good.'

He took a second to glance at Casey and her rhythmic breathing before pacing to the window and staring outside, seeming unaware of the lack of a view now day had switched to night.

'The sample consisted of two kidneys, and liver... I've sent off samples from each for DNA testing, but before that I examined the tissue samples under the microscope.'

Alana wanted to hurry him to the finale, but she knew of old that Dr Mulholland liked his few minutes in the spotlight. Any move on her part to curtail his showmanship always resulted in a curt response.

'As we know the food industry is way ahead in its investigation into the preservation of its produce: prolonging the shelf life of their products is big business,' he continued. 'Freezing is one such way, but it does come with its problems not least the creation of ice crystals, which can alter the microstructure of the product. Basically, what I'm trying to say is that the meat isn't fresh.'

'You mean it was frozen?' Alana said, feeling sick. It would be a very long time before she reached for anything in the freezer aisle that had a whiff of meat about it.

'Exactly. But that's not all. I'm afraid to say that the kidneys had different owners.'

'As in we're looking for more than one victim?' Flynn said, his fingers hovering over his keyboard.

Rusty nodded, turning back to face the room. 'There was also a sign of scorching to one of the kidneys, which leads me to think that we're looking for a budding surgeon.'

'You what?'

Rusty threw back his head and laughed at Flynn's reflexive response only to choke it back in deference to Casey. 'That was my initial thought too.'

He grabbed a marker pen and headed to the whiteboard and the tiny square of space in one corner.

'Basically, our victims both had nephrectomies, another term for surgical removal of the kidney. A simple enough operation but one which does come with the risk of haemorrhaging out, so the surgeon has to be quick with either clipping the blood vessels or using some other method like diathermy.' The diagram was quick and effective, the tubes splayed out in an array of squiggles. 'Here, here and here, there are signs that the organ was removed carefully as opposed to being ripped out in a hurry.'

'And the victims?' Alana asked the question even though she already suspected the answer.

'The victims were probably alive at this point. As we all

know, it's possible to live a full and healthy life with one kidney.'

'But not without two or indeed your liver?'

'Er no, that would have signed their death warrants.'

'So, you're thinking what? Someone operated on them, firstly removing their kidneys before operating on the rest of them,' Lorrie said, looking remarkably calm despite the horrific nature of the conversation.

'That's it in a nutshell,' he replied, returning her gaze. 'Our perp performed procedure after procedure, carrying on even after their patient was dead on the table and the need for diathermy didn't exist.'

'To what end?' Paddy asked, his voice soft, in contrast to his flint-hard expression.

'You've got me there, Paddy, but dip into any history book and you'll quickly see blueprints of how cruel the human race can be. The French feudal lord, Oliver V de Clisson, and his party trick of amputating the arms and legs of his prisoners so that they wouldn't be a threat, while a little closer to home – same fourteenth century – hanging, drawing and quartering was the dish of the day for convicted traitors. I'm not even going to start on the atrocities perpetrated during World War Two – during all wars.'

Alana watched as he grabbed his coat from where he'd placed it on the floor beside the door, his brown satchel-like briefcase on top, a clear prompt that time was racing towards the evening, but by the way he lifted his head and darted her a look, not an end to the conversation. Her stomach knotted at his expression, her mind trying to unravel what was to come.

'I can't provide a motive and I should be horrified by this new development, but sadly that's not the case, Paddy. It's been a long time since I've been shocked by the depravity of others. Two years long, in fact.'

She should be grateful that he hadn't polluted the air with

the killer's name, but it was a little enough reprieve for the sudden tension-filled room, where every member of the team appeared to glance her way only to busy themselves with their work. The Sandman, so named because the victims were found buried in sand, was locked away in a maximum-security prison with no chance of parole, she reminded herself, her free hand sneaking to her stomach and the baby that had once filled her belly. Capturing her nemesis had led to a series of personal repercussions that were life altering as well as life ending. A good day was one where she failed to remember the finer points of everything she'd lost. She would never forget.

TEN

It was past nine o'clock before Alana pulled into her designated parking space in the underground car park, pleased beyond measure that Rusty had insisted on following her, his boot packed solid with more baby equipment than she'd ever seen. He'd also insisted on folding up her wheelchair and plonking it on top, a little kindness that made her want to cry – something she hadn't allowed herself to do since being discharged from the rehabilitation unit in Maynooth following her accident.

Casey had fallen asleep on the short journey between Rusty's smart, beach-fronted property along Maretimo Gardens and Alana's far less smart apartment in Kilmacud, her tummy full of cheesy pasta and her lap full of toy cars, which Lara, Rusty's and Gaby's two-year-old adopted daughter, had insisted she take with her. There was also a squashed Wabbit tucked under her arm – her nose and one ear all that was visible.

Alana was tired, more tired than she could ever remember, but she still managed to put a smile on her face and offer Rusty a drink after he'd helped her set up the travel cot at the side of her bed, and unpack the shopping into the right cupboards.

'Get away with you, Alana. I'm for a large gin with the missus before I drop and, excuse me for saying, but I suggest you do the same.' He made for the door. 'Sleep well and any problems we're only on the end of the phone. I mean it.'

With the door closed and the latch in place, Alana heaved a sigh of relief at the silence after a day filled with noise and tragedy. It wouldn't last. She had a sleeping child to toilet and pop to bed before she could think about the next step and, contrary to Rusty's suggestion, gin wouldn't feature.

Alana manoeuvred the chair across the open-plan lounge into her bedroom, and with a bit of toing and froing managed to arrange a sheet and pillow on the bottom of the travel cot along with a thick blanket. She'd turned on the central heating as soon as they'd arrived home, but it would take a while yet for the rooms to warm.

Waking Casey wasn't easy, but teeth had to be cleaned and the tricky question of borrowed pyjamas navigated with a diplomacy Alana didn't know she possessed.

'No, well, I'm sorry they're not pink but red is the next best thing and a great colour for a car, don't you think?'

Alana was in tune with how desperately sad the girl felt, but there was nothing more she could do for her except hug her to her chest and drop a kiss on top of her head before helping her to clamber into bed.

'Don't forget Wabbit. I'm just outside if you need me, love,' she said, watching in silence as Casey's thumb once again found her mouth, her eyes flickering closed against the warm glow from Alana's bedside lamp.

Back in the lounge, and with a hot chocolate on the table in front of her, Alana opened her notepad and started flipping through the pages, pulling her pencil from the loose knot in the back of her hair, only to spend a second on rearranging it back into its usual style.

In the old days, the days before her marriage to Colm, she used to care about how she looked. Every Friday Kari and her would hit the bars and clubs across Dublin city and party the night away, their hair teased into outlandish styles, their make-up raw and sensual, their clothes glued to their tiny frames, their feet slipped into skyscraper heels despite being on their legs all day. Now her thick black hair was creeping past her shoulders and in need of a trim, but instead of worrying about how it looked, she bundled it up in a clip and used it as a pen holder, the white streak piercing the black a vivid marker of all she'd been through. Marriage to Colm had moderated her image, as had the transition from twenty to thirty, but it was her accident that had done the rest. Clothes were chosen for the ease with which she could put them on, as were her shoes. Function over style was the order of the day as she lay on her bed struggling to navigate her useless legs into what she had in her wardrobe. Item after item landed on the floor, dresses and skirts she used to love to wear. Now her wardrobe consisted of a uniform of easy-to-put-on styles that were comfortable as well as business smart for work, hanging side by side with joggers and stretch tops. Her shoes were flat heeled with hidden supports to prevent foot drop, something that she was prone to now the muscles in her feet had wasted. She'd cried when she'd gathered together her belongings and bagged them up for the local charity drop-off point, but that was a long time ago now. She hadn't shed a tear since.

Damn. Alana scrunched her eyes closed. She'd intended to sit a while in the dim light and think over her day instead of wasting time thinking about the past. It was Colm's fault, of course, she thought, pushing her phone away, the latest in a stream of texts still visible on the suddenly active screen. Seeing him was the last thing she wanted, but perhaps that was what it would take to finally cut him out of her life like the cancer he'd become. She pondered a moment, lost in a past she still wasn't able to let go of. There was also a very good chance that as a child psychiatrist with a string of accolades and research papers into childhood trauma, he was exactly who she needed to help her to find Casey's mother.

ELEVEN

Penny sat in her bedroom and clutched the little pink vest, the colour faded to a shadow of its former vibrant shade, her tears mingling with the fabric.

What kind of a mother deserted her baby into the care of strangers? That was the question that wouldn't be answered, a guilt that wouldn't be assuaged no matter the reasoning behind her actions. Knowing it was for the best and being able to live with that fact were in direct opposition and why she'd hidden away in her bedroom after she'd sorted out the washing.

The worst part was the uncertainty. There'd been no news, nothing in the newspapers or, at least, on the front pages, which was all she was prepared to glance at. She'd asked for them not to trace her. Funny how that added to her distress instead of alleviating it. What if she'd been wrong? What if by leaving her in the supermarket, she'd plonked her into the middle of a far more dangerous situation and without her mother to protect her? There were so many permutations to the end of the story. Penny was half driven mad with thoughts of where she was and who she was with. Were they kind and caring or, or, OR!

With a loud sniff, she dredged the tears back and wiped the

back of her hand across her face, before wiping it against her jeans and standing, the vest now folded into a neat square. It was time to start preparing for bed. Another wedge of the routine in her day. Shower and brushing her teeth before book and bed, and tomorrow she'd have the exact same rigmarole to look forward to. No. There was nothing to look forward to.

Realistically she could walk out of the house and never look back. Mostly he wasn't around to stop her. Within hours she could be reunited with her baby and start again. But she couldn't do that. The chains that tied her to him were inch thick and made of impenetrable steel. He'd told her she'd never escape. That he'd find her if she tried. That her life was worthless, something she knew to be true. Her grandparents had told her so often that she'd started to believe it.

She knew what her brother was capable of. The depths of depravity he'd sunk to. The cruelties, both mammoth and minute, that he carried out. The scars that he'd left on both her flesh and her soul. Yes, she'd removed the girl from his grasp, but that wouldn't stop him if he set out to find her. And what then? No, she couldn't leave, not until she had worked out a way to escape him.

But she was scared, scared about what he'd do if he were ever to find her.

The pain from the last time was a living memory every time she lay on her back, every time she twisted in front of the bathroom mirror to see the damage he'd caused her.

TWELVE

The only thing she was thankful for after her failed runaway attempt was that he allowed her to settle her baby back into bed first. He stood in the doorway, a dark, distant presence, watching, as she gently tucked Wabbit under the covers and dropped a kiss onto the end of her nose.

'Sleep well. It will be all better in the morning.'

'Night, Mammy. Love you.'

Penny lingered a second before turning away, her eyes dry, all emotion wiped clean as she faced up to what came next. Her gaze intent on the girl's thumb as it found her mouth, proof enough that she'd soon be asleep.

The thought that she wouldn't remember a thing tomorrow was the one Penny hugged to herself as he forced her down the stairs and into the kitchen before pushing her into the chair, the legs scraping against the linoleum flooring. Up to now she'd been able to keep the horrors away, determined that her daughter would have the happy childhood she'd been deprived of.

'Strip.'

'What!' Penny glanced over her shoulder, her mouth open, her heart thudding in her chest.

'You heard me. Get undressed.'

'Now look here. You can't mean to—'

'Penny, I won't ask again,' he hissed, a globule of spit landing on the floor by his feet. 'If you're not naked in ten seconds, I'll fetch your brat so she can watch.'

'You can't. You wouldn't. You're my brother.'

'Only your half-brother. Tell someone they're trash and they'll soon believe it. Ten. Nine.'

'You know that wasn't me,' she screamed, trying to get through the wall he'd encased himself in. The thought that he was prepared to... She couldn't even think the word let alone say it. Her brother, for God's sake. There were many names for her but prude wasn't one of them. She didn't have the luxury for such behaviours. Tart, prostitute, whore were far more fitting terms, but intercourse with her brother? She felt sick when the only thing in her stomach was the scrap of bread and cheese she'd had for her lunch.

'Eight, Seven. Six.'

The countdown quickened along with her distress, the tears ravishing her cheeks, her hands starting to shake as she removed her coat and started on her jumper, her back turned to hide her nudity, an acrid smell causing her to wrinkle her nose.

She wasn't wearing much. Soon jeans, knickers and socks lay in a heap by her feet along with her worn trainers, the table in front of her partly concealing her from his eyes, but that wouldn't be for long.

'Keep your back turned.'

Penny heard him moving around her then she felt him, his hand between her shoulder blades as he pushed her across the table, her hands stretched out in front of her, her breasts squashed flat against the wood.

'In the old days I'd have kept a whip,' he said, almost conversationally, pushing her hair aside from where it had been dangling down her back, his fingers soft, tender even. 'Ten of the best from a cat-of-nine-tails. Sadly, I've had to improvise.'

It took about three seconds for the nerve endings in her back to register a complaint with her brain. Two for the smell of burning to reach her nose, but only one for the sound of sizzling flesh, akin to sausages hitting the frying pan, to alert her to what was happening.

'Remember, Penny, that you made me do it and, if you try and run away again, next time it won't be *your* back that gets burnt. Understand!'

He left without further comment or offer of assistance, bloody saliva dribbling from her mouth from where she'd bitten her bottom lip, her heart hammering in her chest, her fingers clawing around the edge of the table.

Her breathing finally slowed along with her pulse, the pain ripping through her nerve endings but manageable now she knew it was over.

Penny had no idea how long she lay there, long enough to give him plenty of time to get out of her way. She'd be damned if she'd let him see her naked, but there was no way she could bear to get dressed. Even the simplest of movements to get her from lying to sitting brought on a fresh glut of pain of an intensity she'd never imagined.

The clock on the oven flashed 3:00 by the time she finally crawled out of the room, her clothes bundled up in front of her, the iron safely back in its place on the edge of the ironing board.

THIRTEEN

Alana loved nothing more than to climb out of bed in the morning and climb straight into her running shorts, reaching for the first T-shirt from the top of the pile.

Running on the beach for her was the best part of the day. The sting of wind on her face. The first deep breath that filled her lungs and energised her soul. The feel of rain on her hair, her cheeks, her back, soaking through all the layers, splashes staining her calves and her white gym socks. The spring of the sand under her feet as she pounded the beach, her stride easy and graceful. It wasn't only the exercise though. She brushed away the wetness with the back of her hand, her attention on the horizon and the slit of red growing into a burnished orange ball of emerging sunlight. The night sky of seconds before now stained with an assortment of shades no colour palette could ever match. The feeling of being a tiny speck among a pile of other specks trying to make a living as well as a mark on the increasingly confused planet. This was complete, unadulterated joy. This was her happy place among all the little unhappiness's that made up much of her day. The untouchable place where no one could reach her...

'Mammy.'

The cry woke her, dragging her from the depths of her dream. From a glorious sunlit sky, with the scent of sea air and tangled seaweed still in her nostrils, to the reality of a dimly lit room, her heart pounding in her chest and a cry on the verge of a scream.

Alana swiped at her cheeks, surprised to find her fingers coming away damp in the dim, shadowy light cast from her bedside lamp.

'Come on, goose. How about climbing into my bed for a bit, eh? It's still a little early to get up,' she said, squinting down at her watch, the little hand resolutely stuck between the four and the five. God, it was going to be a very long day if she couldn't get at least another couple of hours.

'Help.'

'Of course. Here, pass me Wabbit first. There. Right. If you stretch your arms up as far as they'll go... that's my girl.'

With a bit of pushing and tugging, Casey collapsed beside her, her body warm and round as Alana tucked the duvet under her neck.

'There you go, chick. Snooze time then breakfast, then a play around at Lara's. You'll like that.'

''K.'

Alana pressed the button of the lift and watched as the door slid shut with a gentle swish. She wasn't in the best of moods after her disturbed night, and a day in the office when it was meant to be her weekend off was only compounding matters. There was another reason for her frame of mind, one she was trying and failing not to dwell on. The text she'd sent Colm last night before bed and his immediate response, as if he'd been waiting for her to call. The sad thing was that he probably had been.

Instead of heading for her office, and the sight of last night's deli tea still sitting on her desk, she made for the third floor where the Technical Bureau was based, another part of the station with round-the-clock cover – although it was potluck as to who she'd find on duty today.

Luckily, she bumped into Rogene as she exited the lift, Rogene's hands wrapped around a tray of slides, a buff-coloured folder tucked under one arm.

'I see you've copped the short straw, Rog,' she said, offering to take the tray at the sight of the folder starting to slip.

'Cheers. Too much to do and not enough hands. With Ox's cuts it's skeleton staff city here currently. More life in the morgue,' she added, a broad smile breaking as she placed the folder on the reception desk and retrieved the tray from Alana. 'I guess you're here for an update on the bins.'

''Fraid so.'

Alana followed her across the small reception, having to concentrate negotiating the narrow corridor down to Rog's office. In the old days she'd have stopped off before work at the Tesco in Stillorgan Shopping Centre for donuts, but that was when jumping out of the car could be done with speed and finesse. Occasionally she was known to bake chocolate cookies for the staff, but that wasn't today. 'I'm only sorry I couldn't...'

Rogene wiped her comment away with a sweep of her hand. 'I wouldn't be apologising if our positions were reversed, Alana, so can it,' she said, matter of fact from the top of her smooth head to the tip of her sensible shoes. Her brightly coloured striped socks, partly visible under her uniform, were a discordant note, the only visible sign that she wasn't as serious as she first appeared. 'I can give you a précis of the long report into the state of Dublin's bins, which I haven't started on, but which includes seven dirty nappies, six bags of doggie do, fifteen biros and a red wig that's seen better days. What it doesn't include is any other body parts, which is a blessing, don't you think?'

'That depends,' Alana replied with a frown. 'We know we're looking for the bodies of two people – Dr Mulholland has confirmed that the kidneys came from different subjects – so the question is where the hell are they?'

Rogene shrugged. 'Not a lot I can say. We've got a lab full of the contents of the bin and also the bin, thanks to the council, in addition to odds and sods from a sweep of the bins in a half-mile radius.'

'That's a lot of bins.'

'Tell me about it!! I'll let you know if we come up with anything noteworthy, including anything that links back to Aidan Crossey.'

Alana nodded her thanks and started for the door only to stop and turn back. 'What about the note we found in Casey's pocket?'

'Fingerprints aplenty but none that we have on file. Sorry.'

'And the handwriting expert?'

'A good call but not a great deal of help, I'm afraid. As you know, handwriting forensics is based on the key tenet that no two people write alike, which is no help here, as we only have the one sample to work with. Our man has also studied graphology but' – Rogene spread her hands – 'the ability to identify personality traits or even gender from a few words is far from an exact science. All he was able to say for sure was that the person was obviously well-read, based on the word choice, spelling and use of punctuation in that final full stop. Tentative and certainly not court worthy if and when we get to that stage, but it might be of some help in finding her parents.'

The incident room on a Saturday was usually empty, but with body parts floating around the city and a missing mother to contend with, along with the Crossey case, all the desks were full, the room alive with the sound of ringing phones and clattering keyboards, the coffee maker in the corner working overtime, a large box of donuts sitting next to it.

'Whoever brought in the donuts has my debt of thanks,' Alana said, remembering the Weetabix she'd spooned into Casey's mouth, her own breakfast abandoned in the effort of getting the girl to eat. She was surely old enough to find her mouth with her hand, her thumb managed, but that didn't seem to make any difference. 'Anyone want a top-up?'

'We're good, thanks,' Paddy said, joining her. 'Where's the princess?'

'Princess is the right term! Around at Rusty and Gaby's until Gaby drops her off later. I take it there's been no news about her mother, father, guardian or other sundry next-of-kin bashing our doors down?'

'Not a whisper.'

'Poor little mite. What kind of a person would do that to a kid?' Alana said, mirroring Paddy's serious expression as she reached for a mug. 'I've just come from seeing Rogene and it's not great news. No convenient dead body, or indeed bodies littering up the pavements, which means we have a problem on our hands.'

'Thanks.' Paddy raised his eyebrows, meaning anything but. 'So, nothing of use then?'

Alana added two heaped spoons of sugar and milk before taking a tentative sip. 'The best part of my Saturday by far and, no, nothing apart from the handwriting expert about word choice and use of punctuation, as in the writer knew how to wield a full stop.'

'Either well-read or well-educated,' he mused. 'Possibly both.'

'Also, someone who's fallen on hard times.'

'Why do you say that?'

Alana placed her mug down on her desk, her mind drifting back to last night. 'Because of the nature of Casey's clothes.

Washed within an inch of their life, even torn in places but beautifully repaired when fast fashion and cheap imports sounded the death knell on such practices years ago. I'd lay a pound to a penny that they're either second-hand or hand-me-downs.'

'Poor kid.'

'Not so poor, Paddy,' she said, with a note of rebuke. 'If the note is to be believed, someone is trying to protect Casey and poverty doesn't mean that she isn't loved or cared for. We only have to look at children born into wealth to know that money is no protection from the vagaries of their parents, but enough from me and my hobby horse. What have the team been up to?'

'Flynn and Lorrie have been looking through all our missing persons files, while I've concentrated on seeing if there have been any reports of bodies turning up minus any of their key parts. I hope you don't mind but I've also initiated a Black Notice with Interpol to broaden the search from Ireland to worldwide.'

'Good plan. And?'

'And nothing so far. The case is too sickening to contemplate.' He paused to take a bite from a chocolate-covered donut. 'I've saved you the jammy one.'

'Cheers. I don't know where we go from here, except more of the same until Rusty comes up with some DNA.'

'Or we find the bodies that go with the organs.'

FOURTEEN

Penny listened to the news on the small radio in the kitchen, the sound as high as she dared, the door closed despite the house rule. There were rules aplenty in the house, some were remnants from her childhood, some newer ones that held no rhyme or reason to anyone but him. The open-door policy was a nightmare. She never knew when he'd appear out of the blue, his feet silent in his well-worn smooth-soled slippers. His cadaverous head, the skin stretched taut, looming over her when she woke was the worst because she never knew how long he watched her sleep. What thoughts stole across his mind. What plans did he make to the sound of her snores.

She'd taken to wearing high-necked granny nightdresses and pants to bed, and singing in the toilet and the shower. Getting dressed and undressed was a skill she'd had to relearn, threading her arms and legs through her undies in the same way she'd used to do on the beach before her world had dissolved into the narrow frame of rules and retribution.

Oh yes, the retribution, when it came, was quick and merciless. A passing slap along with the threat of the iron. How she'd grown to hate that contraption, even though he'd never repeated the exercise: she'd never given him cause to. The loss of something dear to her. A treasured book picked at random from the motley collection she'd managed to put together from Salvation Army handouts. A favourite item of clothing among her ragbag pile in the old wormy wardrobe that had once housed her mother's possessions. Her child would have been next. It was there in the ensuing madness and the glare of his gaze every time he'd looked at her.

Her eyelids slipped closed a second, her ear close to the radio, the news items burbling in the background as she listened to the newsreader's report. The escalating cost of food and fuel. The latest from the Dáil. It was only when she heard the weather report starting that she pressed the off button and pulled the door open, before quickly shifting back to the table and the Irish stew he'd demanded for his tea. A scrag end of mutton begged from the butcher and a few past their sell-by date carrots, mixed up with half-decent potatoes that she'd managed to negotiate with the seller on Moore Street.

The stallholder had been rough, rougher than the last time. She could still feel the burning between her legs and pain on her breast where he'd grabbed her flesh between his teeth, branding her a whore if his rutting hips and low, grunting piggish groans weren't evidence enough of how low she'd sunk. The vegetable seller was fat and old – she couldn't bear to call him by his name – his belly slapping her thighs as his blackened fingers found purchase in the thin flesh over her bottom, driving in quicker and quicker, but with his wife hovering at the front of the stall, there wasn't time for the finesses. This was quick and dirty. Sex on the floor of his van amongst the smell of underripe bananas and rotting cabbage leaves, all for food and a ten euro note, which she'd stuffed up the lining of her sleeve. The only place she could think of that would be safe from greedy eyes. When the time came, when she had a few more euros squirrelled away – she knew she wouldn't survive another attack – she'd run.

'You're taking your time peeling those carrots,' he said, causing the knife to slip, the tip slicing through the top of her thumb, the blood pumping red and bright.

'See what you've done creeping around like that,' she managed, her hand under the running tap, her breath hitched with the sudden pain.

'Nothing to do with me and make sure you wash them properly. No point in wasting good food over a bit of blood,' he said, wandering out of the room, ignoring his breakfast, his dressing gown belt trailing behind him as he made his way back down to the cellar.

With a piece of kitchen roll wrapped around her thumb, she dropped into the kitchen chair and rested her head in her hands, the carrots forgotten. He hadn't asked any more about his niece. That conversation was now well and truly closed, and with no news on the radio or in the papers, she had to hope that they'd given up on trying to trace her whereabouts. Leaving her baby across town in a supermarket she'd never been to before had all been part of her plan and, along with the carefully penned note in her pocket, so far it seemed to be working. The thought of where the girl was and what she was doing was killing her, but she'd been desperate. She wouldn't lose her daughter too.

Penny couldn't believe how much her life had changed since the car accident that had killed her parents. Life had been good then, or what little of it that she could remember. She'd only been five at the time. Five was old enough to bask in the love of her mam and the adoration of her dad but too young to remember the finer points. There were no photos to prompt, no mementoes from those early days to remind her. Her grandparents had emptied the house and packed away everything for when she was older. She'd been twelve when she'd finally found the courage to climb up to the attic, a room she'd been forbidden to enter. It didn't take her long to realise they'd been lying. The attic was empty. No photo albums or pictures; and her dad had been an artist of some note. Nothing but dust balls and regret. Everything lost except the scantiest of memories. She owed her grandparents nothing but her everlasting hatred.

Taking the bag from the freezer and dumping it in the bin had been a fit of madness.

A cry for help.

Her biggest hope was that it would lead to their salvation. Her biggest fear was that he'd find out. She dreaded that day more than anything that had gone before.

FIFTEEN

Dr Colm Mack had poster-boy looks offset by a smattering of grey sprinkled through his hair, the only indication that he might be older than he first appeared. Forty-six last birthday, Alana recalled as she watched him step into the room and shrug off his heavy cashmere overcoat before taking the seat offered. The coat was new but not what it revealed; his sombre dress code of smart black suit and snowy white cuffed shirt and whichever silk tie came to hand were his daily uniform, but as it was the weekend, he'd swapped it for his usual choice of tailored jeans and button-down shirt with a round-necked cashmere jumper, this one in a complementary shade of blue.

His home was a five-bedroomed house situated in Dalkey's exclusive Knocknacree Park. Up to two years ago it had been one Alana had shared with him, comfortable in the thought that their marriage was for life. How wrong she'd been. She missed the views over Dublin Bay from the terraced garden, but the house had never felt like home. She was far more comfortable in her Kilmacud flat, in spite of the deficits in the garden department, and no views worth speaking of. When she'd left Colm, she'd left everything behind apart from her clothes. All the presents he'd bought over the years. All the artwork and knick-knacks they'd collected together. All the fancy kitchen equipment that he'd filled the cupboards with and expected her to use. Labour-saving devices that were anything but when you factored in how long they took to disassemble and wash after use.

There were still things she missed about her failed marriage, apart from the views, there were bound to be after a relationship that had spanned five years. The companionship and cuddles. Having someone to return home to of an evening instead of a cold and empty apartment. Lazing around in bed on a Sunday with coffee on tap, and the newspapers spread over the duvet as they swapped pages. The worst of it was she knew he'd have her back in an instant. The most difficult part for her was the fact she still loved him despite everything that had happened. She hadn't seen him in months, and she wouldn't have arranged to see him now if it hadn't been for his experience in childhood trauma and cognitive interview techniques.

Alana wasn't unnecessarily cruel. When she'd made the break, it had been a permanent one, with the lawyers left to negotiate the nitty-gritty of the split. There was no acrimony on her part. She'd entered the relationship with nothing and that's the way she wanted to leave it. With some savings in the bank courtesy of her grandparents, she'd put an offer in on the flat within days of being discharged from the rehabilitation unit. The divorce that followed had been a formality of dotting the i's and crossing the t's. The day she'd left the marital home was the true day of her emancipation, not the decree nisi, which she'd stuffed in a drawer when it had arrived. She hadn't looked at it since.

It wasn't easy to know how to act with him in front of a room full of colleagues. It also wasn't easy to know what to say. *Good to see you* when it really wasn't. *How are you?* when she could see for herself by the telling shadows under his eyes and new lines bracketing his mouth. *The weather* when it was the last thing on her mind.

She bypassed the usual social small talk for a more direct route. 'Thank you for agreeing to help us, Colm. You remember Paddy, Lorrie and Tatty? Good. Let me introduce you to Garda William Slattery, who's been seconded to us for a bit. We're about to have a quick catch-up.'

She poured him a coffee, adding only a splash of milk, just the way he liked it, before handing it to him, careful to avoid a clashing of fingers.

'Right then, let's get started.' She swivelled her chair sideways to face the room, her tablet lying flat across her palm, snagged in place by her thumb. 'Basically, we have three cases we're concentrating on currently, Colm, but it's only this last one that we need your input on. Casey is a toddler, two or thereabouts, who was found abandoned, in Clonabee supermarket yesterday. There's been no reports of a missing child and there's very little we know, apart from her first name, and this note we found in her coat pocket,' she said, pointing to the board and the image of the note. 'It's not to scale but you can get the gist.'

She watched him study the sheet before returning to the desk and retaking his seat, his gaze thoughtful.

'How was she?'

Colm had never been a man of many words, something she'd had to get used to when she'd moved in with him. Probably the cleverest man she'd ever get to meet, and one that always got right to the crux of the problem – at least where work was involved.

'Distraught, which I think is how most children would present if in a similar position.'

'Oh, not all but carry on. What else?'

Alana wasn't sure what he was getting at. 'Weepy and clingy. Wanting her mum.'

'And how did she appear? Well cared for or...?'

'Oh well cared for,' she said, relieved for the prompt as she had no idea what he was getting at. 'Her clothes were old, maybe even second-hand. Certainly, well-worn but clean as was she. A plump little thing too.'

'Okay. What about indications of abuse? Bruising. Cigarette burns. Slap or bite marks. Signs of sexual activity?'

Alana blinked, aware that Colm was only doing his job but still shocked by the way he'd expressed himself, his words stark and unadorned. The man came across as detached, neutral, almost uninterested. A discordant note in contrast to the image of Casey still strong in her head, and when she knew he had the capacity for strong feelings – otherwise why would he have responded to her call for assistance when his workload was as heavy as hers? She felt confused and suddenly out of her depth. Incidents of suspected childhood abuse had to be reported to the Garda Domestic Violence and Sexual Assault Investigations Unit, which meant that any dealings by her team were only cursory before being handed over to the experts.

'Absolutely nothing of that sort.'

'And what do you want from me?' he continued, crossing one denim-clad leg over the other. Relaxed and obviously in no hurry.

'We're not sure, to be honest,' Paddy said, coming to her rescue and relieving the tension with his usual impeccable timing. She'd have to return the favour at some point. 'The child's language skills are rudimentary, to say the least, and unlikely to be of any help in finding her parents, so anything really, any clues at all as to where we go to next.'

'I take it there's an obvious associated reluctance for any media involvement because of the note,' Colm said, angling his head towards the whiteboard.

'Exactly. So, do you think you can help? Gaby Mulholland should be dropping her off anytime shortly.'

Alana paused at the sound of running feet outside, accompanied by Gaby's Liverpudlian-hued voice. 'Stop, will you. I can't keep up.' And then. 'Little minx,' said in a much softer tone.

Casey launched herself at Alana, waiting to be helped into her lap before snuggling into her neck, Wabbit tucked under her arm. There were no words from either of them, just the creak from the wheelchair as Alana shifted to accommodate her passenger, conscious of Colm's stare.

'She's been fine, more than fine,' Gaby said, following on behind, Lara clutching onto her hand, her baby-fine mousy hair starting to touch her shoulders. 'Been playing all morning. We've lent her some more things to be going on with. I'll be waiting in reception. Take as long as you like. I have a bagful of cars and trucks to keep this one amused for however long it takes.'

'Thank you so much. We shouldn't be too long.'

Alana watched as Gaby surveyed the scene before making for the door, her mussed plait and reddened cheeks telling as to the busyness of her morning, a brief respite from Colm's continued glare.

There was no appeasing the man and there was no going back on their relationship. Her road to independence had been a long and hard-fought journey. One out-of-place smile or touch and it would all have been for nothing.

With a flick of her fingers she released the brakes and turned the chair to the door. There was too much to do to waste time on thinking about her relationship with her ex.

'This way, Colm.'

Alana had decided to use an empty office for Casey's psychiatric assessment, instead of one of the impersonal interview rooms with the table bolted to the floor. With Casey installed on her lap, there was no difficulty in persuading her to accompany them.

'Leave the talking to me, eh, Alana,' Colm said, shutting the door before reaching for Casey, his briefcase already open on the table, a writing pad and a pencil case beside it.

'I know how it works, but you don't know her and, more importantly, she doesn't know you,' Alana replied, shortly, as she started to free Casey's determined arms from her neck.

'I need you to do me a favour, love, and have a chat to my friend. He'd also like to meet Wabbit.'

'Wabbit?' Colm sounded slightly less confident than moments before.

'Yes. Her rabbit's name. Cute, isn't she?'

'A real stunner and such a pretty colour,' he said, clearly lying through his teeth at the sight of the dirty pink. 'Would you help me to draw a picture of Wabbit, Casey? I'm not very good at colouring,' he went on, fetching the blank pad and childish-looking pencil case.

In the days of their marriage, Alana had wondered why her middle-aged husband always carried a well-stocked Mickey Mouse pencil case in his briefcase, but she'd never got around to asking him. It had become a joke between them when he wasn't really the joking sort. Every Christmas came with a little packet of pencils or crayons. An easy stocking filler, which she hadn't thought of in over two years and she was determined not to dwell on now.

'What a good idea. We can pin it on the fridge at home,' she said, helping Casey to join Colm where he'd set up his art studio on the floor, a fat blue crayon held between his thumb and forefinger.

He shot Alana a startled look, but she wasn't about to explain herself. He'd lost that right a very long time ago.

'That's blue. Pink,' Casey said with a shake of her head, her chubby fingers searching in the pencil case for the right shade, her face scrunched up in concentration.

The ears came first, they nearly filled the top half of the page, followed by a scribble with no discernible features, all accompanied by Colm's gentle probing.

'She's a very special rabbit. Where did you find her?'

'Present.'

'From Mammy?'

'Mammy.' Her head never veered from the page, the pink crayon slashing across the rabbit's body with no consideration for keeping within the lines.

'I'd like a picture of your mammy. Could you do that for me, Casey?'

'This is a bit of a punt, Alana,' he whispered out of Casey's earshot. 'She seems pretty well developed for her age, but a little young for more than basic shapes and lines. What I'm hoping for is colourings and perhaps markings. Something that might help you in your search.'

He sat back on his heels, seemingly unaware of the damage he was doing to his designer jeans while he watched Casey again reach for the pencil case, the picture of Wabbit along with the pink crayon discarded in favour of the brown. A red scribble in the centre of the page followed by a blue larger one below. A pause, her tongue clenched between her teeth as she picked the orange crayon. Another scribble, this time at the bottom corner of the page.

'What a lovely drawing and what a pretty Mammy you have. You've drawn her hair beautifully,' he said, offering her one of his rare smiles. 'Do you have a cat by any chance, Casey?'

She nodded. 'Per.'

'Yes, that's right, sweetheart. Cat's go purr.'

She shook her head, her blonde curls flying. 'Cat Per.'

'Your cat's called Per?'

The drawings continued. The floor quickly filled with a random selection.

'What about where you live?'

A picture of a wonky square. One window and a hovering door ensued.

'Your bedroom. I bet it's blue.'

Two beds side by side followed, one larger than the other. Wabbit prominent in the trail of pink ears. No blue in sight.

And so, it continued, question after question disguised as the drawings piled up. Fists pressed into her eyes and skin bleached white were indication enough that, after an hour, the session was reaching its natural ending. They hadn't discovered much. Hardly anything at all as far as Alana was concerned. An address. A telephone number. A name. Nothing to fill her with any feelings apart from despair at who could do such a thing as abandon their child under any set of circumstances.

Back in the incident room, and with Casey safely in Gaby's competent hands, Alana pinned six of the seven drawings to the noticeboard, all except the first one of Wabbit, which she placed on her desk for later.

'Where's Paddy?' she asked.

'He decided to reinterview Aidan Crossey's neighbour, ma'am,' Flynn piped up, a grin lurking in the depths of his gaze. 'You know. The busybody with an eye on Crossey's bank bAlanace. Said something about sending a search party if he hadn't returned by teatime.'

'Did he indeed. That's just grand so it is,' she said, her words laced with sarcasm. They were short staffed as it was without him going over previously covered ground. She'd remember to have words with him on his return about wasting station resources.

'Right then, gather round as we don't want to squander any

more of Dr Mack's time.' Her voice reverted to neutral as she gestured for Colm to retake his seat, waiting a moment while he folded his frame into the black swivel chair before continuing. 'Thank you again for giving up your time to help us this morning, even if we haven't got the answers we were looking for.'

'Oh, I wouldn't say that, exactly. You need to remember that Forensic Art Therapy is used as a way to encourage the subject, through the medium of drawing, to reveal lived experiences without the risk of having to dwell on them during the process. With Casey, it's an even more useful tool due to her limited vocabulary,' he said, animated where before he'd appeared awkward and uncomfortable, which was understandable given the room full of strangers and his relationship history. 'The session had two purposes. Firstly, to observe Casey in a non-threatening and non-judgemental environment, where she's doing something that all children love: colouring. You remember her relaxed manner, Alana.' He glanced at her before scanning the room, in a way that she used to call *playing to the audience*. Now she knew it was his way of trying to elicit their sympathies. Good luck with that. The one thing she never did was dip into her personal life at work.

'Casey quickly acclimatised in my presence,' he continued, 'despite having only met me moments before. Indications are that she's a well-adjusted child who's used to the company of adults. She was quite confident in contradicting my colour choice for her rabbit. In this the drawings were only secondary to my assessment, but they still made up an important part of my review,' he said, making his way across the room to stand beside the wall of pictures, and causing Alana to reverse to make room.

'The drawing of her mother is telling. The way she dominates the page, positioned front and central, an important presence in Casey's life. Children of this age can't differentiate between body, arms and legs, but we can see the blue at the bottom, topped off with a red scribble for the body. Maybe she's wearing jeans. A lot of people do,' he added, with a wry smile. 'The cat is the one discordant note and, I think, significant. The way "Per", her name for him, barely makes the page. Unless she's scared of animals,' he pondered, seemingly lost in thought for a second. 'I'm not sure. It's not something that I've come across before. With people yes. Abusers and the like, but not animals.'

'What about the house?' Flynn said, pointing to the last picture and the black scribbles surrounded by a wonky square of red. 'I take it that's a window but what's behind?'

'Well spotted. Sorry, what's your name again?'

'Flynn O'Hare.'

'Well, Flynn, Art Therapy isn't an exact science and far more difficult to interpret the younger the artist. All I can say is that whatever lies behind the window is something that scares her. She certainly wouldn't tell us when I questioned her choice of crayon.'

'And the colour is important?'

Colm nodded. 'Outside of the fact young children prefer primary colours, probably related to red and green being the first they can recognise, very. You'll observe that it's the only black used across any of the drawings, which has to be viewed as significant. Some of the artwork produced by severely traumatised children has a complete absence of colour.'

He returned to his seat and folded his arms.

'Of course, it's all subjective until we know more.'

SIXTEEN

SATURDAY, 18TH DECEMBER, 10.15 A.M.

Aidan Crossey lived in a quiet avenue near Dublin Zoo, which featured solid, red-bricked houses built in the fifties and smart gardens. The sort of area where lawns were mowed once a week and washing only pegged out of sight of the road.

Paddy pulled into Crossey's drive, sitting a minute to survey the scene and finding very little to like in the cookie-cutter homes and identikit exteriors, so very different from his two-up, two-down rental in Stoneybatter, only a fifteen-minute walk away. Unlike Crossey, who'd bought the property with the proceeds from the sale of his parents' farm, Paddy had been renting his house ever since he'd started work, with the hope of one day being able to afford the quirky abode, which had character oozing out of every brick and joist. With the way the housing market was going, it was a hope he'd tucked away in a dark corner along with winning the lottery, owning a Porsche and other sundry unachievable dreams. Having his sister living with him was a huge help with the bills, money he religiously squirrelled away each month in a bank account marked *deposit*, but it was barely keeping abreast with the rise in inflation let alone making a dent in the €50,000 initial outlay he reckoned he'd need to secure a mortgage.

Instead of walking across the road to interview the woman in the house opposite, he decided to revisit Aidan's house, very different now the SOCOs had completed their investigations.

If a house could tell a story, he wondered what number six Chestnut Court's would be. He slipped his hand into his pocket and pulled on the pair of disposable gloves he always carried around with him, determined to find out. The first time he'd visited the place was when it had been brimming with members from the Technical Bureau, so many that he could barely find his way round let alone allow his mind to drift on a path of its own making. A pathway to the truth.

He'd always been that way. Eschewing noise and crowds in favour of silence. The quiet to think and the reason the house had dragged him back, even though there was a comprehensive report on his computer about the investigation into Crossey's disappearance. A report that had more gaps than a dentist's waiting room, he thought, pulling up a copy of the man's photo on his mobile. Not a recent one – Crossey hadn't been the sort for selfies and the like – but a true likeness, if his cousin was to be believed and there was no reason to think she was anything other than open and honest.

Paddy stared down at the broad, domed forehead with the swept-back hair and arrogant jawline. The thin lips and wide-spaced gaze. There was something about the name Aidan Crossey that struck a whole host of musical chords in his mind, but he'd swear he'd never seen him before. It was a joke back at the station that he never forgot a name, but as for remembering faces... He might as well go through the course of his day blindfolded for the notice he took of how people looked, which was probably a huge contributing factor to his lack of success with the opposite sex. At least that's what Tatty's theory was, but new hair dos and clothes weren't on his radar no matter how many times they were flaunted in front of him.

No. Faces were Alana's forte, not on the same level as a super recogniser, but not far off, which was another one of the reasons they worked so well together. She recognised them and he pulled their names out of that proverbial hat. It also helped that she never got snitty when he failed to comment on her appearance, but then he wouldn't even if he noticed, which was unlikely. Fear of saying the wrong thing to her was embedded in his veins, a deep-rooted anxiety that stemmed from their initial hostile working relationship.

Last night he'd given up his precious evening, checking his stack of notebooks instead of taking advantage of his sixty-inch television and the box of foreign language art-house movies that were his not-so-secret passion.

Keeping diaries was something he'd done since his mid-teens. Glossy copybooks full of illegible scrawls detailing what he'd had for his tea: cringeworthy information that he looked back on with horror. The glossy notepads had progressed to black-bound diaries and, instead of food, now he detailed the crimes he worked, entries that sat alongside less interesting aspects of his day. His sister thought him obsessional, but jotting down the name of the substitute hairdresser that had trimmed his hair three years ago when his regular barber had been off sick with glandular fever was normal enough behaviour, surely. However, after four hours of reading, he had to admit he'd never come across Crossey in either his day job or his free time, which left only one option: the years before he'd started keeping records. In other words, from his childhood.

Paddy entered the large hall with its reproduction Victorian mirror and black and white tiled floor, his footsteps ringing out in the empty house. It was easy to make an impression of someone from where and how they lived. The pet lovers with that particular scent of wet dog hanging in the air. The fastidious, with a place for everything. The hoarders. The *I don't give a shits to the house proud and show-offs*. He'd come across them all over the years. A melange of styles all merging into a big melting pot of indifference. His only interest in how they lived was in how it influenced the crimes against them. It was all about clues, and in the case of Mr Crossey, clues were the one thing they were short of.

The lounge echoed his impression of the hall. Neat and tidy. *Fastidious* was the report they'd had from Crossey's cousin and next-of-kin. *Obsessive* the term used by his former employee. Paddy could believe both as he surveyed the plain green carpet and matching velour sofa suite. The cushions had been left in an untidy pile in the centre, but he'd seen the photos. The meticulous angle of the plumped-up floral-covered pads, chosen to match the curtains. The books on display arranged in height order. The mantelpiece with a clock right in the centre. Nothing disturbed. Everything as he'd left it – almost as if he'd only stepped out of the room.

The kitchen came next. Old-fashioned cupboards that no housewife would be proud of, but with the same finicky touches in the lined-up tea towel on the bar of the oven. The inside of the fridge with all the labels facing outwards.

Back in the hall Paddy took out his phone, bringing up the report from Rogene and her team, his eyes scanning over the first six pages until he reached the bullet list of key points and the final conclusion drawn at the end. The officers present, the way the scene was processed. The list of items removed from the house for further processing were, at this stage, irrelevant.

- *No fingerprints or footprints in any of the rooms apart from the owner's.*
- *No discernible footprints found on the grounds. Please note the heavy rainfall the night of the disappearance hampered this process.*

- *No tyre tracks.*
- *No body hair, fluid or fibres that can't be traced back to the homeowner.*
- *No blood.*
- *Taking into account eye-witness testimony and the unmade bed, the top cover thrown off, we can deduce that Mr Crossey exited the property sometime between 10.15 p.m. and 7.15 a.m. – the usual time he collected his milk from the doorstep. There is no sign of forced entry and no sign that he was taken under duress. Also, no sign that this was a burglary gone wrong. His passport was found on the premises as well as his wallet, along with his bank cards. The wallet was found to contain forty euros.*

Basically, they'd just fallen short of not typing up what the whole of the station thought: that Aidan Crossey had gone to bed only to disappear into thin bloody air. Either that or the Martians had him.

Paddy shut off his phone and stuffed it back into his trouser pocket, a frown splitting his brow into a myriad of lines as he made for the stairs. The whole scenario was too depressing for words, and time was marching on. If he lingered any longer recapping on the case, he'd have Alana texting him to get his butt back to the office.

In the bathroom he found a box of hair dye in the cabinet above the sink next to a box of denture fixative. An array of aftershaves grouped together on the top shelf, some the same brands as he owned but never used. A reminder that a trip to the local charity shop was well overdue.

The bedroom only reinforced what Paddy had found in the bathroom. The wardrobe with carefully pressed clothes. Shirts and trousers folded into military creases. Socks paired. T-shirts grouped in order of colour. The book that he'd been reading was the first discordant note. The hardback placed face downwards on the bedside table, the bookmark ignored. Crossey didn't strike him as a man to ignore his little routines, unless something had happened to make him, something like an unexpected interruption for example, he thought – a stab of guilt blooming at the way he always turned down the corner of the page to mark his place – before shifting on to the other items on the table. The glass of water beside the book, still full, and a denture pot, which wasn't.

Paddy removed his notebook from his inside pocket and made a quick entry before moving back downstairs. The time of the abduction was important, but with no eye-witness account forthcoming, it was something they'd been struggling with until now. Now Paddy had a scenario building of a man heading for bed, his book tucked under his arm, his glass of water in his hand. A finickity man who'd spend time in the bathroom on his ablutions before making his way to bed, the house secure, the main lights off, the curtains closed. A vain man, if the hair dye was anything to go by, who'd leave his dentures in his mouth until he was about to go to sleep, which was probably early given his previous job as a newsagent: A man who followed his daily routines religiously.

So, something had disturbed him. Something to make him discard his book in annoyance. The sound of the doorbell? The ringing of his phone. No. They'd had the report back from the telephone company and his landline hadn't rung for days. Like most people he seemed to work off his mobile, which they'd also found at the scene and, also, like most people, he'd turned to *one two three four* when deciding on the four-digit code. Annoyingly, the iPhone held nothing of interest. No juicy emails or even juicier photos. Nothing, apart from seemingly innocuous texts and phone numbers, which they were laboriously chasing up back at the station.

Paddy descended the stairs, careful not to either brush

against anything with his jacket or touch anything with his gloved fingers. The additional paperwork was too much bother if, for some reason, the team had to return to carry out further checks.

The front door was dark brown with brass fittings, and with the addition of an eyehole, a useful security feature that Paddy wished more people would think of.

Still in character, he bent slightly, his eye in line with the peephole but not touching.

He's lying in bed reading while he prepares for sleep, only for the doorbell to disturb him. Ditching his book with a sigh of annoyance, he clambers out of bed and into his dressing gown without bothering with his slippers – they'd been found neatly arranged in front of the bedside table.

Paddy was only guessing at the dressing gown, but he seemed the type not to answer the door in his jammies. Once in the hall, he'd have had to switch on the outside light in order to check the peephole. Paddy eyed the light switch, conveniently situated on the right-hand side of the door.

It's dark and cold. The suburban street deserted at that time of night. He's not expecting anyone, but as it's someone he recognises, someone that he knows, someone that he trusts or at least someone he doesn't suspect of causing him immediate harm.

Paddy stooped down and carefully examined the threshold. Tons of staff had traipsed over the span of metal, destroying, and redistributing the evidence, and with Crossey in bare feet... It was useless. What they needed was to inspect the man's feet, but with no body there was little hope of that.

He pulled the door open and exited the house, ensuring that the door was securely fastened behind him before making his way down the path, his gaze examining the gaps and spaces between the brick paving, in the unlikely event that his colleagues had missed anything. They hadn't, which was no surprise at all, he muttered, lifting his head.

. . .

The house directly opposite was a mirror image of Crossey's, down to the small patch of lush green grass and absence of anything to provide character, apart from two carefully positioned Victorian-styled outside lamps, which he did approve of. Anything to detract the burglars and ne'er-do-wells that could be found in any city. Petty crime was on the up just as criminal convictions continued to drop, something which this homeowner had acted on. He only wished others would be as proactive. The gardai needed all the help they could get.

The door was opened after the first knock, the only delay was in the time it took the owner to unravel the security chain, another point in her favour. It made him wonder if she'd already guessed as to the reason for his visit.

'Yes?'

'Mrs Smith?' Paddy stopped, recognising the woman. 'Irene?'

'Hello, Paddy, I wondered if you'd show up. You'd best come in.'

There was nothing of the femme fatale about the woman he'd dated, albeit only the once. It was a disingenuous comment made by one of the younger guards, and completely misleading, Paddy thought as he followed her down the hall and into the bright and airy kitchen at the end, a room so very different from Crossey's pine nightmare that he blinked. White wood featured, clashing beautifully with butter yellow walls and blue accessories.

'Would you like a tea or a coffee, Paddy?' she asked formally, almost as if they were strangers.

'A black coffee, if you have it, but don't go to any trouble.'

'I won't. I was about to make myself one anyway.'

With that she turned her back and started messing about

with mugs and the like, providing him ample opportunity to study her.

Irene was tiny, barely five-foot, and with a thick head of glossy auburn hair framing her face. An understated look he found most attractive.

'There you go.'

'Thank you, that's very kind,' he said, taking a cautious sip before setting the mug back down.

There were plenty of things he'd like to ask her. About her change of name for one. Presumably there was a husband in the offing, but so far, he'd spotted nothing to support that. No ring on her finger. No men's shoes in the rack in the hall, or jackets mingled with her bright red fleece and conservative woollen coat on the hooks above.

Instead, all he said was, 'I'm here to follow up on your statement, in case you've remembered anything else?'

'No sign of him, then.' It was a statement more than a question and one he decided not to expand on apart from a brief *no*. Any trawl of the local papers would be saying the same thing.

She removed her glasses, rubbing the bridge of her nose between her thumb and forefinger briefly before resettling them back in place.

'I'm not sure what else there is to say. I noticed him shutting off his lights and pulling his curtains when I was putting out the bins, and the following morning when the curtains were still shut, and the milk left on the doorstep. That's it.'

'And that's his routine?'

'I really wouldn't know. It's not as if I'm at home a lot to notice. It's no more than a fluke that I happened to spot that much,' she said, with a frankness he believed despite inference made to the contrary by the guard who'd taken her original witness testimony. Irene wasn't the nosy type, and as for her being attracted to Crossey, a man twice her age. It was nonsensical.

'What are you up to now?' he asked, more interested than he should be. The last time he'd heard, she'd left her job and gone travelling and not a whisper since.

'Back at the Royal College of Surgeons, for my sins. Same old job.'

Her answer caught him off guard. Living and working in Dublin as long as he had he'd made a number of contacts among other professions that linked to his role as detective. Primarily lawyers but also social workers, probation officers and prison guards to name a few. Criminal Psychologists were also an important adjunct, co-opted onto the team when they needed a profiler on board. He'd only had dealings with Professor Weaver in that capacity after Irene had left, a backpack in one hand, a tourist guide to Europe in the other.

'Alongside the Prof?'

She inclined her head. 'The one and only.'

'How's he doing? I heard he was a little under the weather.'

'On sick leave but we're hoping he'll be back in the new year.'

'Well, I don't think there's anything else. Thank you again for the coffee, and if you do happen to remember something that might be of help...' He left the end of the sentence hanging, instead punctuating it by pushing one of his business cards towards her.

Back in the hall, he paused, a sudden thought pressing. 'Actually, before I go there is one thing. We might need the assistance of a profiler on another case we're working on, and as the prof is out of action?'

'You'd best have my card,' she replied, pulling open the drawer on the hall table and selecting one from the box. 'All my numbers are there.'

Paddy glanced down at the card with the name *Irene Burden* in blocky script, but before he could say anything she answered his question for him.

'Decided to go back to my maiden name. It was time.'

Paddy didn't exactly have an epiphany about Aidan Crossey when he climbed back into his car. As he started up the engine, his thoughts were taken up in their entirety on Irene and whether he had the nerve to ask her out. Dating a work colleague was something he usually avoided, but he couldn't rely on that as an excuse in this instance. They didn't share an office or an incident room. She didn't even work at the station, so there'd be no embarrassing moments waiting to jump out and catch him unawares. He liked her. He had no idea what she made of him – what man ever did – which was a risk he wasn't in the frame of mind to take currently with his workload being what it was.

Decision made to prevaricate, he flipped through the radio stations on the panel above the heater to find a channel with something to keep his mind busy while he tried to banish thoughts of Irene. The news should do it.

'The gardai are increasingly concerned about the whereabouts of Fergal Cunningham. The thirty-year-old prison guard was last seen leaving his house along Ballinteer Gardens at eight a.m. yesterday morning. Anyone with information as to Fergal's whereabouts are asked to contact Ballinteer Garda Station on 01...'

Fergal Cunningham. The key fit the lock. He didn't even have to bother turning it for a whole host of memories to be released, tumbling over themselves in their need to be heard.

He hadn't thought of him in fifteen years or more. Tall, lanky and with a shock of dark red hair that was the bane of his life. They'd been in the same year at school but that's where the similarities ended. Fergal had been sporty, unlike Paddy, who'd been part of the geek brigade. Instead of bothering with his studies, Fergal could be found on the football pitch kicking a ball around, rain, hail or snow. Paddy, on the other hand, was allergic to sport, all sport.

His interest in foreign language films had stemmed from his love of musical theatre and a talent for languages. If he'd been able to act, he'd have loved nothing more than to try for The Abbey Stage School, but that wasn't to be.

Of course, it might not be the same bloke, he thought, indicating left before pulling into the traffic at the end of the close.

Fergal Cunningham wouldn't be that unusual a name for these parts. Probably relatively common.

But it wasn't the name that had his neurones firing up. It was the man's link to Aidan Crossey.

SEVENTEEN

SATURDAY, 18TH DECEMBER, 10.15 A.M.

Penny couldn't decide which she hated most. The cellar or the front bedroom.

The cellar was out of bounds. The thick wooden door was locked when he was out roaming the streets and bolted from the inside when he was 'working'. He'd even added seals to the frame to stop sound filtering through the gaps, but it hadn't helped. Thankfully the screaming had stopped sometime overnight. A week of wails and moans interspersed with the most horrific cries. Now silence reigned supreme, which was somehow worse.

He'd disappeared after she'd sliced her thumb and she hadn't seen him since, his breakfast left to congeal on the table. She'd tried banging on the door but there'd been no response. With her ear pressed to the panelling she could hear the dull thrumming of the saw, the wood vibrating against her cheek. Pause and stop. Pause and stop. She knew what he was doing. That's what scared her the most and the reason she'd decided to abandon her baby girl. The risk was too great as was the thought that his madness could be catching.

It had to be madness that flowed through his mind. She'd

never raised a hand or her voice to her child, but that hadn't stopped the idea creeping in from the sides. Memories from the past hurtled through the walls of her mind, walls that crumbled to dust, walls that offered no protection from the destructive beasties inside her head.

At one time normality had dominated their home but that had been a long time ago. Before the death of her parents, in a freak car accident with no one to blame, and before her grandparents had offered her a home but not her fourteen-year-old brother. Hell would have had to ice up first before they'd ever accepted Penny's half-bother as part of their little family. The progeny of their son-in-law, though they'd never admit that relationship to anyone. The free-spirited artist who'd been at the steering wheel of the car when their beloved daughter had been killed.

Penny often wondered if her life would have been different if she'd been fostered too, instead of the protected life she'd had to endure. It's unlikely she'd have dropped her knickers quite so quickly when faced with Doug's overtures. She also rationalised that her pregnancy had been the catalyst. The start of Danny's descent into madness simply because he was as powerless to help her as he was himself. At the time he'd been struggling to find work. No one wanted someone with no qualifications. The only thing that kept him off the streets was a surplus of friends, other lost boys he'd been fostered with and had managed to keep in touch with over the years.

When she'd fallen pregnant, he'd gone round to their grandparents to plead on her behalf, and they'd laughed in his face. This inability to help was the crux and the only reason she'd decided to return with him to the grandparents' home when he'd persuaded her as to their change of heart about their great-granddaughter. If she hadn't fallen pregnant. If she hadn't told her grandparents in the naïve belief that they loved her too much to abandon her to her fate. If none of that had happened, he might still be normal.

The front bedroom faced onto the street, the large bay window a feature in the otherwise airless, drab room. The wallpaper was a dull yellow with black mould seeping over the faded pattern: a pincer movement she had neither the money nor wherewithal to stop. The mahogany bed was the main feature. Bought when her grandparents had first moved into the house on their marriage. The mattress stained and bare. The mattress where her mother had been conceived. The mattress she couldn't bear to look at.

Her grandparents sat either side of the window in chairs dragged up from the lounge, their aged faces crumpled and lined. The smell of the embalming fluid heavy, oppressive, overpowering.

The daily ritual had begun. The closing of the curtains to stop prying eyes. The sprucing up in preparation for the day. The changing of their clothes even though there was little point. The caring when that was the very last attitude they'd shown her. She wasn't a nurse. She didn't have any room left for the charity it would take to feel compassion for the two people she despised the most. All her heart and soul were for her baby girl. What was left was duty laced with a heavy dose of fear because she knew what her brother was capable of.

While there might once have been the same blood flowing through her grandparents' veins all that was left was cotton wool and straw bound together with wire and thread. There was no relationship, no love and there never had been. Any initial acts of presumptive kindness had only been meted out in the presence of others.

Penny wasn't either gentle or rough, more ambivalent with a thin layer of disgust. Her movements were firm, decisive, quick as she released them from their bindings and removed their shirts and jumpers... It was a job he made her do; she didn't know why, and she hadn't felt able to ask. The one time she'd broached the subject of why he'd chosen to keep their skin alive instead of leaving them for the maggots, she'd received a punch to the face, which had the desired effect of shutting her up. If she'd have to guess she'd say it was fashioned from the need to deprive them of the only thing they craved: a free pass into nirvana. After all, they'd spent long enough putting in the groundwork with their overt do-gooder charity efforts. Having an unwed mother for a granddaughter would have had them running to the priest in despair, if they hadn't decided to remove the problem first.

After, she redressed them and rearranged their hair, then she pulled back the curtains, the weak winter sun surprisingly light after the dim room.

There were no words of goodbye. No see you later. She folded up the discarded clothing before making for the door and pulling it closed behind her. The chore done. He'd be up later to check on them, to check that she'd done what he demanded. Until then her time was her own.

She scraped the remains of his breakfast into the bin, her thoughts returning to how she could free herself. He'd told her often enough what he'd do to her if she disobeyed him. The burn mark on her back, the skin puckered into an ugly rash of welts, the scar joining the other medley of disfiguring wheals that were older but no less painful. All of her resistance had been beaten out of her. She was planning her escape but for now she had to stay. The only thing that mattered was the safety of her child. She'd do anything and everything to prevent history repeating itself, her mind drawing her back into a past she rarely visited.

'Come out of there, Jasper. If they find us up here we'll be in big trouble.' Penny crawled under the eaves, her hands extended to pick up the fat ginger cat, who didn't want to be picked up.

'There, that's better. We have to be quick. They'll be back soon,' she said, hugging the warm squirming body before letting him run on ahead and take a flying leap onto the landing below. She followed more slowly, taking the short ladder one step at a time unaware of the cobweb clinging to the back of her jumper.

The attic had been a disappointment, another one of the many lies they'd told her over the years. She'd found nothing belonging to either her mother or her father, not even a scrap of wedding photo or the chest of old, mouldy, long-discarded clothes she'd been hoping for.

Penny knew she should be thankful that they'd taken her in – they told her often enough that most people wouldn't have been so charitable – but she wasn't. How could she be when they treated her so badly? There was money enough for the things they wanted. New outfits and hats to wear to church. Bookcases full of the kind of reading material her grandfather thrived on, but never the money for the basics like school clothes or shoes. Having to rummage through the bin at the church for castoffs when all her friends were taken to Hickey's Outfitters in Wexford Street, twice a year, to be kitted out with everything they needed.

She wandered down the hall and into her bedroom, small and pokey when she could have had the larger room at the front, her mother's room. There were no tears on her face or disappointment in her demeanour. *When you hope for nothing then you'll never be disappointed.* Her grandmother's words not hers.

Jasper was nowhere to be seen but that was nothing unusual. He hated her grandparents nearly as much as she did, and had learned the hard way to remain scarce whenever they were around. The garden was his home, and the shed on a cold night. It was a rare occasion she got to sneak him into the house.

The sound of the front door had her scampering across the room to the small, battered table and chair that she had to use as a desk and where her untouched homework sat.

'Penny.' Her grandmother's singsong voice sounded from the bottom of the stairs, a sure sign there was trouble brewing.

'Coming.' Penny couldn't bring herself to call her Gran or Granny. Instead, she got around it by calling her nothing.

She found her in the kitchen, divested of her felt hat and woollen coat, a cup of tea brewing. 'There you are. How's the homework coming on?'

'Not finished yet but I will be by teatime.'

'Remember, dear, we call it supper in this house.' Her voice changed, hardening into a thick rasp, which caused Penny to stiffen. 'Turn around?'

Penny turned. She'd learned a long time ago, within weeks of arriving at the house, that the worst thing possible was to disobey her.

'I know where you've been and I know where you're going.' Her singsong voice was back but accompanied by bony hands grabbing at her shoulders and pushing her out of the kitchen and into the hall, the cellar door gaping open. 'You never learn, child, but then why am I disappointed? Not with a father like yours. Your mother could have had anyone she wanted and yet she threw herself at a useless scoundrel. Your father. Her murderer.'

The cellar was cold and dark. Empty, apart from dusty wine bottles that never got drunk and a thin leather whip hanging up on the wall.

'Jumper and skirt off, dear. You know the drill. Naughty girls need to be taught a lesson.'

Penny didn't speak, she couldn't. She stood there shivering in her thin vest and knickers, arms folded across her chest, her fingers biting into the skin on her arms, her legs set apart, her toes digging into the cardboard insoles that lined her shoes to stop the water from coming in.

'Lift up your vest, dear. Bare skin so you don't get your vest dirty.'

For dirty read blood, blood she'd been forced to wash out in the little sink in the corner of her room.

She didn't cry or yell, not like the first or the second time. That only fed the anger and prolonged the suffering, the promised three of the best turning into five or more.

After, she stood still, her hands clawing around the thin fabric of her vest, her face the pallor of the dead, apart from twin spots of red in her cheeks.

'What do you say, dear?'

'Thank you.'

EIGHTEEN

'I think we've got another one.'

'You think we've got another one of what?' Alana said, manoeuvring her chair back so that she could stare up at him. 'Sorry, I don't get you.'

Paddy had decided to collar her as soon as he returned to the office, his expression and body language a clear warning to Alana that he was about to tell her something she didn't want to hear, or maybe it was a remnant of his displeasure at her having called in Colm to assist them when there were plenty of other child psychiatrists that came with none of the baggage he did. Her ex was a nuisance, but as her junior, he wasn't in a position to mention it.

'Another missing person related to the case.'

'What the...?'

'No, listen up a sec,' he said, broadening his audience by sweeping a glance around the room, his voice slightly raised. 'Did anyone hear about the missing man on the radio earlier? No. Really,' he added, amazed at the sight of the shaking heads. 'I thought listening to the news was something that all guards did but obviously not. Anyways, happens I know him, or I did that is if it's the same bloke. Fergal Cunningham. In my year at school.'

'And how is that relevant to the case?' Alana interrupted. 'People go missing all the time. You know that as well as me. The likelihood is that he's had a row with his missus, and he'll turn up later with his tail between his legs and a headache to rival yours.'

'Not when they're prison guards, they don't. I would have hoped by now that you had a little more faith in me than that,' he finally said, clearly annoyed and not bothering to hide it. How she knew about the slice-and-dice operation currently shredding his brain into wafer-thin slivers was another matter entirely.

Paddy liked Alana as a boss because she was both hard-working and dedicated. She was also smart, which for a detective wasn't a given. He'd worked with far too many muppets over the years to realise that. However, on occasion, like now, she could make him feel ten inches tall. Normally, he'd let it slide over his head. After all, everyone was allowed to have an off day. He was pretty sure that's what he was going through himself – an off day of his own making, and all because of that third beer. Perhaps he was finally growing up. Perhaps he'd taken one too many digs over the two years they'd been working together that he'd finally decided to bite back and bugger the consequences. Perhaps...

'Sorry, Paddy. That came out all wrong,' Alana said, putting an abrupt halt to his internal dialogue. 'I'll make sure to reset my bitch button when I get a chance. Carry on, I really am interested in this Fergal Cunningham. Do you remember him too, Tatty?'

'Different school and year,' she said from the other side of the room. 'Brothers and nuns. Never the twain and all that.'

Paddy was pleased of the short conversational break while

he swallowed back his mood, harder to do than he imagined given that he was usually a little left of laid-back.

'The news item said that he was last seen leaving his house yesterday at eight o'clock, but that's not the reason for my interest,' he said, tucking his hand inside his pockets, his fingers curling around his phone. 'I remember him, you see. We were school mates for a while. With both of our dads coppers it was something the parents encouraged. Then his parents split up and things went a bit haywire for him. I don't remember the details. To be fair, at that age I probably never knew them. Anyway, he was placed in emergency foster for a bit before being adopted. After that we lost touch. In fact, I'd forgotten all about him until this morning's news item.'

He knew she was getting bored; he was getting bored, but the story had to be told his way for all the ends to tie together into a bow of understanding.

'To cut a long story short he was with his foster family for about six months before being placed. I was invited round a few times. A bit of a madhouse with more kids than sense but the mum was nice. I never did get to meet the dad. They had an older son living away but I think I might have met him the once, and what felt like fifty youngsters, but in reality was probably about five. Surname of Crossey.'

'You're sure about this, Pad?' Alana said, taking control of the conversation.

Alana didn't doubt that Paddy believed in the link between Aidan Crossey and this Fergal Cunningham. She'd seen many examples of his phenomenal ability to recall names over the last two years but that didn't change the reality of cross-party workings. Turf wars were as common in policing as they were in crime gangs, and she couldn't just ring the lead detective on this case without first going through Ox Reilly. So many hoops and with little guarantee that they wouldn't be wasting their time. There was a lot of leg work to get through before they could be sure that Cunningham hadn't decided to do a bunk for whatever reason. The one thing she couldn't afford was to waste time when the likelihood was that they had a serial killer on the loose.

Alana curled her fingers around the padded arm of the chair – Rusty's report had removed any doubt of what they were working with. Someone who'd indiscriminately butchered at least two individuals, possibly more, and the reason she was determined to keep that fact confined to the police station for as long as possible.

For some unknown and incredibly bizarre reason the media and the general public differentiated between rapists, paedophiles and serial killers. The former two were societal misfits and miscreants who deserved everything coming to them and more. Serial killers, however, were in a special class of their own. Stuck on a pedestal with mini-series and book deals galore. Alana couldn't comprehend it because as far as she was concerned, they were equally evil: society's substrata band of dross. So far, the gardai had managed to keep the gory findings to themselves, but that wouldn't last. Someone somewhere always blagged to the wrong person about things like this, either intentionally or by mistake. It only took one wrong word in the wrong ear for the vultures to be banging on their doorstep, shoving microphones in their faces. They were lucky they'd got away with it for so long.

'As sure as I can be,' Paddy said, shrugging his shoulders.

He looked like he was about to speak again, but Alana lifted her hand to stop him. She needed a moment to think this new development through, and how she was going to play it, especially in light of Reilly's draconian management style. He'd be the first to stop her because the truth was he was determined to see her fail just as she was determined to succeed.

'Okay, let's back up a bit. What happened around at Crossey's? You were going to speak to the neighbour?'

'Ah. About that. I have a bit of a confession to make.'

Alana paused in the act of retying her hair, unsure of where he was going with this but fearing the worst.

'You know how Reilly feels about profilers?'

'Ah. As in: "All they are is jumped up, overeducated pricks with no common sense and no clue as to the criminal mind, profilers"?' she said, mimicking the DS's tone and expression exactly, an extraordinary skill that she'd discovered by accident the first time she'd tried karaoke.

Paddy laughed. 'That's them. I've said it before, but you do know you're wasted in the Guards.'

'Perhaps at one time,' she said, tapping the arm of her chair, her lips pulled into a lopsided smile as she changed the subject. Sympathy was the last emotion she looked for in others. 'So, what's this about a profiler? I was thinking about contacting the prof.'

'No point, he's still on long-term sick leave but, luckily for us, Crossey's neighbour just so happens to be Irene Burden that was and is again, I might add.'

'Our Irene, from the Royal College of Surgeons?'

'The one and only,' he said, his suddenly neutral tone causing Alana to eye him over the top of her laptop before dropping her head to hide her smirk. It felt good to confirm her suspicion that her number two had the hots for the delectable doctor, even though it wasn't the time or the place for such thoughts.

'Okay. We'll invite her to drop by the station on Monday, although, with no clues, no body as such, no suspects and absolutely nothing to go on we're probably barking up a gumtree without a paddle in sight.'

'Surely that's a crime against idioms, or is that metaphors?' he said, frowning.

'I can never remember. Next, you'll be insisting I use the Oxford ruddy comma, Pad.'

'If only I knew what it was.'

With that, she logged on to the system and opened her emails. 'Oh good. An email from Rusty. He wants me to phone him ASAP. I wonder what's so urgent?' she added, her tone suddenly full of concern. 'Hope it's nothing to do with Casey.'

'Unlikely. Didn't Gaby say he'd had to drop into the office briefly to pick up some file or other he'd forgotten? He probably checked his messages while he was at it,' Paddy said with a gleam, adding, 'I always get a bit worried when pathologists talk about taking their work home.'

'Ha ha, very funny, not,' Alana replied, flicking through her contacts before making the call.

'Hi, Rusty, I'm just going to pop you on loudspeaker, as Paddy's with me.'

'Another boring old fart with no idea what to do with his Saturday, I see,' Rusty said with a chuckle.

'Thanks a bunch, Rusty. I'll have you know I'm missing out on an afternoon showing of Fellini's *La Dolce Vita* at the Irish Film Institute to be here.'

'Rather you than me, mate,' Rusty replied, his chuckle drying up only to be replaced by what Alana recognised as his serious voice.

Her worry escalated.

'Casey's okay, is she?'

'Far as I know. Gabriella was planning on taking her into Dunnes for a bit of retail therapy.'

'That's good of her.'

'Not a bother. Lara needed a few things.' By the sound of his voice, he was obviously only going through the motions, his mind clearly on other things. *'I wouldn't dream of bothering you on a Saturday, but something's come up, something confusing if I'm honest.'*

'Go on.'

'I had to pop back into the office for some notes and I decided

*to check up on a few things while I was at it, which included the
results of the DNA on those organs you very kindly sent my way.
I had a few minutes, so I added them to the DNA database along
with the results of Casey's buccal swab. The thing is, they're a
match.'*

Alana looked across at Paddy, her mouth gaping until she
realised and snapped it shut.

'What do you mean they're a match?'

*'Just what I said, I'm afraid. Casey is a blood relation to both
sets of organs found by Dr Gaunt. Sadly, the database didn't
come up with anything else of use. In fact, the only match was
with the girl, and as we haven't been able to identify her as yet.'*
His voice stalled briefly before continuing. *'You do know what
this means, don't you?'*

Alana's stomach clenched and her mouth dried, moisture
pooling in a sudden sheen of sweat on her brow, her thoughts
swinging to Casey and what was coming next.

*'If someone has killed already, there's every chance that
they'll want to tidy up any witnesses floating around, even if that
happens to be a small child.'*

NINETEEN

SATURDAY, 18TH DECEMBER, 6.00 P.M.

The telephone rang as soon as she got home. She could hear it trilling as she inserted the key in the lock and pushed the door open, Casey racing past her.

'Hello?'

'I really think I should come over. It's not safe on your own.'

Alana raised her eyes heavenwards before dropping her gaze to where Casey was sitting on the rug in front of the television, the remote in her pudgy hand, totally unaware of the panic her presence was instilling.

'Paddy, we've already discussed this.'

'But.'

'No buts. No one knows where she is, and even if they suspect what's happened, they certainly won't guess that some random guard has taken it into her stupid head to look after the little girl until her parent is found.'

'But what if she's been followed. Anything could…'

'Enough already. We can't and won't be going down that road until it's a fait accompli,' she said, lowering her voice. 'I'm ending the call and going to pour myself a ruddy large gin.

You'd be advised to do the same. Have a good evening. See you on Monday.'

She didn't wait for a reply. Instead, she headed for the kitchen, looking for something to eat from the bag of food which Casey's mystery shopper had seen to supply her with.

It was a long time since Alana had eaten fish fingers, so long that she couldn't remember the last time. It was also something she wasn't going to be making a habit of. She dipped the end of one of her pieces of fish in the chilli relish she'd added to the side of her plate, all the time watching as Casey wolfed down her portion. She'd opted for an early tea instead of the gin she'd bragged about, but there would be time for that once the child was tucked up in bed in her new pink unicorn pyjamas.

By seven they were both on the sofa, Wabbit between them. Gaby had suggested seven as a good bedtime, and this had been what Alana was working towards as she started on one of the storybooks that she'd found in the Dunnes carrier bag along with the new pyjamas and a couple of sets of day clothes. One book had become two, but she was comfortable and warm. She couldn't define the feeling. It wasn't quite pleasurable, the sudden burst of joy that all was well with the world, when clearly it wasn't. The feeling was more than that. The sense of achievement at the end of a long and tiring day. The warmth of the squirming body tucked into her side. The smell of freshly washed hair tickling her chin. Even the sensation of a full belly. It was those things and more. It was also a shock of an emotion. An imposter sneaking up on her. A reminder of the last time she'd allowed a breach of her carefully erected defences and the catastrophe that had followed.

Alana viewed herself as one of those wretched people doomed to a life of mediocrity. She'd never felt the need to have a man to define her or a particular drive to have children, until she found herself pregnant. Now that she'd lost both, work made up a huge volume of her life. Not that she needed to be happy in her role, only assured that she was performing at the high standard she expected. Wasn't it chancing fate to even think about allowing happiness back in the fold?

The crash when it came was loud, unexpected and scary given that Alana was stuck on a squidgy sofa, and out of reach of a weapon, even her phone, which she'd left charging in the kitchen.

'What the...?' Alana stopped short, instead swallowing the expletive along with the ball of fear lodged in the back of her throat, contentment forgotten. Why the hell hadn't she taken Paddy up on his offer of acting guard dog? The sofa wasn't long enough to accommodate his rangy frame but surely that was his lookout.

'You stay there and look after Wabbit.'

She grabbed the arms of her wheelchair, heaving her body across the short distance, cracking her hip against the side of the metal arm in the process. The fact that she couldn't feel any pain from the waist down didn't offer any consolation as she swivelled around to face the patio door. There'd be a bruise tomorrow, a reminder of what a fool she'd been.

She hadn't bothered to pull the curtains. The patio door was firmly closed against the cold weather. The flat was well insulated and the small garden bounded on all sides by six-foot walls. Tall enough to deter all intruders, except four-legged ones with a penchant for leaping from the top and tipping over both of the chairs in the process.

The cat was all eyes in a far-too-skinny orange body behind the glass door. Alana didn't know much about animals, hardly anything, but she was able to recognise when one was in difficulty.

'Look, Casey, we have a visitor,' she said, going to the door only to stop, her hand on the latch, astonished at the scream emanating from the child.

'No. No. No...'

'Casey, what is it? It's all right. It's only a stray. A dog-tired little puss by the look of things.'

But Casey was beside herself, her hands to her ears, her eyes scrunched closed, her body bent double, Wabbit discarded on the floor, for once forgotten.

Alana tried to remember her words about the orange blob. Per. That was it.

'The cat's nothing to be frightened of.' She went to the child and pulled her up into the chair, ignoring the ache in her arms and the way Casey was hiding: her face pushed into her side, her small body trembling with what must be a very real fear.

'It's not your cat. It's not Per. Come on. Have a look and see for yourself. It's a poor ol' thing getting soaked while we're warm and cosy. Let's give him some milk, and if you're still scared, I'll make him go away, I promise.'

A promise that was very easy for her to make, less easy to execute if the girl was truly terrified. Colm would know what to do. The thought pinged only to be relegated in the delete bin. There was no way she was going to contact her former husband, not even if her life depended on it.

The cat had slunk into a corner, his fur glued to his skin from the sudden shower of driving rain pelting his back. There was nowhere for him to hide and no way for him to escape now both chairs were upended. Cold. Wet. Pathetic and, like Casey, in need of a little love and attention. Instead of making for the patio door, Alana did an about turn and made for the kitchen and the leftover fish fingers from her plate, which she mashed up with a fork.

'There, you hold this for me, love. I can't manage the chair and the plate,' she said, her voice firm now the screams had stopped. It was all very well being scared of your demons, but there had to be an honest threat and, as far as Alana could tell, the cat appeared far more terrified of them than they could ever be of him.

'Right, hand me the dish and jump down.' She watched as Casey followed her gentle instructions, one eye on the cat and the way it was following the bowl with his large luminescent eyes, seemingly placated at the idea that it wasn't her cat. Interesting.

'That's right. Now, pop the dish by the door and go and fetch Wabbit while I open the door and let him in. You see. Nothing to worry about, eh. Once he's been fed up, he'll be a handsome boy, won't you, fella? You can stroke him if you like,' she said, running her fingers over the bumps of his vertebrae with a gentle hand, her mind running to thoughts of a litter tray and the like. 'Poor puss. I wonder what your story is.' And then. 'No, scratch that. I really don't.'

'Not Per?'

'No, definitely not,' she said, adding the question of the girl's cat to the list of oddities about the case. What on earth had Per done for her to be so scared of it was a question she currently had no answer for. 'In fact, we do need a name. Any ideas?'

'Goose.'

Alana's hand paused a second before resuming her rhythmic stroking, the animal pushing up against her palm before pulling away and concentrating on his plate. She'd been thinking more of Saffron or Marmalade in deference to his colouring, but Goose it was.

It was late but the gin was cold, the ice chinking around the slice of lemon as she held the glass up to the light before taking a small sip, the silence of the room enveloping her in a cloak of steel. A prison for some but not her. She liked music as she did the television but there was a time for both. With Casey in bed, she wanted a cocoon of quiet while she worked on the puzzles laid out in front of her, her notepad off to one side, copies of Casey's drawings spread out in a halo of colour.

Sleep had stolen in when the little girl was still on the sofa, the newly named cat pressed up against her, Wabbit for once forgotten in the thrill of having the cat next to her, her fear forgotten. Alana ignored the guilt about teeth-cleaning. Once wouldn't matter as she lifted the child into her arms before negotiating the door into her bedroom and the travel cot, the cat slinking by her side before jumping up and settling on the foot of her bed. She eyed him uncertainly, but what harm would there be in him staying in her room? As long as he was toilet trained...

Three cases. Two irretrievably linked by the latest information about the genetic association between the bag of body parts and the little girl. The information was useless in its current state, as they had nothing else to hang to it and no way of finding out more. Organised crime was her first thought. Dublin had its fair share of drug cartels slicing up the streets, but how did that involve Casey?

Staring down at her empty pad her only thought was that, as cases went, it was a disaster. They had no starting point to work from. No sight of the parent/guardian deserting the child. No DNA matches on the system apart from the link between the organs and the girl. Not even a body, or two, as she remembered what Rusty had said about the offal belonging to different victims. They didn't even have any suspects. No one to pick up and interview. No one to read their rights to. No one to interrogate. What they had was an unreliable witness with a warning note stuffed in her pocket, seven drawings and an alarming aversion to a cat called Per. They needed more, more information and more time, but with Ox on her heels and the media looming, there was no chance of that.

There was also Crossey's disappearance to consider, a more boring man it would be hard to find. Everyone had a good word to say about the former newsagent, from his previous employee who'd helped him behind the counter, to the customers who'd frequented his shop. A man who went to Mass three times a week, and walked in the Dublin mountains in between times. His neighbour, Irene, had reiterated as much in her statement. For a man like that to dissolve into the middle of the night, and without a clue left at the scene... And then there was Fergal Cunningham to consider...

The ringing of the phone interrupted her thoughts.

'Hello, is that Detective Mack?'

'Speaking.'

'Sorry for the lateness of the hour. It's Molly Stein, the duty social worker. It's just to let you know we've found a temporary foster family for little Casey. They have the added advantage in being experienced in all sorts of childhood trauma. The only downside is that they have a farm over in Glendalough. A bit out of the way but—'

'No, not at all. Thank you for all your trouble, and the Wicklow Mountains will be ideal. All that fresh air,' she said when what she was really thinking was the importance of tucking the child out of sight and out of harm's way until they actually had a bleedin' clue what was going on.

She returned the phone to its cradle after arranging for the social worker to pick Casey up from Gaby's tomorrow. A cowardly act but one she wasn't going to waste any time mulling over. In a day or two the girl would have forgotten all about her.

Alana felt a wave of dark despair flashing across her consciousness, the black demon of her inner mind pushing into the foreground. Depression had been her constant companion since the accident, more faithful than her best friend or any of her colleagues. More demanding than her boss. More damaging than her physical disability. It was always lurking in the background, happy to spread nebulous insecurities like litter on a windy day. This late in the evening, after her brief spell of contentment, it was a war she was too tired to battle, not with a glass of gin bubbling away in her system and the truth laid out before her; the truth that everyone left. Alana had read somewhere, probably in a magazine in her doctor's waiting room, that it was the chemicals in her brain holding her hormones to ransom, but that didn't make it any easier to navigate. Sertraline had only been of limited help. After all, it wasn't a powerful enough drug to turn back the clock and make her legs better, which was the only result that could ever make a difference.

It was too late to work but she still took the time to gather the pictures into a neat pile, placing them on top of her notepad, the pages unmarked. Pristine white. She hummed and hawed over the patio door, weighing up the threat of an intruder over the possibility of a little present left by the cat in the morning. She finally slid the bolt closed and, for once, shut the curtains.

TWENTY

Penny woke and stretched, savouring the final seconds under the nest of blankets before sounds from below had her hurrying out of bed, scrabbling into her clothes under her nightdress, flinging it off and stuffing it under her pillow. It was raining again, a glancing thought as she fastened the top button of her jeans, before whipping back the curtains and staring out of the steamed-up windows onto the road below, puddles forming in the pits and dips of the pavement that ran parallel to their front garden. She called it garden, an optimistic term for the bare stretch unlike her neighbour's impeccable lawn and paved driveway. The only benefit, or disadvantage depending on which side of the fence you were on, was the extensive grounds surrounding the property and the distance from the only other house on the road. She'd been able to let Casey run amok without fear of disturbing the neighbours. It also meant that the house was effectively soundproofed from prying ears, which wasn't so good.

Before she ventured downstairs, she took a moment to check the bottom of her wardrobe to see if he'd found her hiding place. She had money, a growing stash from her fumblings, but that was her security net, her means of escape if and when she finally built up the courage and the funds to leave. When she was completely sure that her daughter was safe. When the threat to her life became too great. She'd starve before she touched a cent for food.

She didn't know what had happened to her grandparents' savings. The last time she'd asked had ended with a black eye, but an empty table would have the same result and, as the cupboard was bare.

The freezer. She had a dim recollection of a loaf of bread and possibly some bacon, enough to placate the twitchiest of fists.

The freezer was another thing she despised, along with Jasper, the cellar, and the front bedroom. It lived in the hall ever since her grandfather had decided to take up fishing more than fifteen years before. The stench of rotting fish heads and guts still remained.

The bag was new, the contents moulded to the side, and with the tip of her finger extended, still soft. It wasn't a surprise. How could it be? when she'd heard the screams punctuating the air long into the night before silence. No, not a surprise but a shock. She'd thought him improved after Jasper and their grand-parents. There'd been months where he'd left roadkill where it was meant to be left, instead of bringing it home and practising what he called his *hobby* for want of a better word. He'd read a mountain of books and even watched the odd programme on the television in the cold and depressing lounge. Those had been the days she'd thought the madness over, the cancer ripped from his mind, but she'd been wrong.

The bread was almost translucent with that speckled frosted finish that comes from far too long in the freezer, but it would have to do, as would the bacon, she thought, picking up the pack of grey, green meat and holding it by the edge of the ridged plastic as she started to close the lid, her hand curled around the metal handle, her gaze hovering on the jumbled remains, thinking again about what was missing before shaking the images away, images too horrific to contemplate.

She'd been to school. She knew how it worked. The dissection of first a slowworm and then a frog, both closely followed by a pig's heart. She'd hated every minute. The smell. The feel of the slimy entrails. The white brain globules. Most of the girls had been the same, all except for Olga Feeney, but with her old man a doctor it was a sure bet that she'd been earmarked for a life trying to follow in the family footsteps.

With the bacon sizzling in the pan, and the bread in the toaster, she allowed her mind to drift. There'd been no news of her baby girl, which was both good and bad. Good for her precious child, which was all that mattered, but that didn't stop doubts creeping in from all sides. The not knowing what had happened once she'd hurried out of the shop. She should have remained, hung about in the back of the car park, but she hadn't wanted to get caught.

When she had a few more euros, enough for the train fare to the west coast, she'd go begging to the authorities, on bended knees if necessary, to get her back. The manager of the mother and baby unit over in Drumcondra would support her and, even if she didn't, Penny would find a way.

There was a step behind her, the soft sound of a slipper scraping against the floor, and without turning, she said, 'Your breakfast is ready.'

He didn't reply and she didn't expect him to. Instead, she piled rasher after rasher between the toast before presenting him with the plate.

Penny didn't sit. She didn't want to watch him eat. Instead, she busied herself with her drink, her attention on the rim of the red mug and the crack that split the ceramic in two, a little like her heart.

The scrape of his knife on the plate. The noise from the

crispy, overcooked bacon setting her teeth on edge. She started to count in her head. *One. Two. Three. Four,* following the crack with her thumb, round and round the edge of the mug. She got to two-hundred-and-five when she heard him pushing back from the table and making for the door.

'Hey. Wait.' There was money beside the plate. Twenty euros or thereabouts in a neat pile.

For food? For her? For what?

'I know I left you short,' he mumbled, his back turned. 'There won't be any more until next week.'

It used to take her forty minutes to walk from Phibsboro to Moore Street, the location of one of Dublin's oldest vegetable markets. Penny knew this because she'd used to time the distance on her watch until the battery stopped. There was never enough money for nonessentials like batteries.

With the door pulled closed, she wrapped the shopper tight in her hand, the plastic gnawing into her palm, but she couldn't risk one of the brats on the North Circular trying to whip it out from under her. She knew it was her last hope at redemption, throwing a quick glance towards the back garden and the sight of the birds swooping and soaring overhead. Homing pigeons. Twelve plump bodies owned by their only neighbour. She could tell the time by their presence so there was no need to mourn the loss of her watch. Nine in the morning and again four in the afternoon before they were called back to roost for the night, not that she could hear them. The secluded nature of the property meant they were completely private and one of the reasons her brother could do what he liked.

She hurried towards the back gate, the thought forgotten, her mind on the walk ahead, the weight of the bag heavy on her arm, ignoring the sound of the birds grunting instead of the soft bills and coos she was used to. Birds meant nothing to her

without her baby girl to point them out to. They were something else she'd rather not think about, along with the contents
of the freezer. The twenty euros wouldn't go far unless Eddie
was up for a quick shag. That was a laugh. She'd never known
him to refuse, even though that hag of a wife of his was getting
suspicious. It was there in the way she stared at her across the
stall, her black beady eyes encased in thick folds of reddened
skin, her mouth compressed into a concertina of wrinkles. Ha,
you'd think she'd be happy. After all, she was doing her a favour.
She was doing them both a favour, the sudden image of the wife
opening her flaccid thighs filling her vision with a picture so
horrific that she blinked.

The scrabble in the back garden continued as she slipped
out of the gate, as did the flapping of wings and sharp pecks.
The battle for the soft white, fatty globules of human flesh. It
was a veritable feast and so very different from the grains and
seeds they were used to.

TWENTY-ONE

'Ah. I was about to ask you to come and see me.'

Alana stiffened in response to Reilly's tone, which screamed his dislike in all the words and syllables. She'd have to be denser than a brick not to realise that he wasn't her biggest fan.

Ox Reilly ran a self-appreciation society with an exclusive membership of one. A firm believer in patriarchy, he was happy to tolerate the men on his team but only as long as they weren't his rivals. As a woman, she had no chance of being treated with either respect or as an equal, but this attitude was different. The way his smarmy grin glued to his fleshy lips and the gleam in his eye told her that he had something on her. She had no idea what was coming only that it wasn't going to entail praise or news about a bonus. Ah shucks!

She took a moment more than necessary positioning her chair so that she was facing him without being blinded by the winter sun streaming in through the window behind his desk. It was probably wrong to take pleasure from outmanoeuvring him in this small way, just as it must gall him that he couldn't play his usual mind games on her like he did with the others.

Ox didn't stand on ceremony, certainly not with her. There

was never any of the conversational paff she'd experienced with other managers and, up to her injury, he'd never asked her to take a seat. Having a readymade chair attached to her bum was another victory, albeit minor, as was her decision early on in their relationship not to open her mouth until she had to. She sat there, her hands folded in her lap, and waited, an expression of polite interest on her face.

'I've had a call from Garda Slattery first thing. He's made a complaint about you.'

Alana maintained her silence, her focus on the man in front of her, her mind running through the list of things she'd like to do to Slattery, none of which were repeatable or doable without stern repercussions. The smarmy little toad.

'You have nothing to say,' he prompted, leaning on his desk in what passed as his intimidating pose.

Instead of being intimidated, she wondered how long the buttons on his jacket would last without popping off under the strain and revealing his vest. She knew he wore one, she'd seen the evidence on the one occasion she'd seen him in his shirt-sleeves. Probably string.

'I'm sorry. I thought you were intending to explain the nature of the complaint,' she parried.

The sound of his sigh filled the room. 'I shouldn't have to explain to you the seriousness of this. The lad has been seconded to us less than a week, and yet he's already clogging up my schedule with talk of bullying and harassment from the senior officer – you.'

'I would have thought that you'd wait to hear my side of the story, instead of taking the word of someone who hasn't darkened our doors more than a couple of days, but what do I know? I take comments about bullying and harassment very seriously. However, in this instance there is no case to answer, as I have witnesses to all of our interactions,' she said, punctuating the *all* with a small smile.

'You're very glib but then you probably don't know who Slattery's father is.'

Oh fuck. Billy Slattery, billionaire mogul and owner of *Clonabee Globe*, Dublin's answer to the *Daily Mail*, *Mirror* and *Sun* newspapers combined. Sex and sleaze for fifty cents along with a daily wordsearch, sports news and page four instead of page three – now place-marked for obituaries. She'd forgotten all about Slattery being his father up to now, probably because it wasn't relevant.

Despite all that, she maintained her silence.

Alana needed this job for more reasons than financial. It was one of the two things that made her tired enough to flake out at night without resorting to the box of sleepers she kept in the bathroom cabinet as a reminder of uglier times. Times when she'd go for weeks without sleep. It was also her sanity switch. Her reason for getting up in the morning instead of drowning in a combination of self-pity and fear for the future.

Ox had clearly become fed up with her silence because he spat out the reply. 'Billy Slattery no less, so you'd best start behaving yourself with his son, missy, because I for one have no intention of coming to your rescue.'

'You mean he still wants to be part of the team?' Alana said, shocked into replying.

The easy option would have been if the lanky guard had decided to shove off to pastures new, preferably out of Clonabee entirely, but it was probably too far away from pater's hillside mansion, with views over Poolbeg's twin towers, she thought nastily. Alana had only met Billy Slattery the once and that was once too many. She didn't move in champagne-swilling (well, more like pig-swilling) circles – and neither did she want to. Before her divorce, she'd been on the fringes, but even Colm had fallen short of the standard expected to garner invites to Slatts Palace, as it was known locally, and thank all the Gods for that.

'Apparently so.'

Alana watched him settle back, well aware of his meaning. The boy must be mad or have an agenda. She knew which one of those she favoured.

'Now that's out of the way—'

'No. You'd best tell Garda Slattery to turn up on time in future, or he'll be in for a rollicking. Perhaps it would be a good time to share your lecture on the importance of punctuality, sir?' she said, firm in the knowledge that he'd starve rather than deigning to do anything to upset Billy Slattery.

'Harrumph. Why did you come to see me, Mack?'

'I think we might have a lead on the case.'

'Which one?'

'There appears to be only one,' she said, going on to explain the forensic links. 'The thing is another man has gone missing. Fergal Cunningham. You might have heard it on the news earlier.' He inclined his head; all he was prepared to give until she'd finished her spiel. 'On the face of it there's not much to go on and, as we know, most missing people turn up eventually, but Detective Quigg knows Cunningham. It was him that made the association with Aidan Crossey.'

'Tenuous at best, Mack. You're expecting me to get in touch with the detective over in Dundrum because Detective Quigg had a revelation. Where are the clues or is this just a fishing trip?'

What could she say? Alana was annoyed with herself for not forging a stronger link between the two men before launching herself at Ox, something that didn't primarily rely on Paddy's memory. A rookie error that had the colour staining her cheeks and Ox visibly salivating at the sight.

'Who's the OIC over there anyway?' he asked, picking up his mobile and checking through his messages with a complete disregard for her presence.

'Detective Brian Buckley, I believe, sir,' she said, watching with interest as his hands flexed around his phone before placing it on the desk and shifting it out of reach.

Reilly was nothing if not predictable, which was one of her biggest disappointments. Alana didn't care about the way he treated her because she had nothing to prove to him or anyone else, for that matter. That coupled with the knowledge that she wasn't going for promotion made her invincible. She could just about cope with the politics of the place without the added responsibility that came with any career advancement. But Brian Buckley was in a completely different situation, and one he could do little about with bigots like Reilly stonewalling his career simply because of the colour of his skin. It was up to the likes of her to engineer a different narrative, one that wouldn't allow Reilly any wriggle room. The reality was if they didn't cooperate with Buckley, they'd be risking the life of Fergal Cunningham, something Reilly wouldn't want on his watch whatever his bias.

'Are you all right, sir?'

'Perfectly.'

'So, I can rely on you to square it with the powers that be before I approach Detective Buckley. I do think it's best to act quickly and tie in any loose ends after. When the media get a whiff that we've got a serial killer on the loose...'

'Now hold on a minute.' His face (apart from his three-Jamesons-a-day Rudolf nose) went from pale to puce in less time than it took her to plan her next strategy if this one wasn't strong enough. A word in the Assistant Commissioner's ear.

Alfred Gaunt had a lot to apologise for and no way of making amends. It was too late to dig up the cases he'd let slip through his fingers, the victims he'd betrayed, the criminals he'd allowed to escape justice – and all for what? An illogical obsession with the bottom of a whisky bottle, the amber liquid more demanding than any job or needy mistress. He'd lost his trophy wife at the first hurdle and his children along with her. Alfred didn't give two hoots about his ex, but his children were a different matter. Not so much children now, he thought, shuffling along the pavement, Terpsichore by his side, his raincoat doing little to stop the raw drizzle soak through his clothing.

The boys were in their late twenties and with families of their own to guide. It wasn't that difficult to keep track of the pair of them. The apples hadn't fallen far from the tree with both having chosen careers in medicine. He'd have liked nothing more than to be able to attend their graduation ceremonies at Trinity College, but there had been no relationship by then, no happy memories left over from the bedtime routine and sleepy cuddles. The trips to the park to kick around a football. The mindlessly boring beach holidays that Marissa had thrived on, him and the boys less so. All of that had been drowned out by the lost nights and absent weekends. The missed birthdays and Christmases. The argument at the school when he'd ended up punching one of the teachers. The embarrassment at having the guards called. Officers he worked with. The messy divorce that had followed, where lies exploded under the weight of Marissa's need for the house and all the trappings that went with it. The grain of truth from the one time he'd almost hit her mushrooming into tales of full-blown physical and mental violence.

He couldn't battle any of those things. Instead, on the day he was due to appear in court for the final ruling, he'd walked out of the family home. It would be wrong to say he'd never looked back. Never a day passed when he didn't regret all of it. The mistakes made. The butchered relationships. How to wreck a life in one easy step. Booze.

The day he'd left was the last day he'd touched a drop, but it had been far too late for that to make any difference except to his failing health. And yet here he was, still alive, still functioning despite a dicky heart and lungs that were finding this winter harder than most.

If he was a betting man – one of the only vices he hadn't subscribed to – he'd say he was heading for the end game. There was something about the way his breath hitched in his chest and the weight falling off his bones, revealing the planes of the man beneath. Cancer at a guess, but he wasn't in a position to get his diagnosis confirmed, just as he wasn't in the frame of mind to fight it. Tooley would be sad, but he'd move on, men like him always did and the likelihood was that he'd look after Terpsichore for him. Alfred didn't have many needs. The future of his faithful friend topped the lot.

He trudged on, skirting Trinity College, memories of his time there flickering in and out, finding no purchase. For all his advantages and stellar career, he'd never been able to ditch the black dog sitting on his shoulder. The imposter inhabiting his body and his shoes. The quiet, unassuming man unable to deal with the sycophants and leeches. If he'd been stronger, but that wasn't in his nature. Marissa had called him a doormat, one of the last words she'd flung at him; the boys, lanky teens by then, following on behind her scrawny body and brassy-blonde locks. It was one of the only times she'd spoken the truth.

Dame Street was busy on a Monday. Too many people. He'd always had a hatred for crowds and today wasn't any different, but he'd decided to see for himself where Tooley had found the bag. It was a whim, a flashback to his former life when he'd worked with the gardai on some of the biggest cases the city had ever seen. He knew he was a stupid old man, well past his sell-by date, but that didn't stop him from hugging the wall, trying to keep out of the way, his attention on the bin and the world carrying on around it.

He propped against the wall, Terpsichore settling by his feet, his tail curled around his body, his nose resting against his paws. It was easy to see that they'd changed the bin for a new one, which was exactly what he'd have done if he'd been involved in the case. It was one of those dark grey, Purple Flag ones that were dotted around the city. The old one would be littering up the lab – he pulled a grin at the pun – the technicians moaning at the stink while they worked through the contents. Fingerprinting. DNA. CCTV footage. That last thought had him lifting his head, his rheumy eyes scanning the buildings for signs of the telltale cameras, but there were none to be seen in this part of the street. If it had been him in charge, he'd have kept a police presence in the area, but staff cuts had obviously put paid to any of the usual, common-sense approaches.

It was the sight of Terpsichore jerking to his feet that first alerted him that something was happening.

'All right, boy.' He stooped, his hand looping through his

collar. 'Easy there,' he placated, his fingers scratching him at the scruff of the neck, his attention on the woman stalled in front of him, a carrier bag swinging through her fingers.

With a flick of her wrist, she deposited the bag in the bin before swivelling around and heading in the opposite direction, her gaze forward, her slim frame weaving between the other pedestrians.

Alfred glanced between her and the bin with a frown before pulling gently on the dog lead. The bin and its contents could wait, unlike the girl. 'Come on, Terp.'

Trying to keep up was a hopeless task. By the time he'd reached the bank of the River Liffey she was out of sight, that is until he spotted her scurrying across the Ha'penny Bridge, or at least he thought it was her. There was something about her slim, almost skeletally thin build and swinging ponytail that made him think that it could be her. There were many places she could be heading, too many to count let alone think about. To continue trying to follow her was madness, but there was nothing else he had to do so he carried on, his breath shallow, his lungs battling with the effort, his left hip and knee throbbing.

He'd lost her by the time he hit Henry Street, the wide pedestrian area a hive of shoppers on the lookout for a bargain. He looked left and right, stepping back a couple of times, turning a deaf ear to some of the less than kindly comments, which were all on a common theme. *Get out-a-my-way and get-an-f'ing-job.*

If only he could, he thought, taking one last glance back down the street, the noise deafening after the quiet he was used to. The Carol singers were at it again and in competition with an out-of-tune busker and not-half-bad fiddler, the stream of glittering lights in the thunder-dark sky a sight to behold in the leaden mist.

'Sorry, boy. We've lost her,' he said, dipping into his

pocket for the bag of chewy sticks he eked out. It wasn't Terpsichore's fault that his owner was a deadbeat loser with a sudden need to make up for his previous failings. An impossible task, which he should have realised before he'd left home that morning. 'Might as well see if we can earn enough for something nice for tea, eh, boy.' With that he shifted along a bit to find the best doorway, somewhere where he wouldn't be trampled on.

He was an expert on Dublin's doorways. From Georgian to glass plate and everything in between, he mused, picking the only one with a mat – softer on his bony bum and with the added advantage of being near to a burger joint – it was also the one with a To Let sign taped to the window, the yellowed paper as telling as the dusty window that he was unlikely to be disturbed anytime soon.

The worst part of being homeless and dependent on the kindness of others was the begging. He wouldn't do it if he didn't have to, a last resort, which made him vulnerable to abuse. Most ignored him. Some were kind enough to drop a few coins or the occasional bite to eat. It was the rare ones that took pleasure in escalating the verbal to a physical level of abuse. That was why he often preferred to go hungry than beg, but some days, like today, he felt too weak to take another step. As a medical man he didn't want to think about what would happen if he collapsed on the street. Of what would happen to Terp. His hand tightened around the lead, the leather rough under his fingers, one of his only purchases in recent times but the dog had the right to look smart. A poor, old, deserted soul that the world had turned their back against. A parallel he couldn't dismiss.

'A burger for you, mister.'

Alfred looked up in time to catch the eye of the man, a swift thanks on his lips.

'Thank you, sir. God bless you,' he said, the trite words

falling out. His automatic response even though he'd lost sight of his own God long ago.

'Look, Terp. Your favourite.'

Time passed. Seconds. Minutes. He couldn't tell. He didn't care. Terp had consumed two burgers in quick succession, leaving him the bread rolls, but it was carbohydrate, which hopefully meant a spurt of energy for the way home. He rested his head back, thinking about closing his eyes but fighting the thought.

She came out of nowhere. A tangle of brown hair escaping from its band. The old raggedy jeans, baggy around the hips. The navy puffer, frayed at the cuff. Dressed like a teen and with the subtle stride that was owned by the young, but still, impossible to age because of her eyes. Wariness of the world set in a face full of grim determination. Alfred had a sudden image intrude of his mother. A no-nonsense Cavan woman with a tart tongue and a stinging slap that he could still feel biting into the back of his legs. A copper's wife who'd used to age a person by their experiences instead of the lines on their face or their numerical tally. The girl hurrying past was probably twenty, could pass for thirty but with the experience of someone twice that age.

'A few coppers for the dog, miss?'

The words came out of their own accord, untethered to any thought of what her response might be. Like him she was obviously down on her luck. The stale air of poverty and deprivation clear to see in both her stooped head and battered demeanour. Life had been cruel to her, which made his request for money all the more confusing, his nutrient-deprived brain unable to bridge the gap between the idea and the possible outcome.

She lifted her head, her eyes hollow in sunken cheeks, her gaze darting from him and down to the dog, the briefest of smiles breaking at the sound of his muffled snores.

'What's his name?' she said, stuffing her hand in her pocket and, after a moment's consideration, picking a fiver out of the crumpled notes on display before holding it out to him. Her voice was soft, hesitant, slightly husky. A smoker's cough without trace of nicotine-stained fingers, his eyes dropping to her hands before returning to her face.

'Terpsichore. It means...'

'It means to dance,' she said, nodding once before turning and carrying on her way.

By the time he'd creaked to his feet she'd disappeared into the crowd. He knew he'd never be able to follow her. Instead, he turned in the opposite direction, Terpsichore prancing by his feet. He was tired now, barely able to keep up with the dog. It was a choice of going back to the bin and retrieving the meat, or leaving it in the hope that it would still be there when he'd alerted the guards.

TWENTY-THREE

'Afternoon, Doctor. Good to see you again,' Alana said, extending her hand and noticing the changes the last couple of days had made to his appearance. Alfred Gaunt clearly wasn't a well man. She was no medic, but she didn't have to be one to notice the tinge of blue to his lips and rasp to his breath. One of the first things she'd done the last time he'd visited was to search him up. The long list of qualifications and citations. A career seeped in accreditations. A man at the height of his profession, which made his fall from grace as tragic as it was unexpected. Seventy-one was old to be living on the streets and, sad though it was to admit, Dr Gaunt wasn't likely to see another Christmas.

She waited for Paddy to place a tray of drinks and a packet of digestives on the table before setting a bowl of water down in front of the dog. It wasn't only her that was becoming soft in her old age.

'Right, now that we're all here. How can we be of help?'

'It's more a case of me helping you, dear lady,' he said, unfolding a tissue to reveal a five euro note, which he set on the table between them. Alana hoped that the reason would be something other than him offering to pay for his drink. 'I was at a loose end earlier, so I decided to take a walk to Dame Street.'

'That's quite a walk, if you don't mind me saying, sir,' Paddy said, gesturing for him to help himself to a biscuit.

Alfred waved away the comment and the biscuit, instead sipping away at the sweetened coffee. 'I happened to be in the right place at the right time. Must be a first,' he added, his chuckle changing to a gut-wrenching cough, a speck of blood on the corner of his mouth, which he wiped away with the back of his hand. 'Sorry about that.'

'No apology necessary. You were saying about being in the right place at the right time, Doctor?' she prompted, placing a box of tissues in front of him. There was little else she could think to do for him apart from offering a gentle smile.

'You might want to get the Tech Bureau to take the replacement bin into custody,' he said, sipping again on his coffee. 'I'm not going anywhere.'

'Right on it.' Paddy leapt to his feet, his mobile already in his hand. 'Be back in a jiff.'

'There's more, isn't there?'

'I saw her,' he said, almost conversationally, the empty mug set on the table, a biscuit in its place. 'A young slip of a thing scarcely out of the schoolroom. Twenty or thereabouts but with the weight of the world on her shoulders. She placed the bag in the bin mid-stride before carrying on her way. I thought I'd lost her until I spotted her again in Henry Street.' He nodded to the fiver. 'Her fingers are all over that. Mine too, but they should still be on your system from when I was working.'

Alana matched his smile. 'As are mine, also only for elimination purposes, in case you were wondering,' she said. 'They've yet to find the skeleton in the back of my cupboard.'

'And, like most doctors I buried all of my mistakes,' Alfred replied, colour blooming his cheeks, a spark igniting at the twist in the conversation.

Alana liked this man; she liked him a lot. His humility. His bravery. His steadfastness. A man who had a lot to offer despite his past, and someone not too proud or scared to get himself involved with something that wasn't any of his business. *Once a doctor always a doctor* was one of Rusty's stock phrases but the same mantra was as true for coppers. Never a day went by when she wasn't thinking about work and, if not her work, then crime in general. Gardai were trained to be observant and there hadn't been the on-off lever invented yet that would allow her to switch from cop to civilian when she was in need of some downtime.

'I hope not too many,' she finally said, wondering if he'd allow her to help him, even though she already knew the answer. 'I'd like to get started on an EvoFIT.'

'Ah, the new facial recognition software, or, at least, new to me. I've never been any good at art, but I'll help if I can. My dog?'

'Your dog is fine here. I'll get someone from the team to come to you. It's all laptop based,' she said, starting to move away from the table. 'You've been a great help. If there's anything we can do to...?'

He waved her comment away for a second time. 'All I'm in need of is another coffee.'

TWENTY-FOUR

MONDAY, 20TH DECEMBER, 4.00 P.M.

'Settle down, everyone. We have a lot to get through if you want to see the top side of your pillowcase anytime soon.' Alana waited a moment for the chairs to fill. The room was full now that Rogene, Rusty and Garda Slattery had joined them. She was far from sure about Slattery, but he was all Ox had offered and they needed all the help they could get. They'd also managed to prevail on Irene Burden attending despite the late notice.

'Right then, as you know earlier on today Dr Gaunt came across another bag of body parts being dropped off in the same location by, until we know any different, the same individual.' She rested back in her chair, casting a glance in Rusty's direction.

'Liver, two kidneys and, this time a heart, too, something that was missing from the first bag.'

'Is that significant?'

'Probably, but at this stage only to the murderer,' he continued. 'Unless anyone has any bright ideas, but we can discuss that later. The key issue is that in this case the body parts appear to be from the same man: Aidan Crossey.'

'A bit soon for DNA, surely?'

'We don't need DNA, Rogene. Not when Crossey is in possession of the rarest of blood groups. I won't bore you with the finer details of his H antigen deficiency, but basically there's one in a million chance that this is our man. Pretty strong odds given the set of circumstances.'

The room fell silent for a beat only for pandemonium to break out, everyone speaking at once.

'Silence. I can't hear myself think with you lot rabbiting on,' Alana said.

On paper no one was as squeaky clean as Crossey, which could only mean one thing: they hadn't been looking in the right places to discover his secrets. She made a quick entry on the board, which was beginning to resemble Spaghetti Junction. There were too many strands to the three cases, three cases that were now somehow linked. If this carried on, they'd be in need of a bigger incident room. 'Run through the DNA again for me, Rogene. Anything else of interest in the bin?'

Rogene dropped her spectacles from the top of her head and onto her nose, her flyaway black hair curving around her cheeks. 'It's early days but nothing so far, except that my team are up to their neck in Dublin's grimiest rubbish. With the four-hour lead-in to process the DNA, we were obviously going to prioritise the organs recovered from the scene, in addition to the five euro note. You'll be the first to know on all counts.'

'There's another interesting fact about the organs,' Rusty said, slouching against the wall, his arms folded across his chest. 'With no evidence of crystallisation, these ones are definitely fresh but, more importantly, there was also none of the breakdown I was expecting to see.'

'Breakdown? What do you mean by that?'

'Crossey has been missing for ten days, right?'

'Well, heading for eleven.'

He nodded in affirmation. 'A body hanging around that long

will have gone through the process of putrefaction, which means a deterioration in the—'

Alana stopped him. 'I think we all know what that means, Rusty.' She gave him one of her lopsided smiles. 'So, he's been dead how long?'

'Twenty-four hours or thereabouts at a guess.'

'God.' Alana lifted her hands to her ponytail to secure the band, only stopping when the sharp sting of tightened hair hit. The man had been alive all that time, and despite their best efforts, which had included television appeals and an all-ports warning, they hadn't been able to trace him before someone had decided to gut him like a fish and spread his body parts across the city. The worst of it was they wouldn't be able to keep this from the media, not with Ox hounding them. The butchering of a fine upstanding member of the community was going to feature on the front pages of the *Irish Times* and *Clonabee Globe* for days to come, which was bound to panic the public. Having their telephone lines jammed by concerned citizens was all they needed. It would also encourage Ox to remove them from the case, something she wasn't prepared to let happen. She took no comfort in the thought that she'd been right about having a serial killer in their midst. Someone who roamed the same streets, visited the same shops and pubs and breathed the same air. It could be anyone – even one of them, God forbid.

'Rogene, back to you. What about the fiver Dr Gaunt handed in? I hope you're not going to tell me some crap about polymer bank notes and the impossibility of processing them, are you?' she asked, focusing her thoughts along with her gaze. There would be enough fearmongering in the streets as it was without Rogene adding blocks to the investigation.

'Ha. You've been reading the same articles as me in your spare time about the reduction in microorganism activity with the new notes, due to the plastic surface. I must admit that it's made the collection of fingerprinting a challenge. However, we've developed some highly exciting technology, which involves sticky-back plastic, a hard bristled brush and some of our renowned black powder.' She carried on speaking as laughter filled the room. 'We were able to pull fifty partial prints, along with six full, two of which we eliminated as belonging to Dr Gaunt. Of the remaining four, we matched two on the database, while two are still outstanding—'

'The two you were able to match?' Alana said, shifting the conversation forward, a sharp look at the grin still lingering on Paddy's face.

'Both belong to sixty-three-year-old Eddie Murch,' Rogene read from her phone. 'You might remember that investigation a few years back into break-ins at sheltered accommodation. Thought to be the gang leader and the receiver of stolen goods. Couldn't prove anything in the end, but not before the judge had called him one of the most despicable of lowlifes it had ever been his misfortune to come up against. Justly deserved, too, if the part he played in those burglaries was true and there's no reason to presume otherwise. I read the report earlier, almost turned my stomach.' Her jaw tightened. 'Most were conducted at knife point and on a group of society ill-prepared to defend themselves. Many of the old folk refused to return back home after, and he got off scot-free, although his henchmen were less lucky. I've emailed you details of the case as an aide memoire.'

'Thanks. I think I remember it. What about the two outstanding?'

Rogene lifted her head, her tone changing. 'They both match the fingerprints we took off the note found in the child's pocket.'

'That's a turn-up for the books. So, let's see if I've got this right. We have an abandoned two-year-old found with a note telling us not to try and trace her parent/guardian. The same child who is related to the bag of organs found in the bin along Dame Street last Friday—'

'Can I interrupt, ma'am,' Garda Slattery said.

'You just have but don't let that stop you.' Alana wasn't of a mind to give any quarter to someone who ran to the Super for any little perceived or actual slight or hiccup in their working relationship. She treated everyone the same, or at least that had always been her plan.

'If my thoughts aren't welcome.' He pushed up from his chair and started for the door.

'Sit back down and don't be so sensitive.'

Alana was surprised at the way he turned and stared before retaking his seat, more of a glare, which made her think she might have been a little over the top, but then so was his response. There was no room in her department for belligerent gobshites with a touch of the arrogant around the edges. He'd learn or he wouldn't. If he didn't, he'd be off the team quicker than flicking a turd from her shoe, she thought, deliberately ignoring her recent conversation with Reilly. It was her managing the team and not him.

'I was going to mention the shopping the mother provided, which surely must be an indicator that she was only thinking of the child's well-being when she abandoned her.'

'Good point, although we don't know if it was the mother, eh? Yes, I agree it's probable but not something we can prove until we're able to trace her, but a good point all the same, so thank you.' She smiled briefly before addressing the room in general. 'To continue, we also have a match with the finger-prints from the note left with Casey and the fiver given to Dr Gaunt. At the same time, we have organs from two different people who are both linked via their DNA to the child. Finally, we have a new set of organs, discovered by Dr Gaunt, which match that of Aidan Crossey, our retired newsagent who's been missing now for ten days. I think that's all.'

'I can't help thinking the child is key,' Irene Burden said,

drawing the attention of the room, her bright red lipstick a startling contrast against the white of her teeth.

'In what way?' Alana replied, shifting her gaze from the
woman's mouth to her eyes, partially hidden behind a pair of
black-framed glasses that dwarfed her face.

'She's the common denominator between all three cases. A
relative of the first two deceased individuals, and linked to
Crossey by nature of the fact his organs were disposed of by the
woman whose note was found in her pocket.'

'A common denominator. I like that. I'd like it even more if
we had a way of extracting any useful information from the
mind of a two-year-old,' she said, her tone dry. 'We know that
she's terrified of animals, or she was. One animal in particular.
A cat she calls Per.'

Alana made for her desk and, after a little shuffling, found
the copies she'd made of the drawings and set them out on the
table.

'Apart from the note, these are all we have to go on.'

She wheeled out of the way, watching as Irene went
through the pictures, one after the other.

'There's not a lot, is there?' Irene said, staring down at the
orange squiggle, her hand flat on the table, her nails painted the
same shade of red as her lips. 'Although I'll stick with my guns
and say that she's still the key to all of this.'

'What about the chances of a profile?' Paddy asked. 'I know
there's a lot of unknowns...'

'You could say that. It's difficult, made more difficult that we
don't know who the first two victims were.' Irene shot her
glasses back up her nose. 'But I should be able to come up with
something useful for Crossey's murder.'

'Thank you.' Alana glanced back at the whiteboard and the
scribbled mess, which she'd like to rework before she called it a
night. It was the time when the office was empty that she found
links and patterns in their work. Connecting dots was always

more difficult for her in a packed room full of bodies and banter. There wasn't a lot more they could do anyway, and it was well past five. She'd send them off to the pub and stay awhile. There was no rush. She had no intention of joining them.

'Okay. We have a lot to get through tomorrow. I've scheduled an early catch-up meeting with Detective Buckley over in Dundrum.' Alana glanced at Paddy. 'I'd like you to accompany me. In the meantime there's enough for you two to get on with, Lorrie and Flynn. We need to chase up Dr Gaunt's EvoFIT of the girl. Let's hope the image they come up with is a passing likeness, unlike the last time we used it, eh! We also need to check on Eddie Murch and start to track down the other foster kids staying with Crossey's parents.'

'I'm happy to start on that now...' Paddy said.

'And, I'd prefer if you had a good night's sleep, Detective Quigg. We have a lot to get through tomorrow as it is without you coming in under par.'

Paddy inclined his head. 'Don't know about you but I fancy a drink after the day we've had?'

'Sounds like a great idea. It's a shame I already have plans,' Alana replied. Plans that included a date with her notes and a cat called Goose, but they weren't to know that. 'Off you go and enjoy yourself.'

TWENTY-FIVE

Penny was sitting in the kitchen when she heard the front door slam and the sound of feet clomping down the hallway. She spent most of her spare time in her favourite chair, a book propped on the table in front of her, the radio tuned to whichever station was playing the best music. She didn't know what she'd do if she didn't have access to reading materials. There were no books left in the house that she hadn't read until the pages had loosened from the spine, apart from the Bible and that wasn't something she was ever likely to read. She'd been brought up in a religious house. Prayers at the table before they were allowed to eat. Prayers at bedtime, kneeling on the stone-cold floor shivering in her nightie. Attending Mass on Saturdays and religious days. No meat on Friday. All of the things that were meant to show the world what a good Catholic family they were. So good that at the first sign of trouble, they'd turfed her out on her ear with only the possessions on her back. No, instead of the Bible, she took it upon herself to walk along the Royal Canal Bank and across Blacquiere Bridge to visit Phibsboro library once a week to stock up on books. She wasn't fussy as long as it was escapist. Something to dive into up to her neck.

Something to drown in. She jumped from the classics to crime, romance to short stories and essays. She wasn't a purist. She didn't have time for all that nonsense.

By the time he entered the kitchen, she was standing in front of the kettle waiting for it to boil, the latest Samantha Tonge novel hidden by a carefully draped tea towel – it wouldn't be the first time he'd snatched her library book only for her never to see it again. It was a good job the librarian was a saint, suspicious and unbelieving when she'd said the cat had eaten it, but there was nothing she could do about that. The truth of a mad brother who turned humans into full-sized puppets was as unbelievable as blaming the cat.

'Did you close the curtains?'

A simple enough question with a simple enough answer, but one she was scared to give all the same. *No, do it yourself* would mean repercussions that she wasn't prepared to invite.

'I'll do it now.'

'And be sharp about it. You remember the last time, don't you, Penny?'

How could I ever forget! She ran her fingers along the raft of bruises running across her chest, shoulder and left arm, the colours faded to an insipid yellowy-brown. There'd been no trace of her brother, the boy he'd once been, when he'd turned on her. The shift from mental torture to physical attacks had been the impetus she needed to remove her daughter from an increasingly fraught situation. If only she was able to do the same. It didn't take a genius to recognise the time was coming when the ability to choose would be taken from her. Deep down she knew she couldn't save him, but her vein of guilt, a yawning cavernous pit of despair, kept her where she was. If his ma hadn't died then his father wouldn't have met and married her mother and they wouldn't be in this position. Penny knew she couldn't be blamed for something that had happened before she'd been born, but that didn't stop her from feeling guilty at

the way her grandparents had treated him. Oh, they'd treated
her as badly, but at least they'd provided a home, of sorts, until
she'd made the fatal mistake of falling pregnant. No, Penny
owed him; a debt she could never repay even if her life
depended on it.

The hall was cold, the coldest room in the house but it was
relative. All the rooms were cold. There wasn't the money to
heat them. The only heating they had was a two-bar electric
fire, which they tried to limit to an hour or two in the evenings,
but then she was used to the cold. 'Spare the rod and spoil the
child' had been her grandmother's refrain. A little bit of hard-
ship to oil the Pearly Gates for her unworthy soul to slip
through. No thought that a little spoiling on occasion would
have inured her to the overtures when they eventually came.
There was no protection, no knowledge, no experience to
protect her from the flattery aimed at her burgeoning body. She
was as ripe and as innocent as a soft, moist plum ready to drop
onto the ground – and drop she did. Bruised and battered,
unaware of the seed, planted deep, until it was far too late to do
anything about it. The catalyst for her grandparents' ultimate
betrayal.

Jasper was sitting on her grandmother's lap. Cold, still,
unmoving. Penny hated touching him. The spikiness of his
orange fur, the icy-cold of his body, the rigidity of his frame.
There was no softness, no give, nothing of the cat he'd once
been. She hated touching him far more than she hated touching
her grandparents. It was simple enough to understand. Jasper
had been her friend and confidant. The only one that she could
trust. This aberration wasn't him. It might look like him, up to a
point, but her Jasper had long gone. The only place he resided
now was in the darkness of her mind when she lay in bed
thinking about the past and all she'd lost.

She edged her way in front of the chairs to reach the
curtains, taking a moment to glance down at the road below, the

streetlamps forming pools of light from which to make out the occasional pedestrian weaving their way home. Phibsborough was a busy residential area, all the busier due to its proximity to the city centre. Their house was on a quiet lane off Avondale Avenue. She could even see the tall gothic spire of the iconic St Peter's Church looming over the rooftops like a benevolent aunt, although she'd never found anything benevolent inside those doors. It had taken her a long time to realise that churches were only a man-made extension. If there was no charity and love at home, then she was unlikely to find it inside the doors of the parish church.

'What's keeping you? I want my tea,' he said, his voice a hollow echo from the bottom of the stairs.

'Never a minutes' fucking peace.'

Penny tugged at the curtains, taking a great deal of relish in swearing in front of her grandparents, not that they'd notice. She wasn't prepared to look at them. She couldn't. At times she felt he hated her because there surely couldn't be any love left in the way he made her look after them, and all for what? It was obscene and terrifying. Changing them into different outfits, and all because he was worried about what any passers-by would think. The only people to use their lane regularly were the postman and the refuse collectors and they wouldn't notice. It's not as if the old couple had gone out of their way to slip something into their hands at Christmas.

It would have been better to lie. A quick comment about having had to move them into a home for their own good would have sufficed. It's not as if anyone would have checked up on them. Instead, he made her manhandle them into an array of clothing, to perpetuate the lie, their bodies as cold, still and unmoving as the cat.

'Had a good night, Pad?'

'Home by eight thirty, if that's what you're asking?'

'As if!'

'Flynn and Lorrie seemed on fine form and as for William...'

'What about him?' Alana said quickly, glancing up from where she was fastening her seatbelt.

'Well, let's put it this way. If he doesn't have a hangover this morning, there's no justice in the world.'

'God, I remember those days well but he's probably young enough to wear it. Did Irene go in the end?'

Alana didn't expect much of an answer but more than the deep grunt of an affirmation he gave her. There'd always been an atmosphere between those two, one which screamed of unfinished business. It was nothing to do with her, but that had never stopped her from teasing him in the past. However, this time she changed the subject back to the case, a conversation that lasted them until they pulled up outside Dundrum station.

Detective Brian Buckley came to meet them in reception. A giant of a man. Six-foot-six with broad swimmer shoulders and even broader thighs but it was his broken nose, protruding jaw and wide-spaced, dark brown soulful eyes that got him the nickname Bulldog, or so Paddy had told her on the way over.

'Sorry for rocking up like this but we've three cases on the go, which may or may not be linked to the disappearance of your Fergal Cunningham,' she said, after the usual pleasantries.

'Is that right.' It wasn't a question. 'You'd best come with me then,' he said, gesturing for them to follow him down the corridor and into one of the interview rooms.

'Coffee? Tea? I wouldn't recommend either. The vegetable soup is as good as it gets,' he said as soon as he'd closed the door and lumbered around to the far side of the room, after removing the spare chair out of the way so she could slide into the empty space.

Alana laughed as did Paddy, the tension slipping out of the room along with any preconceived fears that Bulldog was going to put barriers in their way. Grousing about the station drinks machine was a guard's way of discussing the weather or the traffic. She'd used it herself on more than one occasion.

'No, but thanks anyway.'

'Cunningham is an interesting case so any help in that regard,' he said, cutting out all the conversational corners. 'I take it that it's to do with that little problem over in Dame Street?'

Alana wasn't surprised that the news had spread. The gardai grapevine was renowned for the speed and accuracy of its dissemination of information. She'd have been far more surprised if he didn't know what was going on.

'The rumour mill has been busy!'

She watched him remove his phone from his pocket and swipe through the apps before setting it down in front of her.

'Sadly, the rumour mill has nothing to do with it.'

Dustbin Butcher at Large in Dublin Central

Our reporter, Dave Moss, has learned of a worrying set of developments that link the disappearance of local man, Aidan Crossey, with the discovery of a bag of human organs along Dame Street. More news as we get it.

It only took a second for her to process what she was looking at. Two seconds for a sliver of bile to escape, filling her mouth with burning acid. Three seconds for her to exchange a look with Paddy before she pushed the phone away as if it was tainted, a brief but all-encompassing look that said it all. They had a mole in the office. All bets were off as to who.

'Shit.' There were other words lined up but she didn't have the heart to spill them. Bulldog would get the message.

'I don't normally swear in front of a lady, but shit is right,' he said, shutting the phone and replacing it deep within his pocket. 'I take it you weren't aware—' He stopped mid-sentence, all eyes now diverted to the frantic ringing of her mobile, the name of *Ox Reilly* lighting up the screen. 'I'll leave you to...'

'You might as well stay. I'll be as quick as I can.'

The phone call was short but far from sweet. Alana was left in no doubt as to Reilly's displeasure at having the case splashed all over the *Clonabee Globe*. There was nothing she could do to calm him other than palm him off with a promise that she'd find whoever the loose-lipped bastard was before the day was out. It wouldn't take long, she thought, already scheduling in a trip to the *Globe*'s head office on the way home. After all, she had a pretty good idea there was a Slattery at the bottom of it. The only question – which one? She knew it would only have been a matter of time before the story came out, but she'd at least have liked some warning if only to get her act together. They'd have questions and, as of now, there were still no answers.

'Sorry about that,' she said, taking a second to arrange her thoughts. 'Right, two things: what can you tell us about Cunningham; and do you have a problem with us getting involved?'

Alana watched him eyeing her from his position of safety on the other side of the table as he weighed up the pros and cons of sharing the burden of the case. It made sense but perhaps only to her.

'The name's Bulldog,' he finally said, pushing to his feet. 'I was about to visit Cunningham's wife along with the lads from the Tech Bureau. You're welcome to join me.' He stopped a second, looking awkward. 'I thought we could catch-up on the way, but I drive a Mini, so er...'

'So, no problem.' Paddy joined him in standing. 'You take Alana and I'll follow on behind with her chair.'

The Cunninghams lived in Blackberry Drive, a small close off Ballinteer Road, almost opposite the entrance to Wesley College Secondary School.

'Eight in the morning is an interesting time to disappear given the close proximity to a school that accommodates nigh on a thousand pupils not to mention teachers and other ancillary staff, but what do I know,' Bulldog said, clicking on his indicator before turning into Blackberry Drive.

'I take it no one saw anything unusual?' Alana stared around at the other six houses. Typical suburban close. Quiet, calm and empty at this time of the morning. No doubt they were being watched. There was always a neighbour eager to see what next door was up to, whatever the time. It would take minutes they didn't have, along with offers of drinks they didn't want, to discover what secrets lurked behind the assorted curtains and slatted blinds.

'Too busy with their own lives to bother with anyone else's,' he replied, swinging in front of a cream-painted semi with neat lawn and a Skoda Yeti parked in the drive.

Alana disagreed. There was always someone who saw

something. It was part of the copper's skill to prise the lid open on the tin of beans and spill the contents, but now wasn't the time to interrupt the detective's train of thought.

'Our man walked out of the house between eight and ten past only to vanish into thin air,' he went on, punctuating the words with a waft of his fingers flying in all directions.

'He didn't take the car,' Paddy said, walking around the pristine grey vehicle. He placed a hand on the bonnet, wiped the dew off his palm with a tissue and joined them at the front door.

'That's the wife's. He rides a Ducati, which is still in the garage.'

'So, he leaves the premises – or is taken off the premises – without anyone noticing, not even his missus,' she repeated, trying to wrap her mind around the fact no one had reported him missing; a married man living on a small close.

'That's about it. You can ask her yourself,' Bulldog said, indicating with a nod of his head the distorted shadow appearing through the etched glass panel in the doorframe.

Marian Cunningham was a surprise not that Alana had made any preconceived notions as to her appearance. She was far more interested in why she hadn't taken account of her husband's whereabouts until his work colleagues had phoned in, looking for him. At first glance the woman didn't appear her age, which Alana knew, at thirty-nine, was nine years older than Fergal. Slim and with a shock of curly hair that was either natural or a perm gone wrong. Dressed in jeans and with one of those yoke Fair Isle jumpers that were suddenly back in fashion. Alana had nearly ordered one online last week, in a particularly fetching shade of blue. The item was still in her shopping basket, but not for long.

She puzzled over her sudden decision not to purchase it as Paddy helped her chair over the threshold. She didn't usually judge someone so quickly, but there was something about

Cunningham's wife that she didn't like, something that had nothing to do with her fashion sense or hairstyle. Probably related to her apparent lack of concern over her husband's whereabouts, Alana speculated. Only time and careful detecting would tell her if she was right.

The lounge was small and featured a simulated fire, laminated flooring, and a three-piece white leather suite with lots of cushions arranged with a flair for the dramatic. Alana liked the odd cushion but the amount on display was ridiculous. A show house as opposed to a home. A room where a man might feel superfluous. Colm would certainly have had a thing or six to say if she'd gone on a crazy cushion spree, while Paddy was always moaning about the amount of clutter that his sister had brought with her.

The men sat on the sofa, Alana pulling up alongside them. Marian perched on the edge of the chair opposite, quiet, still, questionless when there surely must be a dozen to be asked.

'I know we've gone through this before, Mrs Cunningham, but I'd like you to tell me again about the events of yesterday.'

She rolled her eyes. 'As I already told your officer, I last saw Fergal the night before last and he was fine then, the same as usual. I knew he was on an early shift, so I didn't think anything of it when he wasn't around when I came downstairs.'

'What time was that?'

'Quarter past eight, same as it is every morning,' she replied, shifting back and crossing one leg over the other.

'And you didn't hear or see anything unusual, Mrs Cunningham?' Alana said, speaking for the first time. 'What about the doorbell ringing or signs that he'd had a visitor? His breakfast dishes?'

'Nope. Nothing. Fergal is housetrained to the nth degree. Able to make his own breakfast and clear up after himself.' Her mouth thinned, any thinner and it would disappear into her gums. 'It's a pattern that works for us.'

'So, you didn't think anything was amiss until one of his colleagues from the prison rang asking where he was?'

'Exactly. I tried his phone only for it to go straight to voice-mail, which is highly unusual. I knew there was something up when I saw his motorbike still in the garage.'

'If you can show us his room.' Bulldog stood to emphasise that it wasn't a request. 'And, as I said on the phone, the forensic team would like to take another look round.'

She sniffed her displeasure as she made for the door. 'I've arranged to meet a friend for a coffee while they're here.'

'A cold fish if ever there was one,' Alana whispered to Paddy as they followed on behind.

'And too many cushions!'

Alana snorted, managing to change the sound to a cough in time to meet Marian's glare. 'Sorry, think I swallowed a fly.' Not the best of excuses in December Dublin, but the only one she could come up with at short notice.

'I'll be upstairs getting ready if you need me.'

Alana turned to an astonished Paddy and an equally surprised looking Bulldog. She was feeling a tad flabbergasted herself as she surveyed the depressing sight ahead from the safety of the doorway. A large proportion of domestic crimes were ones of passion but there was little to feel passionate about in Fergal's room, with its old, scarred furniture and battered bed settee. She'd never met the man, she didn't know the first thing about him or his relationship with his missus, but she did have a growing list of questions along with a possible suspect. Either Cunningham had decided to walk out of his home, or someone had made him leave. His wife was in the running for both roles.

TWENTY-EIGHT

Penny didn't read the newspapers. There wasn't the money to waste on luxuries and papers fell into the same category as magazines, out of reach. She could still remember her brother's face when she'd come back from the market with a bundle of brightly coloured magazines on top of her shopper. It had taken a careful explanation about how she'd found them sticking out one of the recycle bins along the North Circular Road to placate him. It was also the last time she'd repeated the exercise. The lecture had been accompanied by a stinging slap, the first time he'd hit her. The first time she'd realised how different the man had become from the boy she'd once known.

The magazines were in a well-thumbed pile under her bed. Old friends, even if she knew the stories and fashions off by heart. She couldn't bear to part with this small slice of normality. Glamorous people parading around in diamonds and silk instead of the old tat she had to resort to. Her last link to the world outside her doorstep, one she didn't breach unless he gave her permission and that was only when the food cupboard was bare. He went out, he went out all the time. She didn't know where or what he did. She didn't want to know. The thought didn't register that he might have access to newspapers, that her secret would be splashed across the front page of the most popular paper in Dublin. Instead, she concentrated on peeling the spuds, digging out the eyes and chopping off the green parts before plopping them into the boiling water, white scum starting to cling to the side of the pan.

He was out now. There was something in the way the air shifted and pooled in the house, the absence of creaking joists. She might not be able to hear him sneaking up on her, but she always knew when he'd left. There was nothing she could do with the information. Nowhere she could go to run and hide. The neighbours would be no help. The old ones who'd known her grandparents had moved away, replaced with a young upwardly mobile city slicker couple with their fancy accents and posh cars to match. She never saw them unless it was from the safety of peering round the curtains when they passed her house, but she knew they were there. The roar of their cars as they raced along the lane. The wine and champagne bottles piled high in the recycling bins at the end of their driveway. She was on her own and with nowhere to go. In the dark of night, she prayed to the God that had long since moved to pastures new, in her mind at least. She prayed that her daughter was safe and, on the next breath, she prayed for salvation.

Her favourite books from the library were the ones that featured handsome heroes saving the damsel from distress. She gobbled them up like sweets. The only perfect moments in her life now that she'd abandoned her child. Part of her wished that she could walk out the door and start a new life, but it was far too late to seek redemption. She knew how it worked. Someone had to pay the price for their sins. It wouldn't be him because wasn't she equally to blame?

With the saucepan lid in place, she rinsed her hands under the running tap and dried them on the tea towel. There was nothing else for her to do until he came back, except sit and read and watch that the pan didn't boil over. Instead, she lowered the dial on the cooker and went out into the hall and the door that was always locked. The door to the cellar. She felt like a naughty child when she touched the brass doorknob. Disobedient but defiant. She had nothing to fear, nothing to feel ashamed about. After all, wasn't it her house to do with what she wanted? That included going into all the rooms. He could do his worst because it couldn't be as bad as what he'd done already.

The handle turned though the door wouldn't move, but then she hadn't expected it to. The large iron key was what she needed, the one that surely must be too big to carry around with him. She'd searched before to no avail. His bedroom at the top of the stairs, the double bed tucked next to the wall. The large old-fashioned mahogany wardrobe. The matching chest of drawers. She'd searched them all. Pockets and corners. High shelves and the gap where the carpet met the skirting board.

Taking a step back, she frowned, her eyes travelling the narrow hall with its dated pendant light fitting and tiled flooring. The stair carpet held in place by brass rods. The edges fraying, the pattern faded to a dingy grey. The slight gap where the carpet was starting to lift. It only took a second for her to pull the key from its hiding place. She couldn't believe her luck.

The cellar was a place she hadn't been since she was a child, a dark, scary place, the place that featured in her nightmares. The place that her grandmother used to banish her to as a form of punishment, the place her grandfather had released her from. The place she hated over all others. She'd used to think that he was the kinder of the two. Balding, with a comb-over fringe of only a few hairs, and with kindly blue eyes, eyes that had hardened to steel when she'd fallen pregnant. She'd always known what her grandmother was but not him, right until that last moment, the moment when he'd punched her in the stomach before pushing her out the door, an eerie smile on his lips. A wolf was always a wolf even when dressed like a sheep. As a lesson it had been a difficult one to learn and one impossible to forget.

The memories of a child were very different to the memories of an adult, she thought as she pulled open the door and fumbled on the wall for the light switch. They were also of no use to her now. Her parents were long dead, and her grandparents had followed suit. Now she had to worry about the living.

The cellar looked larger, somehow, from her position at the top of the stairs, the shelves and wine racks empty, the floor brushed clean, the long-handled sweeping brush propped up against the rough-hewn wall. With her hand on the railing, she started down the uneven steps, almost scared to look over the rickety banister. A rack full of paint pots and another with a jumble of tools. Files, saws, large brown bottles lined up along the top shelf along with tubs of paraffin wax. Bundles of wire and mesh. Two black bin sacks tied and waiting disposal. A pile of rags in the corner. The smell of damp and decay overlaid by something darker, an odour she couldn't put a name to. Spicy. Vinegary. Bloody. Stale. Death but not death. Unexplainable. And rounding the corner, she found the explanation right in front of her. Another one of his undeads forever condemned to their prison of wax.

The skin but not skin. At best an attempt, an imitation, a waxy sheen to coat the frailties of human flesh, her gaze skittering across to the tubs of wax and back again, her heart thumping in her chest at what he'd done. The hair was the best thing about the human dummy, clearly a professional wig and, along with the supplies, reason enough why there was never enough money in the house for the basics.

She didn't know how long she stood staring at the wax-like figure. Too long. With a swift turn she headed for the stairs only to pause at a sound behind her. A tap tapping coming from the pile of rags, the ones she'd discounted in her search for the truth.

A mouse. A monster. A man. She turned her back when every muscle, cell and bone shouted stay. But it was too late now, too late to do anything other than run up the stairs and recoup, remembering to switch the light off before gently pulling the door shut and slipping the key back in place.

'What are you doing?'

The sound made her jump, her organs rearranging themselves around flesh and bone, her heart stretching before pinging back to shape; her mind working overtime as she wondered how much he'd seen, how much he'd heard. The thought made her angry, furious – but at herself. How bloody stupid could she be? Time and again he'd sneaked up on her, scaring her witless and yet she'd allowed it to happen again. The only thing for it was to bluff it out.

'Feck's sake. You scared me half to death.'

Penny went to shove past him, but he grabbed her by the arm and propelled her into the kitchen, his fetid breath warm on her cheek; the smell of burning potatoes filling the air.

'I asked what you were doing?'

'Nothing. All right.'

'Are you sure about that, Penny.' He clutched her by the back of the neck, driving her head forward towards the table and the newspaper spread out across the surface.

Serial Killer at Large in Dublin Central

'A bag of body parts, Penny. I wonder where they got them from, eh?'

'Please stop. You're hurting me.'

'I'll hurt you a lot more if you don't tell me the truth.'

TWENTY-NINE

'I can't believe you intend to see Billy Slattery.'

'No time like the present, Paddy,' Alana said, checking her phone before placing it on her lap, the screen face down.

They'd left Bulldog Buckley back in Ballinteer with the intention of heading straight back to Clonabee station, only for Alana to change her mind at the last minute. She was ambivalent to Garda Slattery and his trumped-up charges of bullying, but there was no indecisiveness when it came to having a mole in the camp. His father owned the largest paper in the area, a paper that had managed to run a headline story with no information forthcoming from official sources. Alana was determined to find the leak, and if that meant she would be rid of his vile son, then so be it. He'd only be getting what he was due. A half-an-hour detour would be all that it would take, and as she'd already decided on a sandwich at her desk for her lunch, the additional time was negligible.

They'd be waiting a while for the SOCOs from the Technical Bureau to work their magic on Cunningham's house, and for Rusty to come back with a report on that second bag. Until then it was desk work as they trawled through background

information on both victims, to identify any common denomi-
nators that matched the disappearance of a quiet-living retiree
to that of a thirty-year-old prison guard. So far, the only thing
the men appeared to have in common was their brief contact
over twenty years ago. This time lag made it an unlikely but
obvious place to start looking.

'I doubt if Billy Slattery will agree to see you.'

'That's entirely up to him, but there'll be widespread panic
on the streets if his paper links the disappearance of
Cunningham to that of Crossey,' she said, looking out of the
window at the houses streaming by. 'The man has no idea the
damage he's done by running the story.'

'Probably doesn't care. Have you ever met him? An interesting character by all accounts.'

'Only the once,' she said, bringing up an image of the tall,
powerfully built man to mind. It had been at some work
shindig, shortly after her accident but before her divorce had
been finalised. It wasn't his looks she remembered but the
power and confidence. Someone who knew exactly what he
wanted and demanded that everyone around him jumped to
attention, so he got it. A man's man if ever there was one.
Divorced but a frequent presence in the social columns and
always with the prerequisite blonde clinging to his side.

'How did you find him?' Paddy asked, indicating right
before pulling up in front of an impressive pair of wrought iron
gates, with an S in the shape of a snake threaded through the
bars.

She shrugged. Polite, courteous even. The first man who
wasn't a relative, health care professional or colleague who'd
taken the time to speak to her, albeit briefly. Being newly
disabled hadn't prevented her from realising that she'd suddenly
become invisible to ninety-five per cent of the population.
Whether out of awkwardness or intentionally didn't matter.
Rudeness didn't have to come with an instruction label for it to

offend. 'As you say, an interesting character,' she said, waiting for the guard to approach from his little hut.

'Detective Mack and Detective Quigg to see Mr Slattery,' Paddy said, holding up his ID card.

Paddy was still muttering about how easy it was to gain admittance when he pulled up in front of Slatt Castle. The castle had been transported from the west of Ireland, only to be reassembled, brick by brick.

'You obviously underestimated the power of your card,' she said, opening her door and lifting her legs with her hand so that she was sitting at right angles in preparation for sliding into her chair.

'I don't think the card has anything to do with it,' he replied, paused in the act of positioning her wheelchair into place, his attention on the large Gothic-inspired door studded with black metal nails and the man hurrying to greet them.

'What?' Alana glanced up, her mouth dropping open slightly at the sight of Billy Slattery striding towards them, a broad smile in place. 'What?' she repeated, the sound softer. Puzzled, confused, her mouth snapping closed.

'Looks like you made an impression,' Paddy whispered, leaning close on the pretext of offering his assistance when he already knew that she was well able to breach the small gap.

'Fuck off, Pad.' And on the next breath. 'Hello, Mr Slattery. Sorry for just turning up but there is something important we need to discuss. This is Detective Paddy Quigg by the way.'

'You'd best come in, and do call me Billy,' he said, waiting for her to settle herself in the chair before walking beside her to the front door, ignoring Paddy who trailed on behind.

The castle was a large, impressive grey building that looked to have settled into the landscape for centuries instead of the ten years or so since Slattery had decided on a whim to shift it from Galway. The outside was true to the original, the inside a mishmash of period features interspersed with modern art and an overflowing of bookcases.

He directed her along a wide corridor and into his office. A warm space with dark wood panelling, maroon leather furnishings and an enormous desk stacked with folders, which he proceeded to sit behind.

'I take it this is to do with the piece in this morning's newspaper,' he said, getting straight to the point. 'If so, I could have saved you a trip as I never discuss my sources.'

Alana threw a quick glance towards Paddy, who'd decided to remain standing instead of taking the seat offered.

'I think we know the source, Mr Slattery,' she said – there was no way she was going to call him Billy, despite his sudden frown. 'Your son needs to back off before he gets himself into any more trouble. I can forgive once, because he obviously didn't realise the damage he'd be doing, but if it happens again...'

Billy raised his hand palm facing. 'Stop there, before you say another word. While I'm not in a position to reveal my source, I can tell you that William wasn't it. I can one hundred per cent guarantee that he'd never spout his mouth off about anything confidential to me.'

If it had been anyone else, Alana would have been tempted to believe him but Billy Slattery had a long reputation for bending the truth to meet him own ends. This was just another example.

Instead of answering, she swivelled her chair towards the door.

'Come on, Paddy. He's obviously not going to admit to anything.' She turned her head back only to find Billy barring her way. One second, he'd been leaning forward in his chair the next he'd skirted the desk and placed himself in the doorway. 'What the...?'

'I'm sorry but I can't let you leave until you assure me that

William won't get into any trouble for something he hasn't done.'

'And that's something I cannot give. Your son is old enough to fight his own battles as well as take responsibility for his own actions, Mr Slattery. The truth is your stupid headline has scared half of the population and terrified the other, in addition to informing a seriously troubled individual that we're onto them.' It had also given her a headache-worthy amount of stress and all the extra work involved with having to deal with the media.

'The public have a right to be kept informed.'

'Rubbish. The public have a right to be protected, that's it. If on occasion we ask for your newspaper's cooperation with a case then you should only be too glad to help us, but out of a sense of duty and not the need to profiteer out of someone else's misfortune. Step aside, please. There's nothing you've said to reassure me as to the origins of the story.'

'My son is a twenty-three-year-old idealist who deserves far better than a dad like me,' he said, smoothing his hand over his head. 'Look, I'll grant that the headline wasn't perhaps what you were expecting, but there's no way that William would be involved. I haven't seen him to speak to in five years, not since his mother and I went our separate ways. I'm the very last person he'd go to with a juicy story. The competition. That's another thing entirely.'

Alana stared up at him as she processed his words. As an excuse it was the only one he could have given that would make her believe him, and it was certainly one she intended to check as soon as she returned to the office. If she stayed any longer she'd start to feel sorry for him and that would never do. The likes of Billy Slattery were the enemy of policing and honest journalism alike. It was best she remembered that.

'Okay. Thank you for your honesty and apologies if I drew

the wrong conclusion,' she said, wheeling past him now he'd stepped back out of her way.

'How is he?' The question was forced out as if against his better judgement, a wealth of feeling tucked between the seven letters and six spaces. A question from a desperate man.

There were many things she could say about William. Bolshie. Belligerent. Certainly, a chip off the old block. She decided to go with none of them.

'He's fine. Clever. Intuitive even,' she added, thinking back to Casey's rescue and all that shopping. A bit messed up and possibly in need of a father figure, but she couldn't tell him that. Her inner thoughts were for her alone. 'Thank you once again for your time.'

'If he ever asks about me – here.' She watched him retrieve something from his pocket. 'My details are on there, if you need to get in touch.'

She fingered the plain, white business card. Nothing fancy or ornate. His name. His email. His telephone number. There wasn't an instance where she could ever see herself contacting him, but she pocketed the card all the same, her mind jumping on to other things. If the leak hadn't come from William, then it must have come from someone else on the team. She had no idea whom.

THIRTY

The first person Alana met when she arrived back was William Slattery. He'd obviously just rucked into the station, the very last place he should have been going by the skimmed milk colour of his skin and the shake of his hands. He was also the very last person she had time for after wasting her morning, but she couldn't afford to alienate him any further. His sheepish look said more than a whole host of excuses.

'You head up to the incident room, Pad. We'll have a catch-up shortly,' she said before turning to face William.

'You're looking a little the worse for wear, if you don't mind me saying.'

'Ma'am?'

'Come up to my office for a chat before I send you back to bed to nurse whatever lurgy you've picked up,' she said, not accepting no for an answer despite his clear reluctance to go anywhere with her.

It was obvious that he was hungover, but she wasn't his mother, or father, for that matter, she thought, entering the lift behind him and pressing the button to the second floor. Yes, he probably deserved a telling off for missing work, but it wouldn't be from her.

'Take a seat, William. I can call you William, I take it? You know you can call me Alana. We're all very informal here except when someone officious is visiting, so limit the ma'ams, if you please.'

'That's fine, ma'am. Alana.'

He looked uncomfortable and sounded awkward. He also smelt like the local brewery. Oh, to be young or to know someone she could trust enough to allow her to get pissed and bugger the consequences. She promised there and then to do exactly that if and when they solved the case.

'Right. I'm not here to lecture you or give you a hard time but I have had a word with the DS.' He started to interrupt, but she didn't let him. 'No. Let me have my say then it's your turn,' she said, making sure to meet his gaze as well as offering a small smile. It wasn't returned. His colour had changed from white to sickly green, which had her eyeing the mesh wastepaper bin in alarm. 'Our team is small and therefore relies on each member pulling their weight but also acting part of the team. I don't expect to be your friend, best or otherwise. That's not how it works in the Guards but I do value your input and will try and support you where I can. I think we got off on the wrong foot, something I'm happy to rectify, but only if you're prepared to join me halfway. I also think you have a lot to offer and therefore I'd like you to seriously consider joining us on a firmer basis, after we've put this one to bed.'

'You'd like me to stay despite...?'

'Yes. Look, William, you're obviously not yourself. Go home and think on what I've said. We're not in kindergarten. We're adults who talk when there's a problem. I can't promise not to annoy you on occasion but that works both ways.'

He nodded.

'Okay. Off you scoot. See you in the morning unless you

decide that it's not for you. Just let me know, eh, if that's your decision.'

Alana watched him go before dropping her gaze to the sight of his father's card now tucked under the corner of her mouse mat. She had no responsibility for the lad, which didn't in any way prevent her from feeling sorry for him. It was a dangerous emotion where colleagues were concerned and entirely the fault of his father.

The incident room was a hub of activity on her return, but as the central hub of a murder investigation, she'd have had something to say if it had been otherwise.

Paddy was leaning over his desk in conversation with Flynn and Lorrie when she entered, but he shifted to his feet at the sight of her.

'Here you go, Alana.' He held up her mug, indicating with a tilt of his head the box of chocolate muffins on the side.

'You really shouldn't have.' She watched as he selected a cake and placed it on her desk beside her drink, knowing full well she needed both hands to manoeuvre her chair into place.

'I didn't. They're from Rusty via Gaby. When was the last time you knew me to bake anything?' He chuckled.

'He'd burn water on a good day,' Tatty interrupted, slumping into her chair.

'Anyone want a sister? She's going along with a dowry of ten sheep and three goats to sweeten the deal. Cheap at half the price.'

Everyone laughed, even Tatty, but there was an awkwardness in the sound. A breaking of the ice but threaded with an undercurrent of concern: fear of what they were facing next. The coffee and cake were a nice touch. Now it was time to get down to business.

'Right then.'

'Sorry I'm late.'

Alana looked to the door at the clearly hassled Irene Burden, who was shaking the raindrops from her mac before hanging it on the hook behind the door, her briefcase tucked under her arm.

'Good you could join us, Doctor. Help yourself.' Alana waited a moment while Irene did just that, her briefcase now open on the only spare desk available.

'Back to business. Paddy and I have come from Ballinteer and yesterday's disappearance of Fergal Cunningham, a thirty-year-old prison guard, a detail which may be relevant. What is relevant is that Paddy recognised the name from his childhood as someone we can link to Aidan Crossey,' Alana said, picking up her muffin and peeling off the casing as she tried to decide if it would be greedy to eat two. She was ravenous, which was hardly surprising as she'd missed breakfast and was about to work through lunch. 'It might have been easier if you'd remembered a bit quicker, Pad. Maybe next time, eh?' She took a small bite before continuing. 'It's a crying shame Crossey's parents are no longer with us but at least we have something to go on. Anyway, that's beside the point.' Alana swept her finger across her mouth to dislodge any stray crumbs, her focus on Flynn before switching to Lorrie. 'Any luck with those foster kids' names?'

'Not as yet,' Lorrie said, placing her mug down on the desk. 'We've been having a bit of trouble with the bureaucracy over at IFCA. The Irish Foster Care Association,' she added, for the benefit of Irene's blank look. 'They've forwarded on our request to TUSLA. Apparently The Child and Family Agency have a new tracing service on the back of one of their latest policies, which we have to go through but, surprise surprise, it's not up to date and there's no one available to rummage through the paper files. I've banged off an email in the harshest of terms with my thoughts on the subject.'

'Well done, you. I'll be sure to supply the wine and tissues when the complaint comes through,' Alana said, returning her smile. 'Let me know if there are any more delays. The whole of Dublin now know what we're up against thanks to the effing *Globe*.' She paused to take a long sip from her mug. 'Right then, Paddy and I have met with Cunningham's wife, an interesting individual if ever there was one. Basically, no one saw Fergal leave for work yesterday morning, and with his motorbike still in the garage and no record of him turning up at the prison, we have to conclude that he was abducted from his front doorstep.' She picked up a photo from the desk, holding it up for everyone to see. 'Detective Buckley is leading on the case and cooperating one hundred per cent with our side of things, and that's the way we want it to continue. We all need to remember to copy Buckley into any findings, and I'm including myself in that little nag. No point in upsetting our colleagues.'

'Okey-doke.'

Alana glanced at the board and where she'd made a note of which team member she'd assigned to which task. 'What about the veg stall holder, Eddie Murch? That was you too, Flynn.'

'No luck as yet, I'm afraid. I managed to catch up with him earlier. Said he was too busy to take note of their customers.' He scratched the side of his nose briefly. 'No CCTV to confirm or otherwise, but I have to say I wouldn't trust him one little bit.'

'What about the people working for him? I can't for one minute imagine our Eddie bagging up the sprouts while he waits for the right change to be handed over?'

'He runs it with his wife, probably to keep costs down. He said something about her being at a doctor's appointment.'

'Okay. We really do need to hear what she has to say on the subject. She might have noticed something he didn't. Let's mark him as someone of interest. Speaking of which, how did it go with Dr Gaunt and the EvoFIT, Lorrie?' she said, wiping her fingers on her navy slacks before wrapping her fingers around her mug.

'He was happy with the result, which is one good thing. I've uploaded copies on to the system, so we'll have to see what gives. I take it you still don't want to release the image to the media?' she said, holding up a drawing of a thin, emaciated-looking young woman with dark straggly hair pulled into a lopsided ponytail.

'I'm not so sure. What do you think, Paddy? It goes against the grain after that show-and-tell Slattery ran in his rag, but we also can't afford to risk the life of the person that left the scrap of paper in Casey's pocket. Remember, we can only assume that this woman and Casey's mam are one and the same. I'll agree it's likely but until we have more proof, we can't be positive,' she said, tapping the photocopy of the original note that she'd pinned to the whiteboard.

Paddy pursed his lips, obviously thinking it through. They'd discussed the case on the way back along with his thoughts as to who was drip-feeding information to the papers and, like her, he was of a mind to look no further than the son. It was a risk taking William on the team on a more formal footing, but he was also innocent until proven otherwise. Alana asked herself whether she'd have been quite as accommodating if she hadn't felt so worried about the lad. There was something about him that had made her think twice before sending him back on foot patrol with his tail between his legs. It wasn't something she could put into words. A feeling that all wasn't well with him.

'It's a difficult call. We obviously don't want to put anyone's life in jeopardy; however because of bloody Billy Slattery, the word is already on the streets as to what's happening.' He shrugged, his fingers looped around the waistband of his trousers. 'You could say the damage has already been done and it might prevent another abduction.'

'Another abduction? God, talk about being pessimistic.'

'More like a realist, I'd say,' Dr Burden chipped in, starting to count on her fingers. 'Two unidentified bodies, or body parts if you want to be pedantic, in addition to body parts from Crossey, and now this missing man over in Ballinteer. That's three dead that we know of, possibly a fourth. We can't protect everyone, but is it not our duty to inform the public that there's a lunatic out there?'

Alana sighed, unable to rationalise the implication of the note and what it would mean to Casey. She wasn't prepared to think about the girl and how she was getting on with her foster family over in Glendalough: the wound was too raw for that. She'd known almost from the get-go that she was breaching every ethical code in the book, but it had been impossible to stop the tide of emotion that had swelled and roared. Their relationship had formed between the narrow band of time it had taken for the girl's tears to brim and overflow from her trembling lashes and onto her cheeks. The first hug had only cemented that bond. Ignoring the feeling was the only way forward. She was able to console herself that the gardai over in Wicklow were checking up on the girl's safety. There'd be more drive-bys and visits than the county had ever seen before, due to the tangled case and Casey's importance.

'Okay. I'll think about it,' she said, choosing to shift the conversation to something she wanted to discuss. 'How's the profile going, Irene? Any help we can get would be welcome.'

She watched her cross her legs, her smart black trouser suit obviously designer, as was her tailored cream blouse; the loose scarf knotted at her throat a nice way to soften what was otherwise a severe outfit.

'Oh, definitely a man, for many reasons including the strength needed to immobilise and move both Cunningham and Crossey. I haven't had a chance to give it more than a cursory look, but I suggest you're looking for a loner. Someone who is able to pop across to Ballinteer for before eight, in what must have been busy traffic, without garnering questions while also carrying out a nocturnal visit to my neighbour. However, I must add that—'

'But what about the meat and the girl?' Tatty interrupted. 'Either he gave it to her as a cry to be discovered, or she took it without his permission. Either way, she must have had access to his freezer.'

'A good point and one I was about to address.' Irene sent her a cool look before continuing, a small smile curling her lips. A woman completely in control of the situation. 'Someone can be a loner while also being in a relationship. Take your Fergal Cunningham for one, whose wife was allegedly unaware that he was missing until being informed to the contrary. It's a recognised fact that most serial killers fit into the loner category, less clear is why they'd want to be discovered, if indeed that's what the discarding of some of the body parts is all about. It's been mooted that some killers thrive on notoriety, a theory that's been reinforced time and again by the way they contact and, one could almost say, manipulate the media and public opinion alike. I label this brand of killer narcissistic,' she said, continuing to stare across at Tatty with barely a break to blink. 'Someone superior and with grandiose ideas far outside of their scope merged with a lack of empathy or insight surrounding their actions. That's not the vibe I'm getting here.'

Alana maintained a blank expression as she spoke, even though she had a colleague that fit the narcissist label exactly: Ox Reilly.

'How can you tell?'

'There's nothing in the least showy in the way he abducted the two men. No calling cards left. No contact with either the Guards or the media. I think we can discount the girl too. There's something furtive in her actions. If she is Casey's mother, and there's a good chance that she might be, then leaving her daughter could be seen as a cry for help, as could leaving the organs.'

'You're saying that she could be in danger?'

'Most definitely. After all, we know what he's capable of.'

'So, we're looking for a loner, an empath if you like,' Paddy said, glancing around the room for support. 'That's the opposite of a narcissist, isn't it? Someone in touch with their feelings, perhaps to the point that they've felt driven to act the way they have.'

'You're doing remarkably well, although I wouldn't go quite so far as to call them an empath, Paddy,' Irene replied. 'Performing live organ retrievals is nothing short of barbaric.'

'Would you say then that, as well as a loner, our man would have some medical experience? A doctor or medical student even?' he added.

'Not necessarily.' Her lips contorted into more of a grimace than a smile. 'You'd be quite amazed at what surgeons decide to upload onto YouTube with no thought to the repercussions for the mad among us. I took a quick tour earlier and, while I'm not one hundred per cent confident, I'm pretty sure I could have a stab at it, especially if I wasn't bothered as to the outcome for the patient.'

THIRTY-ONE

Penny had always been scared of the dark. A fear that had started as a small child when her parents had tucked her up in bed one night with promises of seeing her in the morning only to never return. A fear perpetuated by her grandmother when she'd used the cellar as a form of naughty step. The woman had manipulated that raw, visceral, heart-clenching anxiety into something desperate, something frightening.

Bedtime stories never existed in their house. They'd disappeared in a flash of grief along with cuddles and night-time kisses. Instead, her grandmother dropped hints about the boogie man, a fearful, ungodly creature that ate little girls for their supper, stripping flesh only to spit out the bones after. It reached the stage that Penny couldn't walk down the hall without her heart pulsing in her ears and her mouth drying. Her dreams turned into nightmares; her waking moments feeding the images that raced across her mind, night after night.

Before. Before her parents had died, she'd been happy and content. Afterwards, she'd been anything but.

This morning had been the first time she'd visited the cellar since the death of her grandmother, as well as the first time she'd entered of her own volition. Now she was back but this time it was worse, worse than all those previous times rolled up together. It was worse because she wasn't alone and there was nothing she could do about it. There was nothing she could do about any of it.

He'd forced her down the stairs, nearly breaking her ankles in the process of half dragging, half lifting her reluctant body down the steep steps, her fingernails bent back as he'd ripped her clawing hands from the banister, his breath as rank as his body odour. There had been no words, no speeches, nothing after he'd pulled her out of the kitchen, the smell of burnt potatoes lingering in her nostrils long after she'd left the room. He didn't have to tell her that she'd let him down; she'd been letting him down ever since their parents had died, by being the child their grandparents had chosen to keep; one child and not the two on offer. The reality was that, as a five-year-old, there'd been nothing that she'd done to affect their decision. It wasn't her fault that she'd had a mop of white-blonde curls instead of lanky, mouse-coloured locks and a perpetual scowl, or that he was only her half-brother and therefore no relation to her grandparents. None of it was her fault and yet she was the one blamed.

The chair was hard and the ropes tight. Fear caused her mouth to dry; but it wasn't the dark that she was most afraid of. It was the dark combined with the muffled squeaks and groans from the corner. She'd never thought that he'd take it so far. The death of their grandparents was bad enough, but this?

She must have drifted off. Nature's way of shutting down her mind and body to what came next, or something. All she knew was that one second she was trying to figure out what his plans were, the next she'd jerked awake at the sound of the cellar door slamming against its hinges quickly followed by the stomping of feet on the stairs.

There was nothing she could do in her current position

except plead while she tried to rock her chair, but he took no notice. It was as if she wasn't there. All he was interested in was shifting the mannequin into a sitting position before starting to mess about with its hair.

Penny couldn't think of the dummy as a man or even as a corpse. That was the road to insanity, a route she'd been travelling along ever since he'd forced her to return to the family home with cries that it would be different now that her grandparents had decided to change their mind over their great-grandchild. If she'd only realised what he'd done, what he was still doing, she'd have refused his entreaties. He'd planned it out down to the clean clothes and even brushing his hair flat on his head in a style that didn't suit his long, narrow face; but she'd been too pleased to see him to notice the effort he'd made. Before she knew it, she'd agreed to return to the house with him to see her grandparents, in one last attempt to win them over with Casey.

The house had been in darkness, the heavy curtains pulled closed against the cool evening but without the chink of light she'd been expecting. It hadn't taken her long to realise that it wasn't only the lighting that was different. The hall smelt of dirty bodies and dirty dishes with an underscore of something else, something she'd only later realised must be the smell of death.

He'd conned her right up to when he'd directed her to her grandparents' bedroom and she'd seen what he'd done. The misshapen, diminished bodies bundled into ill-fitting clothing. Their shrunken features coated in a shiny film of what she later discovered to be wax. The painted faces and glassy eyes that he'd admitted he'd managed to buy online. It was amazing what you could buy on the internet, he'd enthused, putting out a hand to tap Jasper on top of his icy-cold head. The number of people that wanted to immortalise their pets through taxidermy. Immortalising humans was only one step up, the techniques the same. The skin the only problem he'd found difficult. That, and the disposal of the innards.

He'd been so proud standing there. As eager as a small boy showing off his new toy. The older brother she'd always looked up to until her grandparents had turfed him out to fend for himself. The brother who'd kept in touch by leaving letters for her hidden in the Wendy house. The brother who'd disappeared only to reappear back in her life when he'd found out about Casey. The one constant, the last link to her past.

But Penny had betrayed his trust. Now it was time for retribution.

THIRTY-TWO

Alana finally arrived home at a quarter to eight, a ready meal, a tin of cat food and a bottle of wine balanced across her knees along with her laptop case, hoping against hope that she'd set the timer on the central heating. She only remembered her economy drive when she pushed open the front door to be greeted by an irate cat and a hall that was only missing a set of icicles strung across the ceiling.

'Rats. No, not you, puss. God. I'm talking to myself again, aren't I? No. I'm talking to you. Wait a sec for me to switch on the heating, then I'll see about your tea. Who knew that having a cat gives you permission to be daft, eh.'

She didn't bother to take off her coat, hat and gloves and she wouldn't until the ice had melted from her bones. Instead, she made for the kitchen as promised and set about dishing out fish-flavoured cat food onto the side plate with the chip. The picture taped to the fridge door she ignored, in as much as she knew it was there but shifted her gaze every time her eye muscles wandered in that direction.

The kitchen area was small, too small for a table along with a wheelchair, which meant Alana had to ferry her microwaved spaghetti bolognaise and glass of wine back into the lounge on the clip-on lap tray she'd happened upon on Amazon, an accidental find that had been life changing. Before that, mealtimes had been twice as difficult and taken twice as long. Her wheelchair was her lifeline, the mobility aid that allowed her to function in a world populated by the able-bodied, but after a day of sitting in the same position, she relished the feel of her back and shoulders being cocooned in plush velvet chenille. Goose had disappeared after his feed, but with the front and patio doors both locked and the alarm engaged, she wasn't worried. He'd turn up when he wanted something.

Her emails came first, the majority copied in bulletins that were destined for her junk folder. She didn't bother with anything from Ox. This was her time to do with what she pleased, which didn't include having to read anything that was bound to drop her mood.

The first email she opened was from Rogene. The report of the Technical Bureau findings from the Cunninghams' house, a more disappointing paper she had yet to read. The only thing of interest in the seven-page document were brown marks found in the hall under the door, which on further examination proved to be burn marks.

Alana lifted her hand to adjust the angle of the lamp by the arm of the sofa, a crease forming between her eyes as she tried to work out what the strange matchstick-length strips were only to laugh at the analogy. What better way to get someone to rush to open the door without ringing the bell than to post lit matches through the letter box? She rested her head back against the aqua-coloured sofa and, closing her eyes, imagined the scene.

Fergal walking into the hall from his bed-cum-sitting room. Maybe he'd heard a sound or maybe not. The number of burn marks amounted to twenty or so. Enough to fill the air with the smell of sulphur. Enough to have enticed him out of the house without waking his wife. It would have been an instinctive act with little thought as to the consequences, apart from the need to stop the little shit on his doorstep from setting alight to the hall.

Alana shifted slightly before reaching forward and grabbing her glass, the stem bAlanacing on the arm of the sofa. There'd been no such marks found in Crossey's house, but then he'd lived alone. A ring of the doorbell would have been all it would have taken to drag him from his bed, his book abandoned. The ways to incapacitate were many and varied from a blow on the head, use of chemicals or martial arts.

Replacing her glass on the table without having touched a sip she reached for her phone. It only took seconds to draft a quick email to Paddy and Bulldog about her opinion on the burn marks found in the Cunninghams' hall, her thoughts satelliting in all directions These weren't random abductions. They were deliberate acts. Men targeted in their own homes. They knew the relationship between Cunningham and Crossey, but that's where the trail ended. It would take time to drill through the list of fellow foster kids if and when TULSA delivered the goods, time they didn't have.

THIRTY-THREE

Paddy had always been an early riser which, unlike Alana and her morning jog, had nothing to do with exercise and everything to do with being brought up in a household that appreciated the beauty and stillness to be found while the rest of the world slept. Keeping hens was also a factor or, rather, the cockerel that had come as part of a job lot from the closest farm.

It had been years since he'd lived at home, but the old ways continued. Ten to five each morning found him lying in bed with his nose in a book. He was far too lazy to think of getting up at that time. By six, invariably he was sitting at the kitchen table with a slice of marmalade-slathered toast on one side and a mug of tea on the other, his phone in the middle, the radio on in the background – but not today. For the first time in ages, instead of breakfast, he'd scrawled a hasty note for Tatty before pulling the front door closed quietly behind him. Tatty wasn't an early riser, despite their common parentage and similar upbringing. Some days he thought she must have been adopted, that or left by aliens. The only thing they had in common... Scratch that. There was nothing they had in common apart from their father, the kindest, saddest widower

in County Dublin. He started the engine. Sharing a father. It
was enough.

Half past seven and Moore Street Market was alive with
sounds and smells. Trucks backing up to unload crate after crate
of fruits and vegetables. Sellers shouting across the narrow
street in an array of accents from Dubliner, Corkonian and
beyond. Prices scribbled in thick felt pen. Red, green and
yellow apples vying for pole position alongside juicy pears and
underripe bananas.

Paddy chose an apple from the display and passed over his
money.

'There you go, luv. Need a bag with that?'

He shook his head in reply, rubbing the waxy skin along the
leg of his trousers before taking a large bite, his gaze shifting to
the stall opposite, to where Eddie Murch was leaning against
his van watching, presumably, his wife unload trays of vegetables, a cigarette in one grimy hand, his mobile in the other, his
T-shirt stretched tight across his hanging belly. The wife, by
comparison, was thin, scrawny even, but by the way she was
carting around boxes it was hardly surprising. Eddie looked like
a right one standing there, his eyes darting about. Restless. On
edge. Waiting for something to happen. The question was
what? Maybe he suspected something after Flynn's visit
yesterday.

Paddy didn't know why he'd come out of his way apart from
the nagging doubt about why someone who appeared down on
their luck, would head for the market, which wasn't known to
be the cheapest way to buy food. There was quality on display,
but quality like this didn't come cheap. Fifty cents or more
loaded onto the price for the benefit of the tourists who flocked
to the area for a slice of Ireland, a slice that wasn't for sale at any
price, he thought, chewing the soft flesh. The apple was too
round and red to have been grown locally, and it lacked the
sharpness he preferred from the organic fruit and vegetables he

favoured. There were things he was prepared to compromise on in order to save money, like lowering the central heating thermostat and washing at thirty degrees, but cutting back on his food bill wasn't one of them, he remembered, discarding the half-finished apple in the nearest bin before approaching Eddie, his hand already in his pocket to pull out his ID card.

'Aw, what are you bothering me again for?' Eddie said, going on the defensive as he ground his cigarette end into the pavement with the heel of his shoe. 'Put that away, would you? Bad for business, not that you'd care.'

'You're right there.'

'What?'

Paddy watched him take a step back or try to; there was no room to manoeuvre with his backside rammed against the side of the van.

'I don't care,' he reiterated, hiding a smirk. 'Not one iota, Eddie. Yesterday you gave one of my guards the runaround, but that's not going to happen today. Now, here's the thing. We can do this the easy way, which is a nice chat out in the open while you let your missus do all the work, or the hard way back at the nick.'

'Now, here's the thing,' Eddie mimicked, back in his stride. 'I know my way around the legal system and you hassling me in the street is against my human rights. You have no grounds to target me and no reason to make me go anywhere, either voluntarily or otherwise. I've cooperated fully and have nothing to add. I don't know how my print got on that fiver and the truth is I don't care.' He waved a hand at the odd straggler or two starting to appear despite the earliness of the hour. 'No one would expect me to remember with the amount of footfall we get.'

Paddy knew he could force the issue just as he knew that the outcome would be the same. Eddie Murch was a career criminal who probably understood the Guard rules and regulations better than he did himself. He was also as guilty as sin, but Paddy couldn't prove a thing. A guard's instinct was as inadmissible in court as voodoo dolls and soothsayers.

With a sigh, he returned his ID card to his pocket and replaced it with a photo of the girl and one of his business cards.

'Let's cut through the crap, Eddie. A girl's life could depend on it,' he said, handing him the photo and card in spite of his unwillingness to take them. 'All I'm asking is for you to take a good look, eh.'

'On my mother's grave I've never seen her before in my life,' he replied, trying to thrust them back.

'No, you keep them. You never know, you might remember something.'

With that he turned his back and headed the way he'd come, his shoulders hunched into his jacket, his fingers pushed deep within his pockets, the rain starting to fall on his uncovered head and trickle down his neck and under his collar. Paddy imagined Eddie scrunching up the paper and flinging it in the nearest bin, perhaps the same one as his discarded apple.

By the time he'd reached his car, he was disillusioned with the whole investigation. The only highlight, the only thing to look forward to was his takeout coffee and box of Danish pastries that he'd picked up from Ann's Bakery on his way to his parking place.

His phone pinged through a message almost as soon as he'd slid behind the wheel and peeled back the lid of his cup. The swear was as full-blown as it was inventive.

This is Eddie's wife. What's he been up to now?

She'd followed the message with a whole row of angry face emojis, which made him smile. Eddie must have ditched the card only for his missus to immediately go looking for it. Praise be for small mercies and nosy wives. He just needed his luck to hold out for a bit longer. The wife was probably brewing for a fight, which made it the perfect condition for her to be tapped for information about her errant husband.

He took his time in forming the right reply before clicking send.

Hello, Mrs Murch. I'm Detective Quigg. Nothing that I know of. I was asking Eddie about one of his customers and what he could tell me about them, if anything. I'm afraid it was a waste of time though as he didn't recognise her.

Have a photo?

Paddy's smile broadened, a picture of a sand eel coming to mind. A sand eel dangling on the end of a fishing hook.

Wasn't there one with the card?

Nothing.

What on earth was Eddie up to?

Okay, sending one over. It's only an artist impression but meant to be a good likeness.

What's she done?

I'm sure you know I can't tell you that, Mrs Murch, but it is important that we trace her whereabouts.

And that kid of hers. Poor poppet, with a tart for a mother.

Paddy slapped the steering wheel with his palm before tapping out a reply.

Mrs Murch, please, if there's anything you can tell me. I promise to keep your name out of it.

Don't know much. Penny something or other. Lives Northside. Spreads her legs for cash.

Paddy ended the message with a *thank you* and, ignoring his coffee, phoned Alana.

They'd finally agreed to launch the media appeal for eight o'clock that morning, the time chosen to catch commuters on their way into the city. Alana and Paddy arrived at the office at ten past the hour to find Flynn and Lorrie on their phones, fielding a shedload of calls.

'Right, listen up everyone. Eddie Murch's wife has come up trumps by giving our EvoFIT a name, so please tell me a Penny has featured in one of your conversations. Don't all speak at once,' she continued after a couple of seconds, growing disillusioned at their silence.

'Sorry. Every name under the sun except Penny, but then it's not all that popular.'

Alana knew Flynn was right but that didn't stop her from slamming her hand down against the nearest desk in annoyance, her palm stinging from the movement. So near and yet so far. They'd done everything, thought of everything, spoken to everyone relevant but they'd obviously not tried hard enough. They had a name and an eFit but nothing they could do with either, apart from an extensive door-to-door that would need a level of manpower they didn't have. The Northside was no help. A hindrance if anything. As useful as saying she inhabited the planet earth.

Dublin was split down the middle by the River Liffey into the Northside and the Southside, each part spanning an area difficult to quantify, but with a combined population of over two million inhabitants, they were fighting a war that had probably already been won and not by them. Serial killers were known to speed up and not slow down, which meant that the likelihood of Fergal still being alive was minimal.

'So, there's been nothing useful, at all?'

'Not as yet,' Lorrie replied. 'Mainly the usual nutjobs looking for their five minutes of fame, a couple of names worth following up but that's about it. What we do now have, finally, is the list of Crossey's parents' foster kids, which I was just about to start on.'

'That is good news. You'll have to provide lessons on the art of writing snooty emails. Ping it across. William and I will split it, while Flynn and Paddy man the phone lines. In the meantime I have another job for you.'

'Ma'am?'

'If Murch's wife is to be believed our Penny drops her panties for cash. So, I'd like you to concentrate on the prostitute angle. Phone Detective Chief Inspector Una O'Neil from the Organised Prostitution Investigation Unit and take it from there. If that doesn't reveal anything, we might have to make a trip to Parkgate Street after dark to chat to some of the ladies and gentlemen parading their wares. I'd rather not, but we might not have a choice in the matter.'

'Right on it.'

Alana nodded briefly, diverted by the sight of William shrugging off his jacket and removing his woolly cap, a hand lifted to smooth back his hair.

'All right, William?'

'Fine, thanks.'

He didn't look fine. The sight of his pale skin tightly drawn across hollow cheeks and eyes that couldn't quite meet her gaze added to her guilt of not having dropped his dad a quick line last night, but she wasn't his keeper. She didn't even trust him, and she wouldn't until she'd discounted him from her investigation into the leak, but that didn't prevent her from feeling in some way responsible. She'd spend the morning working with him and think again as to what she was going to do about the situation, if anything, her attention on her phone case and the business card that she'd decided to keep.

'Grab yourself a coffee and pull up a chair,' she finally said, ignoring his look of alarm. They had a killer on the loose and a missing man to find.

The list from Lorrie was presented in a PDF format. Four columns with the briefest of information. The name of the child followed by their date of birth and the dates of their stay at the Crosseys'. Twenty-one names to locate and eliminate from their enquiries. They couldn't even narrow it down to a specific time frame, as their son, Aidan Crossey, would have had exposure to every one of their charges.

'Right, here's what we're going to do, William,' she said, pointing to the screen and the name of *Angela Poole* halfway down the list. 'You look up all the names up to Poole and I'll do the same for the rest. We need to find out their current location, convictions, if any, as well as anything out of the ordinary. Boring as hell but it's in the tedium that we usually find those nuggets of gold.' She paused a beat, suddenly noticing the way his left hand was curled around his right, his fingernails digging into his skin, little indents forming to a depth that must be hurting. 'Any problems or questions, William?'

'No. Happy enough.'

Which was a lie on any measurement scale, but Alana had to let it go. Any more from her and she'd be at risk of mollycoddling him. Either that or have another bullying and harassment chat with Ox heading her way.

'Okay. If you find anything at all you think odd let me know, eh, and we'll bash it out together.'

Alana started on the list, one ear listening in on the conversations swirling around the office, the tempo and pattern the same. Someone they thought they'd seen. A face in a crowd. No name. No location. No use.

The socio-economic and educational disadvantages of looked-after children meant that many at some point in their lives intersected with the police and that's where Alana headed first, hardening her heart to the devastation that she knew she'd find. While the best of intentions ran through every policy and protocol to protect the young and innocent, the stark truth was that there wasn't enough money or staff to make the differences needed. These kids had seen far too much at too young an age not to be affected by it, and the resulting damaged children were easy prey to the criminal fraternity, the likes of which would exploit their granny if given the chance.

Of the eleven on her part of the list two were dead, two missing and presumed dead, while another four were currently being housed at the pleasure of the Office of the Department of Justice. That left two to find as the final one had attained a law degree from Trinity College and was now working in Switzerland for the World Health Organisation.

She smiled at that. It was easier for her to focus on the positives and not on the eight lives failed by the system set up to protect them. It also brought her full circle back to Casey, who'd been mopped up and placed with the best of intentions by a body as well-meaning as it was flawed.

Where the girl would end up in five, ten, fifteen years' time was a question too frightening to contemplate. It was impossible not to dwell on the kind of life she'd have been exposed to with a prostitute for a mother. Alana had enough scare stories in her repertoire of horrendous crimes to know the dangers the children of streetwalkers faced. Vulnerable to abuse and often left alone for long periods of time while their mothers were out. At least she was safe for now, she thought, leaning back in her chair and stretching.

Her spine clicked at the sudden change in position, causing a stabbing pain to shoot up her back, which had her pulling the top drawer of her desk open and downing a couple of paracetamol before wheeling her way around the room and collecting a variety of empty mugs. Being head of the team didn't come with a gold-plated certificate that excluded the bearer from the more mundane of activities. Though delivering drinks might be an impossibility without the threat of her suffering from third-degree burns, it didn't mean that she was completely helpless. While there wasn't much she could do in the tearing around catching criminals department, at least she could boil the kettle and splash a bit of milk into a mug.

'Hands up for tea,' she shouted. 'Now hands up for coffee.' And, a few minutes later. 'Come and get it.'

'Thanks, Alana,' Paddy said, picking up his Chelsea mug, a birthday joke from Alana for the man allergic to anything more energetic than tying his shoelaces. 'If I have to hear another caller tell me to get off my arse instead of sitting answering calls, I'll top myself.'

'Well, if you think I'm going to offer to spell you for a bit you've got another thing coming,' she replied, glancing out the window at what looked like storm clouds building. The weather forecast had mentioned snow, which she'd pooh-poohed at the time. Now her thoughts shifted to Alfred and Tooley, as she handed Flynn his mug, and how she could ever start to repay a little of the help they'd provided on the case.

'How are you managing? Any luck at all?' she said, turning back to William and where he was struggling to meet her gaze.

'All a bit depressing, isn't it?'

'My thoughts exactly. How many did you manage to find?'

'Does it count if they're locked up?' He flicked her a glance before continuing his perusal of the top of his tea and the single escapee of a tea leaf floating on top.

'Sadly yes. It also means that we're going to have to interview them.'

He raised his brows at that. 'Then two still outstanding and no clue as to where to start.'

'The easiest place, I've found, is always the beginning. So, who was the last person to see them and take it from there. Then there's their social security number. If that doesn't flag anything there's the RSA to see if any of them have a driving licence,' Alana said, on a roll, the missing person policy flying through her mind. She'd read it often enough to quote it verbatim in parts. 'Remember too that they could be incarcerated in a place other than prison, for instance sectioned under the 2001 Mental Health Act. Finally there's the internet, social media, and Interpol. We only tend to go down the spiritualist route as a last resort.'

'You what!'

'Sorry, my little joke. We don't need to start bothering Interpol unless everything else pans out.' She sent him a small smile to mitigate her words. 'So, who have you got in prison?'

Alana watched him as he returned to his desk to get his notebook, the hand tucked into his trouser pocket clearly clenched into a fist. As much as she wanted to help him, she didn't have a clue where to start. Keeping him busy and under her eye was all she'd come up with.

'An Alex O'Hagan and Benny O'Connell. Both at Arbour Hill Prison.'

'That's interesting but also a bit annoying.' She drained her mug and placed it back on her desk, her mobile in her hand.

'Why annoying?'

'Because we're going to have to brave the weather and visit

them, whereas my two inmates are housed between Cork and
Castlerea, and that means I can get the local plod to do my work
for me. Come on, grab your coat. I'll phone Arbour Hill on my
way to the car so that we're not left hanging around.' She picked
up her leather bag and rested it across her knee, her phone on
top as she pulled her hat on and started on her jacket.

'Why interesting?'

'Excuse me?' She lifted her head, one hand in her puffer
jacket and the other struggling to find the armhole.

'You said interesting as well as annoying. Why interesting?'

'Because Arbour Hill is where Cunningham works as
prison guard.'

THIRTY-FIVE

Arbour Hill Prison could pass for a private gentleman's residence, except for the large wall surrounding the building and the large sign declaring its purpose to anyone who might not already be aware.

Alana manoeuvred her Volkswagen Polo into the car park and pulled to a halt in the disabled bay to the left of the main entrance, before turning off the engine and unclipping her seat-belt. William, silent by her side, copied her. He had maintained a dignified silence for most of the journey over. Oh, he'd answered when spoken to or when she'd asked a question, but she could count on the fingers of one hand his monosyllabic yes, no replies.

'If you could get my chair from the boot, please,' she said, keeping to the point as she pushed open her door and lifted her legs out until her feet were positioned on the ground. She'd made small talk on the journey from Clonabee to Stoneybatter, but it was like prising a whelk from its shell the response she got. If it hadn't been for reading about his home life yesterday she'd have given up by now.

With the chair in place and the brakes engaged, he stood

back, watching as she slid across the seat before slamming the door, ignoring the dents that ran the length of both doors.

'I have a friend who's a panel beater. I'm sure he'd—'

It was the first kindly thing he'd said, another sign that he was making an effort and she had to turn him down.

'That's very good of you, William, but there's no point. It's not that I'm a bad driver, in fact I'm quite good, but I'm not so good at dismantling this blessed contraption yet and heaving it in the car, wheel by wheel, especially when I'm in a rush.'

His face flooded with colour right up to the tips of his ears. 'Sorry, I didn't think.'

'No need to be sorry. It is what it is. Now let's get this over, shall we?'

'No. No comment. No fucking comment.'

'Well, he was a complete waste of time.'

'You're being far too kind, William,' Alana said, plonking her pen on the table and running her hands down her face in frustration as soon as the door had closed behind them.

They'd been directed to Arbour Hill's interview room twenty minutes before with great hopes for a breakthrough, hopes that turned to dust at the sight of Benny O'Connell with his hands shackled behind him and the prison guard refusing to leave the room. If they got two words out of the prisoner that weren't swears, they were lucky, and nothing of relevance about Aidan Crossey. They couldn't make him talk, which was all the more annoying because Alana was convinced that he knew more than he was saying.

'An effing arsehole with knobs on would be how I'd put it myself but each to their own,' she continued, lifting her head at the sound of his chuckle, the first sign of a thawing in the ice of their relationship.

Alana knew that some people lacked a sense of humour

gene – Ox Reilly for one – but as far as she was concerned it
was a prerequisite of the job. Most days the ability to take the
mick was the only thing that kept her sane, that and the thought
of flopping back in bed at the end of her shift and hoping for a
dream-free sleep. There was little enough pleasure in her life
for her not to embrace the things that made her happy. Humour
was part of that.

'So, what do we know about the next one?' she asked, reluctantly returning to the schedule after joining him in a quick
smirk. The slight change in their relationship was tenuous at
best, especially when compared with the weight of his
complaint to Reilly and the question of his honesty still
looming.

'Alex O'Hagan, age twenty-eight.' He read from his notes.
'Resided with the Crosseys from age three to eleven, which
coincided with his father's release from prison.'

'Ah. Not a great start for him.'

'No although he was doing all right until his marriage broke
up last year. Had a job as a mechanic, which was fine until his
wife shacked up with his boss. Ended up living rough and petty
thieving to make ends meet,' he said, still reading from his notes.
'Sent down last month for twelve weeks on a charge of vagrancy
and petty theft.'

'Ah,' she repeated, staring at him across the expanse of desk,
the sound of feet parading outside before coming to an abrupt
stop. 'The difficult choice of freezing to death on the streets or
three square meals a day, hot showers on tap and Sky Sports all
courtesy of the Irish Prison Service.'

'You mean people actually...?'

'Wouldn't you? It's a complete no-brainer, all apart from
Sky Sports. I much prefer a bit of *Strictly* myself,' she said, her
attention on the short, square man being escorted into the room,
the air of defeat clear to see in the drop of his shoulders and
inability to forge eye contact. A broken man and, as much as she

wished it were different, there was nothing she could do to change that. He'd be mopped up on discharge by some homeless charity or other and provided with the rudiments for survival. A sterile bed in a shelter where he'd be scared to close his eyes at night let alone allow himself the luxury of sleep. Life was cruel but crueller for some, more than others. The Benny O'Connells of this world would always make sure they were all right, but the same couldn't be said for the man sliding into the chair opposite, his hands tucked out of sight under his armpits. A protective measure if ever there was one.

'Hello, Alex, I can call you Alex? I'm Detective Alana Mack and this is Garda William Slattery. Thank you for agreeing to speak to us.'

He hadn't been given the choice, but Alana skimmed over that part as she tried to work on how she was going to play it. She'd been tempted to lead up to the subject gently only to change her mind. Alex looked dazed, probably still trying to work out how his life could have gone off the rails in such a spectacular fashion. She needed to grab his attention and keep it grabbed. Pussyfooting around the edges wasn't going to be enough. It was a risk, as she'd be revealing more than she wanted to, but with the media on the story it wouldn't be long before everyone knew that they had a madman roaming the streets of Dublin.

'We're investigating the disappearance of Fergal Cunningham, Alex. He was fostered at around the same time as yourself? We think it's in relation to the murder of Aidan Crossey.'

'What?'

Alana leashed her smile against her teeth at the way he'd jerked back in his seat as if someone had stuck him with a cattle prod. There could be no excuses that he'd failed to recognise the name, which was a common trick among prisoners unwilling to give away their secrets.

'I see you know who I'm talking about, Alex? Remember,

this chat is just between the three of us, but there's a killer on the loose that we really must find,' she said, leaning forward, her head dipping as she tried to catch his eye. 'Crossey's murder was particularly unsavoury. Can you help at all?'

'How unsavoury?'

She paused at that, aware that William had shifted in his chair at the words and hoping that he wouldn't say anything to interrupt the flow of conversation. 'I'm sure you can appreciate that I can't go into details, but on a scale of one to ten, probably eleven.'

'Good.'

It wasn't the answer she was expecting but there was a wealth of meaning in that single word to make a longer explanation unnecessary. Alex loathed Crossey. It was there in his expression and tone. The way his hands loosened from under his arms. A relaxation in his posture as if someone had removed a huge burden from his shoulders. It was up to her to tease out the details.

'Why's that, Alex?'

'Aidan was an evil little shit that deserved everything that was coming to him and more.'

An interesting opinion made all the more interesting by their lack of evidence from the investigation to either confirm or deny his protestation. That Aidan had been cleaner than the inside of her pseudo-perfect, ex-mother-in-law's oven, had been an itch that Alana hadn't been able to eliminate with any degree of effectiveness.

She felt the blood swell in her arteries and veins in anticipation, but managed to dampen down any signs of excitement. The worst thing possible would be for the man in front of her to realise the importance of what came next. With Reilly as her boss, she didn't have any bargaining chips to work with, no promises on offer. Nothing except a thirst for information with no quenching drink to give in return.

Instead of asking the obvious, she decided on a roundabout approach.

'And what about Fergal, Alex. What did he deserve?'

The rigidity returned but the keenness in his expression remained. 'Fergal's not dead, is he?'

'Not that we know of. Is that a good thing?'

She watched him nod.

'Tried to protect me a bit when I arrived here, though I hadn't seen him in years. He was going to help me get back on my feet too. Fat chance of that now.'

'So, you wouldn't know if he had any enemies then?'

His answer was a shrug, his interest waning.

'And what about Crossey, Alex?' she asked, cajoling. 'You called him an evil little shit.'

'Doesn't matter now, does it? The man's dead.'

'But if it will help us to find Fergal, mate. Friends watch out for their friends, right?' William said, joining the conversation, his fingers still holding on to his pen as he recorded the interview, word for word, on the notebook in front of him.

'Especially when they might have something they're feeling guilty about.'

'Fergal had something to feel guilty about?'

'I'm not saying he did and I'm not saying he didn't, but friends look out for other friends in care. They watch their fronts as well as their backs particularly from sexual predators and the like.'

Alana's glance sharpened at his words, the strands of the case knitting together into a ribbon of explanation that made complete sense. 'So, you're saying Crossey was a sexual predator then?'

'Of the worst type.'

'I hope he won't get into any trouble over the interview.'

'I think the opposite is true, William. Remember, with Fergal having worked here, the rest of the prison guards will have good reason to look after him now,' she said, slamming her car door shut and waiting for him to buckle up. 'People like Alex don't really belong in prison, you know. All we're doing by locking him up is putting him in danger from the other inmates. Benny O'Connell for one.'

'So, what do we do about it?'

'There's not a lot we can do. As much as it hurts to say it, we can't save them all.'

'No. but...'

'There's no buts about it, William.' She picked up her ringing phone from her lap, striving for a patience she wasn't feeling. Yes, it was good that William was sensitive to what Alex must be going through, but now wasn't the time to act Good Samaritan. 'With Fergal still missing, and Casey's mum to find, we have more than enough problems to think about,' she said, turning her attention to her mobile and Paddy's voice repeating her name for the third time.

'Don't blow a gasket, Pad. I'm here.'

'Okay. Just wondering how you got on at the prison?'

'It looks like Crossey was into fiddling with little boys, which is as good a reason as any for murdering him. Ask the Tech Bureau to take another look at what they took from Crossey's house, in particular his phone and laptop. I know they were meant to be clean but there has to be something in the house. Paedos tend to keep some sort of trophy of their crimes. Remember, we'll need it if and when we have our day in court. Oh, another thing. We also need to take another long hard look at the remaining foster kids on the list, Paddy. We still have three to track down, and the likelihood is that one's our man. I'll be back at two. Round up all the usual suspects for a briefing, would you?'

THIRTY-SIX

WEDNESDAY, 22ND DECEMBER, 11.00 A.M.

It was the light that woke her. The harsh florescent strip whipping under her eyelids and powering up her brain, her sensations revving up along with her heartbeat. The feel of the wooden chair biting into the underside of her thighs. The ache in her back and her neck. The trickle of wet dribble on her chin in stark contrast to the dryness of her throat and sore, chapped lips. The chill of her skin as the biting cold infiltrated the thin layer of her jumper and jeans. The sudden realisation of where she was. The fear of what was coming next. The sound of the scream wrenching through the air no more than a breath away, interspersed by the soft crooning tone of her brother in a voice she'd never heard before.

'You brought it upon yourself, Fergal, so there's no point in moaning now,' he said, the words a complete disconnect with the continual scream of pain. Raw. Guttural. Almost feral in its intensity. An animal cornered and with all escape routes closed off.

'No. Stop. Please. Why are you doing this?'

'Why? You ask why when you did nothing to help.'

'I couldn't. How could I? I was in the exact same position as you.'

'And yet Crossey left you alone. Day after day. Night after night he crawled in beside me with you only a few feet away. You knew and you did nothing.'

'Please. What could I have done? I was a kid, for Christ's sake. There wasn't anything...' The last word ended in a screech, the tip of the blade pressing.

If Penny's hands hadn't been strapped behind her back, she'd have placed her fingers in her ears. There was nothing to divert attention away from what was being played out next to her, just as there was nothing to stop her from turning her head and focusing her gaze. There was also nothing to stop the tears filling her eyes and running down her cheeks in a steady stream at her brother's words – blurring her vision and damning her soul. She'd be lying if she'd never suspected that something had been going on. The way he changed almost overnight from the loving, caring older brother, who used to leave notes and little bags of sweeties in the playhouse in the garden, right under the eyes of her unsuspecting grandparents. In that first year it had been the one thing that had kept her from running away from her grandmother's petty tyrannies. In the second the missives stopped abruptly. All sorts of thoughts ripped through her six-year-old mind, primarily that he didn't love her any more. To her young, unformed self it seemed the simplest of answers. She used to cry herself to sleep, her face pressed into the pillow to muffle the sound. Unlovable Penny, who everyone left in the end. She didn't see or hear from him for a whole year after that and then only sporadically, until he'd come to find her as an adult.

Now she knew why.

There was no thought for the position she was in. No hopes and prayers. She was long past believing in fairy tales with their happy ever afters. Her grandparents had drummed into her long and hard the power of the Church and the repentant soul, only to fling her on the scrapheap the one and only time she'd fallen off the path of righteousness. She'd been wasting away on that scrapheap ever since.

The man was stretched out on his side on the workbench, his feet dangling over the edge, ugly bruises running up his shins where the leather straps tied him to the top. She skipped over his flaccid penis and the redness of his testicles against the pallor of his flesh, her face blooming at the sight. It had been nearly three years since she'd seen a man in his true form, since she'd experienced the draw of a warm smile and a comforting embrace. The likes of Eddie Murch pummelling into her from behind didn't even flicker across her mind as being part of the same thought. A means to an end. Payment for services rendered. Sex when what she'd sought had been love, and the home life that had been denied her. She'd found neither in Doug's arms.

This man was no Doug with his inked sleeves and winning ways, she recalled as she scrolled past the man's pasty white skin and up to the circle around his throat, where a ring of tan lingered in spite of the time of year. His neck was extended, revealing thick ropes of muscle and a knobble of Adam's apple. She couldn't see his face, his eyes, his expression but she knew what they'd tell her. Desperation. Hopelessness. Resignation. It wasn't hard to guess. She'd experienced all three at various times since being invited back home, her baby girl in a third-hand stroller with a wobbly wheel and stained seat.

Her brother was bending over him, his fringe flopping over his eyes, the crown of his head revealing where the hair was starting to thin, his thumb and forefinger pressing on the man's side as if in search of something. In his other hand was a thin knife, the sheen of steel glistening in the light and causing her to blink, even though she knew what came next. There were no missing pages to the story, no censured paragraphs, nothing to protect her from her mind racing ahead, the man's skin rippling while waiting for the blade to strike.

The scream as the tip punctured the flesh before plunging deep. The gush of rosy red spreading out across the plane of white. The smell of iron punctuating the air. The drip of blood as it reached the edge of the table and slipped onto the floor. The growing silence apart from the rasp of her brother's breath, death clinging to all sides.

The next time she woke it was dark, a darkness like she'd never experienced before. A thick wall of black, a heavy weight that made no sense to her muddled mind. Even in the middle of the night, she could still make out the shape of the wardrobe in the corner of her room and the fall of the raggedy curtains draping the window. The barest gleam from the streetlamp combined with the stars and a fair bit of light pollution, if she'd had to come up with a reason that is, which she didn't. This was different. A consuming black that nibbled away at her common sense and caused a scream to build. The black of a shroud. The black of a sealed coffin. The black that comes with death.

She drew a breath and then another. There was no indication that he was in the room waiting to pounce.

No, he'd be back upstairs by now eating those burnt spuds. *Bet he doesn't remember to soak the pan.*

She knew she was on the cusp of hysteria, a wave of panic rippling across her cold skin. Why else would she think about a saucepan when there were so many other things to think about? The man dying inches away from her for one. There was also her own death. It couldn't be far away, but she wasn't going to allow her thoughts to veer off in that direction.

Escape.

That's where she'd go in her mind. A wander through all the possibilities. Something to warm her against the bite of the cold and the ripple of fear. Her only hope was someone coming to a house that no one visited apart from the bin men and postie. By tomorrow night she'd be long dead, if not by his hand, then from dehydration. There was no one to save her and, with her hands and feet bound, no way to save herself.

All was quiet and still, all apart from the sound of another breath, slow and rhythmic, a sound she'd been trying to blank out because of the memories it drew. The man on the work-bench. Asleep and not dead, which was a relief, although there wasn't anything she could do with the information.

She'd watched what her brother had done right up until she'd squeezed her eyes tight, tears managing to push through the gap to streak down her face.

The tears were forged from guilt, her own guilt at allowing it to go so far, for it to get to the point where there was nothing she could do to stop him.

'I blame myself for not realising what was going on sooner,' Paddy said, collaring Alana as soon as she returned to the office. 'I mean, I went to his parents' home. I would have sat at the same table while I ate my tea. I didn't suspect a thing.'

'You were only a kid and, on your own admission, far more interested in trying to get into stage school than in what was playing out around you.'

She placed her hand on his arm briefly before working on unwrapping her scarf, her gaze on William slipping into his seat and staring into space without having bothered to remove his coat. She hadn't managed to get much out of him on the way back despite her plan to get him to open up, but there was nothing she could do about that now. Paddy was in need of reassurance, which was a unique enough experience for her to want to provide it.

'Don't take this the wrong way, but I think it would have taken a better person than you to know what he was up to. For Crossey to have got away with it for so long means that he was adept at hiding his true character long before the likes of you came on the scene. God only knows how many victims he's left behind,' she added, tucking her hair behind her ears and checking that her stud earrings hadn't come adrift with the removal of her scarf. 'That's a strand we'll have to knit into the investigation when we track down both Cunningham and his abductor.'

'You think we'll be able to find them before history repeats itself?'

She shrugged, her fists clenching under the tangle of scarf layered across her lap. 'No idea but here's hoping. So, what about Eddie Murch's wife then? A bit of a turn-up,' she said, deciding to shift the conversation to a topic that she could control. There was nothing she could do to change Paddy's past except to concentrate on the investigation and catch the killer.

'I must admit to being gobsmacked when her message came through. I didn't for a minute think that anything good would come of my early morning visit. Eddie Murch is such a disparate individual, while she struck me as a meek sort of person. Certainly not the sort to break ranks.'

'We may never know what pushed her over the edge, and it doesn't really matter either way if it leads us to Casey's mother.'

'It's not going to be as easy as all that. Penny What's Her Name doesn't give us much to narrow it down with any degree of accuracy.'

Alana laughed, but without any humour laced between the waves of sound. 'What, you mean a name and an EvoFIT aren't enough? I was expecting her address, date of birth and shoe size by now.'

'Ha bloody ha and she doesn't wear shoes, remember? Grubby trainers, if Dr Gaunt is to be believed.'

'And there's no reason not to,' she said, manoeuvring her chair towards the front of the room and where the team were starting to gather, Paddy walking beside her. 'He's proved his worth in all the ways possible. I only wish there was something he'd let us do in return.'

'Too much pride for that.'

'Pride is made up of fool's gold coated with a layer of arrogance but a deeper one of insecurities. It can't feed or warm him and it certainly can't replace his family, the three things he needs more than anything.' Alana darted a glance out the window and the thick yellowy clouds, laden with snow. She'd listened to the news bulletin on the way back, anything to interrupt the silence of the car, only to be greeted by the promise of snow flurries, which was all they needed.

'Oh, I don't know about that. What he needs or what you think he needs? The line separating the two is only sliver thin.'

Which was food for thought as she waited for everyone to settle in their seats. Dr Gaunt was a niggle that wouldn't go away. She couldn't in all conscience leave him to his fate, but there was nothing she could do that he'd accept. That didn't mean she wasn't prepared to let the problem rest, she mused, picking up her phone and adding a quick note to her to-do list. It was a very long list made longer by Christmas looming on the horizon.

Paddy had managed to fill the room with all the key personnel on the case, which meant a shortage of chairs with Rusty, Flynn and William propping up the far wall in copycat stances, their arms folded across their chests. Lorrie and Tatty were sharing a desk to make room for Rogene and Irene. The only person absent was Ox Reilly – he wasn't missed. The phones were quiet – the calls diverted to the two uniformed officers stationed in a spare interview room.

Alana glanced at the clock above the door. She'd called the meeting for two. It was ten seconds past when she started to speak.

'Thank you for attending at such short notice but it's imperative we do everything we can to find Cunningham before it's too late.' Her smile was fleeting. With her tablet in her hand she connected to the white board and rapidly bulleted the events of the last twenty-four hours, explaining each additional point with her soft burr of an accent.

'Aidan Crossey, paedophile with a predilection for young boys, which he found readily available at his parents' house. It's, at least, a strong motivator for murder, especially as Cunningham was one of those foster kids. The reason for the prison guard's abduction is less clear.' She looked over her shoulder briefly, catching each set of eyes in turn before returning to the board. 'Rogene, please tell me you've found something that will stand up in court about Crossey. I'm not fussy as to what it is.'

Rogene shook her head. 'I'm afraid I can't do that. As you already know Crossey's laptop and phone were left at the scene, but they're both squeaky clean. We can link Crossey to both through fingerprint analysis, so it's not as if they weren't his. I also had our Digital Forensic Officer look for any patterns with Crossey's mobile phone usage, but there's nothing significant. It seems as if he only used it to take and receive calls and messages, all of which we can track back to the original owner, mainly family and with the odd dental and doctor appointment. The laptop tells the same story. Used for bank reconciliations mainly – our Mr Crossey liked to keep track of his spending – certainly no signs that he used it to access the internet.'

'Which is odd, don't you think?' Alana said, her palms shifting to her wheels, which she gently rotated forward and backwards. 'Hands up anyone here who doesn't have an Amazon account?' she went on, compressing her lips at the stillness in the group. 'Just as I thought. That's unusual and, as you know, I don't like unusual.'

'Actually, I think you're onto something.' It was Irene's turn to interrupt. 'I can't be one hundred per cent sure, but I do recall on one or two occasions the postman delivering packages. Who orders packages these days, if not online?'

'So, what are we saying? That he had another device for all his dirty little secrets. Rogene?'

'We've turned the place upside down, but I'll get the team to have another look.'

'Hang on. Before you mobilise anyone let's get in touch with his network provider to see if he had more than one device in his name. Worth a punt surely and a much better use of manpower.'

Rogene gave a sharp nod of thanks in Paddy's direction for the suggestion, her phone in her hand, her index finger swiping at the screen. 'If there is one it's likely to be a PAYG burner but you never know. I'll get right on it.'

'Great. Let's move on. Anything new from you, Rusty?'

'Nothing, without a body to work on. I'm not touting for business you understand.' He punctuated the words with a lopsided pull of his lips. 'But you have to appreciate that there's a limit to what a heart, liver or kidney can tell us.'

'If we come across any random corpses, you'll be the first to know. Now, what about the woman that dumped off the organs? This Penny Whatever from the Northside.' Alana spread her hands as she repeated the name. 'Penny, such a pretty name. It could take weeks to run her to ground unless you lot have any bright ideas. Who was working on the prostitute angle?'

'Me,' Lorrie piped up. 'Detective Chief Inspector O'Neil was most helpful, although I wouldn't have her job for the world.'

'It certainly takes a special kind of person to act part copper, part social worker, part therapist and with a touch of medical experience thrown in for good measure. So, what did you find out?'

'After all that, nothing of any importance, I'm afraid. Penny isn't someone she recognises. She's happy to ask around on our behalf though, which…'

'Saves us a shedload of work,' Alana continued. 'What are we missing then if we can't find her on the streets? Come on, one of you must have something?'

'Didn't someone mention that they thought she was well-read?'

'They did indeed, William. The handwriting expert for one.'

'And Dr Gaunt too,' Paddy interrupted, recrossing his arms in the opposite direction. 'Something about her recognising the origins of his dog's name.'

'That's right. I'd forgotten. Named him after one of the Greek Muses, as you do,' she said, thinking of Goose, a wry smile brewing. 'So, where does someone like Penny Whatever have access to books then, as I'm guessing it wouldn't be the local library.'

'Why not the library?' William looked confused and well he might because it was the obvious of answers.

It was also a carefully laid trap, one which he'd fallen straight into. While Alana didn't for a minute think that they'd find anything of use trawling around Dublin in search of a literary type named Penny, it was still a box that needed ticking. It was just a shame that they couldn't phone instead. If she heard someone spout on about GDPR regulations again she might scream. Visiting in person was a waste of everyone's time but essential if they were to have any chance at finding out about Penny. 'I take it you attend the library yourself then?'

'Attend the library myself,' he repeated, consternation in both his tone and expression. 'Doesn't everyone?'

'Not necessarily. I prefer reading on my Kindle, and Paddy here is more into movies than the written word, which means you're the ideal person for the job.'

Slow realisation dawned as she watched him turn around to

look out of the window and the first flakes of soft snow splattering against the pane. The weather forecast on the way back to the station had intimated heavy snowfall right into the night and beyond, and warnings galore about no unnecessary travel, which was a huge worry during an investigation of such magnitude.

'I'd better start now so.' He picked up his coat and phone before heading for the door, all surly looks and negative body language, only to pause at the sound of his name.

'Here, you'd best take this,' Lorrie said, rushing to his side with a sheet of paper she'd pulled out of the printer.

'What is it?'

'A list of all the libraries. There's twenty-one in all.'

'Bloody great.'

The words were muffled but still clearly audible across the room, and they lingered for a couple of seconds after the door had slammed behind him.

'You think he'll manage?'

'We'll soon find out, Paddy,' Alana replied, pushing away any ideas that she'd made the wrong decision in sending him off on his own.

It was a simple enough brief to show around Penny's photo and ring back any results. It was also another chance for the lad to prove himself, not that he needed it. William had a good brain and a guard's instinct for getting to the truth. If only he could get rid of the chip on his shoulder.

But what if he failed? The thought appeared out of nowhere along with the image of his father and the telling off she'd had from Ox. If he failed she'd be in the wrong and that would never do, not in the climate she was forced to work in. Ox would escalate William's original complaint, and Billy. Well, she'd never liked the idea of appearing in the *Globe*.

'Actually, run after him, would you? Tell him whatever you

like to make it right. I don't want him on my conscience and, thank you, Pad. I owe you one.'

'Right then, what about these three missing men? Jack Mauger, Chris Conlan and Danny Devlin,' she continued, one eye on Paddy as he raced out the room, his coat and phone bundled in his hand, and the other on her phone, which had just bleeped through a royal summons from Ox Reilly.

THIRTY-EIGHT

'I had expected you earlier, Mack, but then I am only the detective superintendent.'

'I have been busy, sir.' Alana slipped on her brakes and lifted her head to make eye contact. She was quite happy to call him sir, it was expected, but she'd be blowed if she'd apologise for only doing her job.

'If you can't organise your workload sufficiently in order to keep me abreast of developments in a timely fashion, then I'll have to rethink our little arrangement,' he said, interrupting her thoughts as he pointedly looked at his watch.

What arrangement? Oh yeah. The one where you've allowed a cripple, and a female one at that, to lead the team. She rolled her eyes.

'Just get on with the update, Mack.' He used his index finger to pull back his cuff a second time. A hot date with his missus then, Alana thought, managing not to smile at the image of the far-from-hot Mrs Reilly, even with a bucketload of Botox and more fillers than could be found in the nearest DIY shop.

'We've managed to eliminate all bar three of the children fostered with Crossey's parents from our enquiries. A Jack

Mauger, Chris Conlan and Danny Devlin. They're the last three to be ruled out and therefore there is a strong possibility that one might be the man we're looking for. The only thing is their trails have gone cold.'

'I take it you've issued a Yellow Notice through Interpol as well as looked at kinship matching?'

Alana looked pained at his suggestion. The first thing she'd done when she realised the possible importance of the missing trio was pull the policy and work though each of the steps in case she omitted any, easy to do when the document was seventeen pages long. However, the Yellow Notice was a no-brainer and certainly not something she needed the policy for. It was just one of the six global alerts that allowed for worldwide corporation on key and urgent issues, the Yellow One pertaining to missing persons.

'Yes, to the Yellow Notice but not the kinship matching. We'd have to have a source of his DNA in order to match with any relatives for that.' She'd have liked to add what a stupid suggestion it had been from the stupidest man imaginable, but that would be one step too far over the line and the one thing she couldn't afford to do was lose her job.

He waved away her clarification in the same way he would a fly. Alana knew she was an irritant. The stone in his shoe that wouldn't be shifted until she was good and ready to move on. Little did he know that she was on the countdown – to retirement, which was currently set at fifty-five. By that time, she'd hope that he'd be long retired, or promoted. God forbid. The damage he could do as a detective chief superintendent, or even higher was more frightening than the thought of having to work under someone of his calibre for the next fifteen years or so.

'What else?'

'We're looking into the possibility of Crossey leaving some kind of calling card as to his predilections. You know, trophies, photos. At least then we'll have proof as to the kind of man he was. Apart from that—'

'You have nothing,' he spat out, a bead of spittle lingering on his fleshy lower lip, which he swiped away with his sleeve. 'We have one man missing, three dead, in addition to that abandoned kid and you have fuck-all apart from a wild goose chase to find the mother and those three former foster kids, who more than likely aren't relevant. The DCS will be most displeased when I tell her.'

He recapped his fountain pen before placing it carefully across the few notes he'd been taking. It was black with a gold cap and the one that he religiously filled each morning from the pot of India ink that sat on the edge of the desk. A little ritual that separated him from the rest of the biro brigade that worked twice as hard for less than half the pay. One day she was going to rip the pot from its gold-plated holder and smear it across his pristine blotter, and maybe a little on his chair too. It was the very least she could do to repay all the petty insults flung her way over the last two years. For now, she watched as he stared down at his meagre notes, waiting for him to speak.

'She also asked me to pass on a message, Detective. Any more shenanigans from the media and she'll have your badge. Now get out of my sight.'

THIRTY-NINE

He was back. The sound of the door creaking. His footfall on the steps. A sudden flare of brightness where before there was black, a black as thick as soup no matter how wide she opened her lids to find a glimmer of light. Penny squeezed her eyes shut, water starting to gather and stream at the unexpected glare. The pain almost a physical thing as her vision adjusted to the shift in light. Tilting her head, she checked on the man on the bench beside her. Motionless. His skin waxy white. Dead or nearly so. It wouldn't be long and there was nothing she could do to change that. She'd be dead herself if she didn't get a drink of some sort soon.

Her brother ignored them both as he knelt on the floor and ripped back an old sheet, one of the sheets that used to cover her grandparents' bed – she'd had to make it often enough. She'd wondered where it had gone, not that she'd have ever used it. It was a random thought slotted into the other one-hundred-and-one other random thoughts that fluttered around her head in any one day, like the worry over her child.

Who she was with. Was she safe? Was she even still alive? Desperate thoughts that slashed her heart in two, gushing blood from its tattered edges and bringing a trail of memories along with its congealed mass of grief. Her tiny hand within hers; her sweet breath against her cheek; the pressure from her lips as she planted a kiss against the tip of her nose, a game Penny had started when she was a baby and one they continued.

The feel of a tear dribbling into the edge of her mouth dragged her from her pity party, spitting her back into the reality of the cellar and the horrors within. The man whose screams had wrenched through the air for ten days and ten nights in wave after wave of agonising belts was now silent. The man she hadn't heard from since.

She saw him now. His naked body a criss-cross of scars. The skin a mottled blueish green. The face. A face but not a face. No eyes. No smile. The sheen from the coat of wax. She couldn't be sure how long he'd been held captive. Time was irrelevant to someone in her position, someone with no watch and no source of light to guesstimate the shift in the sun across the sky. It could have been hours, days or weeks since she'd been held prisoner. No, not weeks, she amended. She'd have been long dead if it had been weeks. She'd read somewhere that humans could only go for about three days without water, although she'd also come across true-life accounts of people far surpassing that tally.

Her mind filled with the image of a flowing stream, but it disappeared with a jolt at the sight of her brother starting to drag the man across the floor on the sheet.

'Water.'

Was that the sound of her voice, that croak? It must be because there wasn't anyone else capable. She hadn't been planning to speak. She hadn't been planning on alerting him to her presence, even though he was the reason for her current predicament.

Penny knew her brother, and she was far from stupid.

Those two facts should have maintained her silence. It was desperation that made her speak. She tried again.

'Please, Danny.'

He stopped, his hands clenching tight around the edge of the sheet before lowering the man to the ground and forcing his fingers to unfurl. She followed him with her eyes as he made his way across the space, his stride slow and measured, his gaze fixed on hers.

'You let me down, Penny. You, of all people.'

What makes you think I'd be complicit in this madness? was what she'd like to have said to him if she hadn't had a mouth full of what felt like sawdust and ashes.

She should have seen the depths of his madness on that first day when she'd agreed to go back to the house and see their grandparents. She'd been homeless and destitute, having to rely on the women's shelter for the clothes on their backs and the food in their bellies. It was this hope for a better future, and the promise of a reconciliation with her grandparents, that had led her to grab their paltry possessions and follow him.

It had been easy then for her to rationalise the horrors. The preservation of Jasper because he'd thought it would make her happy. She couldn't tell him then that she'd been revolted by the sight of her beloved cat; and it was far too late by the time he'd led her to the front bedroom to see what he'd done to her grandparents. He'd taken her silence for agreement in all that he'd done, and she'd let him. He'd tricked her back to the house with his promise of a secure future, and he had continued to trick her for the first three months, until the madman had finally come out of his secret hiding place and revealed the depth and breadth of his insanity.

FORTY

William Slattery drew his beany low over his ears before working the top button of his overcoat closed and tucking the ends of his scarf under the collar, his attention switching between the yellow half-light of the sky above and the thick snowflakes smearing the pavement outside the station.

He'd reached his car by the time Paddy caught up with him, the keys in his hand along with the list of libraries and a pile of Penny's eFits.

'I thought I'd come along with a bit of moral support, William.'

'So she's sent you to spy on me. Wonderful!' he said, unable to mask his annoyance and it must be said, disappointment. It had been a pain in the arse when she'd set him up to trawl the libraries, but this lack of belief in his abilities was much worse.

'You should know us better than that, lad. The weather's shit and we're dealing with the worst kind of git imaginable. You have the list so, where do you reckon we start?'

Penny What's-her-name lived on the Northside, so William had immediately discounted all the libraries located south of the River Liffey on the stairs down – who'd travel across the river to grab a book which was freely available on their doorstep! That left the Dublin Central Library and the one over in Phibsborough, both of which were within walking distance of Penny's sighting by Dr Gaunt. However, the latter one had the added advantage of being firmly set in the middle of a popular residential area instead of in the centre of the city.

'Phibsborough. It makes sense.'

'Agreed. That's near me so no need to fiddle with the satnav. I'll drive.'

William resigned himself to spending time cooped up beside the senior officer but that didn't mean he had to speak to him. He wasn't in the mood for conversation despite Paddy's efforts and, after the first few uncomfortable minutes, they both sank into silence.

The Public Library in Phibsborough was an attractive Art Deco-styled building that had William reach for his phone to take a quick photo before approaching the Georgian arched doorway. Inside was a hive of activity, with what looked like a parent and toddler reading circle in full swing. It was a good enough incentive for William to produce his shiny new ID card to whoever would care to look at it, aware that Paddy was keeping to his word and letting him do all the talking. He decided on the middle-aged woman in head-to-toe floral with a serious smile and an armful of books.

'Did you want a hand with that?' he said, which he thought as good an opening as any.

'I'm fine, thanks.' She set them down on the trolley in front of her and turned back to him. 'I take it you're not here to see Santa then?'

He could feel the tide of blush rise from under his collar and strike for his forehead, the bane of his life ever since he'd reached puberty.

'Afraid not.' He opened his palm to reveal his ID card, a trickle of sweat running down the back of his neck. The next time he'd keep it inside his pocket, instead of clutching it in his hand like a schoolboy heading to the shops with the rounded coins pressed into his skin. 'I'd like to ask you a couple of questions, if I may?'

'Come with me. We wouldn't want to upset the children now, would we? Not with the promise of the big man in the red suit divvying up presents,' she said, leading them into a small office.

'Now, how can I be of help?'

'We're looking for a woman called Penny as a matter of urgency, and there's some thought that she might be a prolific reader.' It sounded a flimsy excuse for a visit, he thought, nudging the eFit across the desk, the creases from having folded it into four before tucking it into his pocket causing her to raise her eyebrows. Next time he'd make sure he came better prepared, if there was a next time.

The librarian was called Sue, or that's what her name badge stated, but he was far more interested in the way she barely glanced at the picture before pushing it towards him and leaning back in her chair, her arms folded across her chest, her gaze sharp behind a pair of red-framed glasses. If he was a betting man, he'd sink a small fortune in her having recognised the girl. In the same way he also knew that she wasn't about to tell him anything of use.

William had heard about the copper's instinct, but it was the first time he'd actually experienced it. Her next words confirmed his worst fears, and he didn't think there was a thing he could do about it.

'With GDPR we're not allowed give out that sort of information.'

The last thing that William knew how to deal with was an uncooperative witness hiding behind Data Protection legislation he knew very little about. He glanced across at Paddy, who threw him a wink.

'Actually, GDPR doesn't prevent you from disclosing information to us in this instance, Sue.'

'Really? I'm still not sure that I should tell you.' The sound of shrieks from the excited children had suddenly stopped, cut off mid-squeal, which could only mean one thing. The arrival of Santa.

William knew they only had a few seconds before she made some excuse to leave the room but that didn't stop him from glancing down at Penny's image, the first time he'd studied it in detail. The hair was different, but it was like looking at Casey, Casey in twenty years or so. The heart-shaped face and feathered brows. The wide eyes and bow-shaped lips. His fingers smoothed out the image before carefully folding it along the same lines and returning it into his inside pocket, his smile not a smile at all as he lifted his head to meet Sue's sudden look of interest.

'I'm only pleased that some kiddies will get to enjoy their Christmas.'

'What do you mean by that?' Her tone was now as sharp as her expression, her fingers curled into her palms as she stood by the closed door.

'Only what I said. You must know as well as I do that life isn't easy for some young mothers and Christmas can be especially difficult. I was really hoping to reunite one little family in time for the big day, but it's obviously not meant to be.'

Too much? Not enough? He'd certainly laid it on thick enough to need a trowel. He could see she was weakening in the way her feet weren't quite sure which way to move. Towards the door or back to the desk and the desktop computer that filled one corner.

'That was pure genius. Well done, William. I couldn't have done better myself. Most people think that we're a hard-boiled lot, but the job requires a degree of sensitivity and the ability to treat everyone with a degree of difference, tailored to their individual personalities and circumstances. You have the makings of a very fine guard indeed.'

William felt a glow of warm pleasure burst somewhere in the vicinity of his solar plexus and radiating across his abdomen and down his arms, not that he gave any response apart from a sharp nod. His mother called him a cold fish who only cared for himself. His father... He didn't know what his father thought of him. He wished he didn't care so much about that.

'What's next?'

'I'll phone Alana from the car; I think it's likely we'll go in once we've called for backup.'

'How long will that take?' William slid into his seat and fastened his belt, watching as Paddy did the same.

'The snow is the main problem. We don't want to waste time but we can't go in unprepared. God only knows what we'll find.'

Paddy pressed the ignition only to groan at the sound of the engine failing to turn over.

'I don't bloody believe it. A flat battery is all we need. You stay here. I'm just going to ask if they have such a thing as a set of jump leads. I'll phone Alana while I'm at it. There's no time to lose.'

'That was Paddy on the phone. They've found her,' Alana said, tapping away on her keyboard and quickly embellishing on the information. 'Bingo. Penelope Katherine Claire Devlin, aged 19. Registered as having stayed at that specialist mother and baby hostel over in Drumcondra from the 3rd of July last year until the 1st of September this one. Current address unknown and nothing on the system, but I have managed to trace her birth certificate which tells us she was born on the 3rd of September 2003 to Michael Peter Devlin and Katherine Claire Devlin, deceased. She also has a daughter who it appears she named after her mother...'

'As in Katherine with a K, or Catherine with a C?' Lorrie interrupted.

'K for kilo. Why?'

Lorrie slapped her head in frustration as she jumped ahead to the punchline. 'Katherine Claire or, KC for short. What a lot of numpties we are. Carry on. What else?'

'An elder half-brother. Danny Devlin, aged 29. Same father, different mother.'

Alana stared across at the whiteboard, silently cursing that she hadn't hit on the idea of joining Penny's name to each of the surnames of the three men they'd shortlisted. 'So, what do we know about the brother then?'

'Nothing that I can discover since his stay at the Crosseys',' Flynn said, peering at his screen. 'I'm afraid. their parents were killed in an RTA. Wait a sec.' He flipped through a couple of screens. 'Ah, yes. Here it is, road traffic accident fourteen years ago, when Penny would have been five.'

'And her brother fifteen, but she wasn't farmed out to the same foster parents. Does it say why?'

'I don't give a flying fuck why, Mack,' the door banging open to reveal an irate DS Reilly, almost frothing at the mouth. The man was so distressed that, if he'd been a horse instead of an ox, Alana would have considered calling in the vet. 'What I want to know is which one of you little shits has been speaking to the *Clonabee Globe*, again, I might add,' he spluttered, waving a copy of the newspaper in the air.

Alana jerked her head, a feeling of dread in the pit of her stomach. Had she been stupid when she'd convinced herself that William had been innocent, or had Billy been leading her down the bloody garden path? She raised a hand to her forehead, fingers icy against her suddenly flushed skin. Flushed from annoyance and not embarrassment. The one thing she didn't have time for was this crap when she had Cunningham still missing and a murderer on the loose.

'Sir, I fully appreciate your concern; we have just had a breakthrough on the case, and—'

'I don't care what you've got. I want this sorted now,' he said, slamming the newspaper face up on the desk in front of her, the headlines clear to see.

Jack Mauger, Chris Conlan and Danny Devlin Wanted in Connection with the Dustbin Butcher Murders

Alana's eyes widened at the headline, her fingers itching to pick up the paper and absorb every word, but she didn't have the time for that.

'So, let me get this straight, sir. You want me to prioritise this story' – she flicked the edge of the paper with her finger to emphasise the point – 'over finding Cunningham, when we have a pretty much guaranteed lead that should result in his safe recovery.' There was nothing Ox Reilly liked more than a feel-good story about Clonabee police station. As a fish/hook angle it was perfect.

Ox darted her a look which was as calculating as it was full of loathing. 'This isn't over, Mack. Not by a long shot.'

'Yes, sir,' she said, ignoring her ringing phone until he'd slammed out of the room.

'What's up, Pad? I've just had Ox...' She stopped speaking at his next words, her face losing all trace of colour.

'William's done a bunk.'

'What do you mean he's done a bunk?'

'Left me on my tod outside Phibsboro library with a dead battery. The thing is we know who and where Penny is.'

'So do we. Okay. Hold on a minute. I'll ask the team.' She lifted her head. 'Anyone heard from William?' Then, after a second. 'No? Shit.' She marshalled her thoughts, pushing aside the feeling of dread that was starting to take over every cell and neurone. 'Try and follow him Pad but for God's sake, go carefully. We don't know what we'll find. I'll be with you as soon as.' Alana blinked, overwriting the words with a coating of common sense. It was snowing. She was a wheelchair user, with a brilliant team more than capable of being let off the leash without her clucking around their ankles like a mother hen.

'No, scratch that. I'm best staying here organising things this end. There's the digital forensics on William's phone for a start,' she said, feeling the need to qualify her decision. 'Lorrie, you're the better driver.' She glanced at Flynn briefly, noting his belligerent expression but there was nothing she could do about that now. 'Go on then. Vamoose.'

She watched them hurry out of the office, but not for long. There was no time for regrets. A team had many parts, she was only one of them. Calling for backup was first then a call to Rogene to try and trace William's phone. There was also the background on both Danny and Penny. Did they have any priors or even a record? Alana made a brief list on her pad, her mind fact checking what they knew with what they still needed to find out. Informing Ox Reilly was only added as an afterthought.

FORTY-TWO

WEDNESDAY, 22ND DECEMBER, 3.30 P.M.

Avondale Lane was a narrow stretch of road that ran between Avondale Avenue and the North Circular Road. It was also only six minutes on foot, or it would have been under normal conditions. With the snow clinging to every surface in increasingly heavy drifts, William quickly cursed his decision to desert Paddy at the back of the library. It had made sense at the time to get to the property without further delay. Cunningham's life could depend on it, and he might be able to add a bit of extra context to some random name and address by the time the cavalry arrived. His plan was to check out the place and perhaps knock on a few doors, ask the neighbours. That sort of thing.

It was a decision he regretted halfway into his journey, his smart black work shoes – bought specially for his new role – slipping and sliding across the frost-ridden pavement. There was no one else about. No other idiot risking a broken leg or worse. Just him and his stupid idea of making a name for himself.

By the time he'd reached Avondale Lane, his shoes were

ruined, the leather letting in icy sludge and drenching his socks. His fingers and toes were freezing as were his nose and cheeks, the blustery conditions accompanied by gale-force winds with enough sting in the air to make a mockery of his warm clothing. And the possibility that he might have to do the same on his return was the most depressing thought of all. Paddy was alright, nicer to him than he probably deserved but that didn't mean he'd have been happy to be left on his own back at the library. Would he follow him on foot or wait for assistance? It was a bit too late to be worrying about that now. Everything depended on what he found around at Penny's.

The houses in the area were of a pattern. Uniform red brick terraced with brightly coloured front doors and a variety of curtains at the windows, blinds, nets and, in one case, shutters. Avondale Lane was different. The two properties were the same red brick, but that was the only similarity. Instead of buttressing their neighbours the houses were detached and set back from the road with curved semi-circular driveways and two gated entrances, presumably one to enter and one to exit. Two houses bordering one side of the lane and a high wall the other.

William hurried past the first one as quickly as he dared, casting only a cursory look at the smartly finished residence with box planters flanking the front door. The drive was empty and, with no lights shining in the windows despite the darkening sky, he didn't think there was anyone home. With time pressing, he made the judgement call to move on to the next property.

Penny Devlin lived at The Lodge. The only other house on the long lane, the back of the acre-long garden bordering the North Circular Road. There were no fancy planters. No plants whatsoever apart from the weeds poking through the snow in the path up to the front door. The air of neglect and desertion had William pull out his ringing phone, but instead of answering the latest in a spate of calls, he swiped to his camera app and ran off a string of photos. The rusty railings. The chained padlock fastened in place. The guttering that had come away from the wall. The windows...

He stepped back, his head tilted to see over the top of the gate to the first-floor window, his fingers stretching the image to maximum as he continued to click at the two people staring back at him. An old couple. A fat woman with a bad wig and a scrawny man with glasses and a receding hairline. There was also what looked to be a cat.

Per.

Another step back, then another, his attention on the motionless animal and not on where he was placing his feet, which suddenly shifted from under him and his phone with them. Crack went his hip as he hit the pavement, the covering of snow the only thing that prevented him from smashing his thigh. Snap went his head as it jerked back against his neck before bumping off the road, his hat sailing off into a snow drift. Crunch went his phone as his flying left foot slammed against the edge of the kerb, his heel engaging with the screen and the inner workings.

Shit. Fuck. Wank: the run of expletives wrenched from his lips as he tucked the pieces of his useless mobile into his pocket with one hand, the other massaging the back of his head as he tried to stand.

It took him three attempts and many heaving breaths to down the nausea climbing up the back of his throat and remove the greyish-white film clouding his vision before making to his feet. There was nothing he could do about the sudden banging headache or the wobbly legs. He could barely put two thoughts together as he staggered around to the side of the house and the wooden door set into the back wall, his hand relying on the bricks for support, his fingers leaving a trail of blood dripping in the virgin snow. He knew what he'd been trying to do. To find Penny Devlin. That pushed him along, one foot after the other. Find Penny and the rest would follow.

FORTY-THREE

'What now?'

Alana wasn't surprised at his terse response to her knock. She usually had to be dragged by her wheels into his office, and she had only spoken to him ten minutes before, but this was an emergency.

'We appear to have lost Garda Slattery, sir.' The 'we' was deliberate. She couldn't blame Paddy for what had happened, even if it had been his idea to accompany him in the first place. Now she had a missing guard to find and a tricky conversation about the size of the backup team to negotiate, which included an airborne response as well as a firearm one. Hopefully it was overkill. She'd worry about the cost to the Irish economy if and when she was proved wrong.

'You seem to have lost Garda Slattery,' he gobbled, his eyes taking on a frog-like bulge. 'What the hell do you mean you've lost him? He's not a parcel.'

A parcel would be easier to track but that wasn't a thought for now.

'I sent him out to trace Penny, with Paddy to accompany him I might add, but he seems to have slipped the net. The likelihood is that he's on her trail, as we now have a name and address.'

'You do know the implications if anything happens to him?'

'Which is why I need extra bums on seats to help with the grunt work, sir, and I need them now!' She started to turn away. 'If you need me I'm on my mobile.'

He threw back his head and laughed, an ugly sound with no humour. 'What! Don't tell me you're thinking of joining in the search? Remember what happened last time you ventured into the field?'

Alana could hardly forget given that they'd ended up having to mobilise the coastguard to save her. No, she'd learnt her lesson and the reason she was resigned to directing operations from the comfort of the office.

She swallowed back the words pulverising her tongue and headed for the door. It was either that or risk losing her job by telling him what she thought of him.

FORTY-FOUR

Left foot. Right foot. Left foot. Right foot.

William's head was swimming and his thoughts in a muddle, so much so that he didn't question when he discovered that the door to the back garden opened under his touch. Common sense would have insisted that there was no point in even trying the handle, but common sense didn't have a place inside William's thick skull, not so thick now he had a gaping gash oozing thick globules of red blood down his head and onto the collar of his coat.

The lane bordered the North Circular Road, which had a bit of a dodgy reputation at the best of times. It certainly wasn't the kind of place he'd like to walk alone on a cold dark evening and, with the day one of the shortest of the year – and the time stretching towards four – it had an evening quality about it. During the day it was fine. There were even parts along the North Circular that were a joy. Tidy road-fronted dwellings owned by people that cared about where they lived, but night was a different scenario. At any other time, he'd have headed back the way he'd come, in search of assistance. This was the

one occasion where there was no arsenal left in his tired mind to
stop him from carrying on.

The door revealed a path up to the back of the house. If he'd
looked carefully enough, he'd have noticed the dim impression
of footprints pressed into the snow, but William's self-preserva-
tion button was stuck in the off position, his brain sluggish, his
bAlanace that of a drunk weaving his way home from the pub.
He had one goal and that was the back door. The rest of the
garden didn't get a glance. The curved driveway with a small,
Ford Fiesta heaped with snow. The workshop with an array of
tools dangling in the windows. The washing line strung across
the width. The solitary monkey puzzle tree standing erect in
the centre of the garden – the top tall enough to peek over the
ridge of the roof.

William saw none of this as he lurched to the door which, as
if by magic, opened under his touch.

The kitchen was a throwback from the nineteen seventies,
with garish wallpaper in orange and green warring with sliding
door cabinets in a particularly gruesome shade of avocado.

'Shush. Must be quiet,' he slurred, swaying to the sink and
knocking into the table in the process, sending the solitary mug
to its final resting place; shattered into five irretrievable pieces.

'Oops.' His left hand clenched onto the sink closely
followed by his right, the room doing a remarkable impression of
The Spins. Closing his eyes didn't help and opening them made
it worse, the vomit pressing up against the back wall of his
oesophagus lurching one step closer.

'Oh God.'

'Well now, he's not going to help you, is He?' said the voice
in his ear, or was it in his head? He couldn't be sure of anything
any more.

William neither knew nor cared as the remaining lights
switched off inside his head, one by one, until all that was left

was a dim parody with no shape or colour. Dusky grey then black. Then nothing.

Alana decided to check on her emails, her attention split between her mobile, the messages from Flynn regarding their progress and the first of the forty-one emails waiting for her attention, all bar one marked urgent. Twenty-four were deleted unread, including the allegedly urgent one which wasn't, and fourteen saved for later while she knuckled down to the remaining five in the order in which they appeared in her inbox.

Alana

An apology. The telephone company came up trumps with a second phone registered in the name of Aidan Crossey. The usual course of events would have been to trade in with a money back offer when his contract was up last year but that's not what happened. I returned to his house and lo and behold we found it hidden in the bottom of a box of soap powder, which one of the team had neglected to tip out. Obviously not trained in the domestic side of life! The bad news is that it's locked – there's a surprise – but Mitch, from digital forensics is on the case.

Rog

It would be because Crossey had something to hide, and Alana had a horrible suspicion as to what it might reveal.

Brilliant work, Rog. Keep me up to date

she typed before swiping to the next message.

Alana

No news this end with regards to Cunningham's disappearance. Our door-to-door was fruitless as were our interviews with his work colleagues. The bloke has disappeared into thin air. How's your side of the investigation going?

Bulldog

Alana's fingers flew across the screen, not that she had much to give him apart from her thanks. She'd religiously followed her own advice by copying him in to all her communications about the missing prison officer, including their findings about Crossey's suspected abuse. In fact she'd have slipped past the message, not bothering to respond until much later, if she didn't have a great deal of respect for the man and the way he'd gone out of his way to help her. That didn't stop her thoughts already turning to the next message by the time she'd hit send.

They needed a breakthrough and quickly if they were to save Cunningham, because there was no guarantee that Penny would know of his whereabouts. However, as much as she embraced criminal profiling, Alana wasn't confident that Irene's report, which came next, would contain the hallelujah moment they all needed. Profiling was one of those soft skills which always seemed more useful after the event, the trail only turning neon bright with the power of hindsight. Alana didn't need a crystal ball to tell her that it would take a miracle to find Cunningham before it was too late, and Irene didn't seem the sort to be able to deliver the goods. She might be wrong but...

Detective,

The full profile is taking longer than I would have hoped due to the absence of useful information, for example a body!

'No shit, Sherlock,' Alana muttered.

However, I have managed to put together the following, mainly based on information received from the SOCOs, and using the premise that Cunningham is also a victim. I hope you find the following useful.

'That's my girl. Okay, Irene Burden, let's see what you're made of.' Alana continued reading, unaware that she was decimating her thumb nail in the process.

Location
Using Crime Mapping techniques, we know that the victims' location wasn't a factor in their selection. It is a well recorded fact that most criminals offend close to home but this doesn't appear to apply to both Crossey and Cunningham, one on the Northside of Dublin, the other on the South. We can deduct from this two things. Firstly, that the offender specifically targeted both individuals and secondly that he was in possession of a vehicle at the time, in order to transport his victims. Whether he would also be in possession of the relevant documents, car insurance, driving licence, is impossible to say.
Organised V Disorganised
There are many studies that attest that most serial killers fall in

the organised category. The lack of clues left at both crime scenes/abductions suggest that this is also the case here and is something that will need to be recognised when he is eventually captured. More on this later.

Employment

The disparity in the times between the abduction of Crossey, assumed late evening, and Cunningham, early morning, is interesting but it is impossible to draw any conclusions due to the limited data. It's likely that regular employment would be difficult for the offender given the time he must have needed to plan and execute the abductions, and the three dissections that we know of. There might be a history of ad hoc employment to cover the bills, etc. It's likely that this is all under the counter casual labour. I am more comfortable with this opinion as it's supported by Jack Mauger, Chris Conlan and Danny Devlin not appearing on any government portals such as Social Security and what have you.

Age

Due to the lack of any physical evidence, his age is impossible to determine but probably somewhere between early twenties and mid-thirties, based on FBI statistical analysis.

Appearance

With no DNA and no material witnesses I'm afraid his appearance continues to remain a blank canvas. However, statistically, he is more likely to be a white male.

Interview advice

Based on all the research available surrounding an organised offender, you are dealing with a highly intelligent individual who will be anticipating your every action and reaction. He will most certainly be acquainted with police techniques and will be well read in topics such as forensics and crime scene manipulation. Surprise will be a useful element in his capture but don't count on him not being pre-prepared. Also, these are abhorrent crimes, which does beg the question as to his sanity. It is impossible to

assess either his mental capacity or cognitive function but it is important to note that he may react, if threatened, in a way that might surprise you. Therefore, backup will be essential in protecting those trying to capture him. I am going to reiterate that I still think his sister is key. If there is any lucidity left, then using her as a bargaining chip might buy you some time.
I hope these pointers are of use. Sorry I can't tell you more.

Regards,

Irene Burden, MSc, PgDip, PhD

'So, we're looking for a white male, aged somewhere in his twenties or thirties, possibly unemployed or working under the radar, which could mean upward of five or so thousand men in the Dublin area. Great.' Alana rubbed her hands across her face, not really surprised at the report, which in truth had nothing to do with Irene Burden's ability as a profiler and everything to do with the small number of clues they'd provided her with. At least she'd been able to offer some guidance on how to treat him, if they ever got that far.

The next email was from Molly Stein, the duty social worker who had found temporary accommodation for Casey over in Glendalough.

Dear Detective Mack,

I hope you are well.
Just to say that Casey is thriving over in Glendalough and that I have managed to secure a longer-term placement with the family in case it's needed. If you can keep me abreast of developments in this regard.

Best wishes,

Molly

What developments! Alana thought as she banged off a quick reply before eyeing the last email in the same way she would an unexploded bomb with a ticking clock and no disposal expert in sight. She'd been in two minds as to whether to contact Billy Slattery about William's disappearance, but had decided to leave things as they were purely out of cowardice. She wouldn't know what to say. It wasn't as if he was William's next-of-kin, so there was no sense of duty involved. There was also the issue of the identity of his informant and an unwillingness on his part to reveal his source. It was a game with only one winner and that wasn't her. The email also raised an interesting question as to how he'd obtained her contact details when she'd never provided them. The fact that he'd have had to go out of his way to obtain them piqued her interest enough to open his email along with the, as yet, unanswered text she'd sent his son. Either William was ignoring her, his phone was out of battery, or he was in trouble. Either way, she needed to track him down.

Dear Alana,

Please excuse this unsolicited email but, when William arrives, get him to phone his mother. She's frantic with worry as he's not returning her calls.

Many thanks,

Billy

'Oh, for God's sake. I'm running a flipping creche now, am I?'

'What's the joke?' Tatty asked, removing her coat to a shower of snowflakes.

'Nothing at all, Tatty.'

'Where are the others?'

'Off on a wild goose chase, probably,' Alana said, going on to explain the situation and the work that still needed to be done.

'Well, that's easy. You check in with Flynn while I look into the Devlin's. No arguments.'

'You're a saint!'

'You might change your mind when I don't find anything.'

Alana laughed, already dialling up Flynn only to find they were still a mile away, the snow hampering their every move. She spent ten minutes relaying the main points from her recent emails before ending the call only to find Tatty by the side of the desk, her notepad in her hand, a broad smile in place.

'That was quick. What you got?'

'The house is owned by a Mary and Sheamus McSweeney, seventy-four and seventy-five respectively, He's Professor of Modern Greek and Byzantine History at TCD, or he was. Retired due to ill-health but only a couple of years ago. There's lots on him. Research papers and the like but nothing recent. The house is mortgage free and all the taxes are up to date.'

'So, nothing of interest then except why Penny ended up in a mother and baby unit when she had well-to-do grandparents waiting in the wings. A story, if only we had the time to follow it up.'

'There is one thing that's a bit fishy.'

'Go on.'

'Up until December last year the McSweeneys used to collect their pension in person in the local post office. They subsequently submitted a request for this to be changed to an Electric Funds Transfer, or EFT, directly into their bank on account of their deteriorating health.'

'Not too fishy given their age, surely?'

'No. It's the next bit where the stink comes in. The DSP have been trying to arrange a face-to-face meeting to confirm the arrangements and, during this time, not a cent of pension has been collected.'

'Ah. Now that is a tad smelly. Anything else? What about Danny?'

'Not much but I'm still working on it. No driving licence or passport in his name, no official records at all, not even social insurance.'

'So, he's someone that's always lived under the grid, which will make him impossible to find. It also makes Penny our top priority.'

FORTY-SIX

William knew something was happening, but he wasn't sure what. His mind was refusing to process new information in the same way his legs refused to work, and his arms dangled by his side, useless. The only things working were his vision and his hearing, although not to the level he'd grown accustomed to over the last twenty-three years. It was like being underwater. Blurred, muffled, distorted. If he'd been in different company, he'd have cracked a joke about taking his body back and demanding a refund, but there was no space for humour inside his head. Just as he knew he was on the move; the voice in his left ear was screaming at him to shift his lazy arse, and he knew he was in trouble. Not the same kind of trouble he'd got himself into in the past. Those scraps and scrapes were inconsequential in comparison to this living nightmare.

The room changed from light to dark. The floor from flat to complex. Now there were stairs to negotiate when he could barely manage to place his feet on the ground. If it wasn't for the steel arm banded across his back, pushing and dragging, he'd have dropped to his knees unable to move another step.

What must have been only a few seconds felt like hours, but suddenly it was over as his feet stopped moving.

'Sit there and shut up.'

The ground was hard, and cold, the brickwork behind him uneven and uncomfortable, but a big improvement on being frogmarched to God only knew where with his head spinning and his mind as blank as a newborn lamb's.

William closed his eyes, the back of his eyelids preferable to the sight of the dark, grim space highlighted by the single strip of light stretched across the middle of the ceiling. He was also trying to ignore the man crouching in front of him, which was far more difficult, as he was searching through his pockets.

'A fucking copper. I knew it! Well, Mr Fucking Copper, see how you like the pleasures of my humble home, as you seemed so determined to enter without an invitation.'

By the time the words were out, William was in shutdown mode, his batteries spent and without a charging port in sight. He didn't hear the man clump back up the stairs or even realise that he'd switched off the light, leaving him in perpetual darkness. William was in a world of his own, his brain taking the opportunity to recover as was his body.

This was payback for all the early morning starts when William had dragged his reluctant limbs out of bed for a jog, and the evenings after work when he'd made for the gym instead of heading to the pub. The truth was that William wasn't a fitness fanatic, far from it. With no friends to speak of and only a fractured family to look forward to, it was one of the only things in his life that he could control. His mother had turned to alcohol in her search for her own personal nirvana, while his father enjoyed the company of a bevy of beauties. Neither had brought them any long-term happiness.

His breathing slowed along with his pulse, giving time for the blood oozing on the back of his head to form a fine mesh, a microscopic net in which to catch the specialised clot-forming cells released to plug the gap. And with the clot came sleep.

William woke fifteen minutes later. He was still confused as to where he was or what had happened; his memory since his fall sketchy at best but his memory wasn't his first priority. His pulse had quickened on waking, causing the blood in his arteries and veins to expand, filling his limbs and thus setting off a chain of reactions, which resulted in the worst case of cramp he'd ever experienced. William wasn't new to pain, shin splints were a frequent visitor, but the tight shooting pain circling his calves was worse than the worst agony imaginable.

With the breath heaving in his lungs and his toes twitching forwards and backwards in order to mitigate the pain, he closed his eyes, waiting for the circulation to return and the agony to fade. His body, wracked with pain, was begging for him to stay put, but he'd never been one for taking the easy road. He'd have forgiven his father a long time ago if that had been the case.

He rolled onto his knees, his hands bound in front of him, his head starting to swim, a bolt of vomit hurtling up his neck and spurting out on the ground ahead. He hadn't had anything to eat since yesterday but the dry heaves continued, wave upon wave of retching where he thought his skull was going to split open and spew out his brains. Finally, the vomiting stopped, or he hoped it had stopped. He spat out a couple of times, squishing the saliva around his teeth, his tongue sweeping his cheeks for any unwanted debris, disgusted at the smell of bile only a footstep away, but he was also feeling better than at any time since his fall.

Without the use of his hands, rising to his feet took a couple of attempts, resulting in grazed elbows and knees. He bAlanaced against the wall briefly to regain his equilibrium and consider his options. There weren't any unless he could free himself.

With his shoulders hunched forward and his elbows bent, he gathered the fabric of his coat between his fingers to ease the material towards him. He couldn't remember the day of the week just as he couldn't remember what he had in his pockets when he'd left the station. A used tissue maybe. What he found wasn't much better. Car keys without a getaway car. A packet of gum. Some loose change, useless unless his assailant was short of fifty cents for the meter. No torch. No pocketknife. No lighter, but it wasn't over until he'd performed the laborious process with the other pocket, he told himself, letting the fabric go and repeating the exercise. His fingers closed around the broken casing of his mobile phone. A broken phone was as useless as an umbrella in a snowstorm, except that he didn't want to call anyone. The time for calling had been when he'd left the library. What a stupid fool. A fool to the end. He'd been so desperate to make an impression that he'd dismissed any rogue thought of waiting for Paddy. It would be unlikely he'd even get a reception on the off chance he could get it working again.

What he needed was an idea he could work with, something that would make a difference, he thought, running the edge of his nail over the razor-sharp shard of screen glass. He'd free his hands then he'd investigate.

FORTY-SEVEN

Flynn squinted out of the windscreen, trying to make out whether he recognised the man in the distance, his head bowed against the driving snow, his bare head and shoulders coated in white icing.

'It must be Paddy, only fools, coppers and dog walkers would be out in this weather and there's no sign of a dog. He doesn't look happy,' he said, winding down his window.

'All right, Pad?'

'About bleedin' time too. I've been freezing my whatnots off here,' Paddy said, stamping his feet and rubbing his hands for emphasis before climbing into the back.

'You're lucky we spotted you. I thought you'd be there by now?'

'Not in these shoes.'

'Hah, serves you right for putting the aesthetics ahead of functionality. I made sure to bring a pair of hiking boots with me just in case.'

Paddy snorted. 'Any news about William?'

'I've just come off the phone from Alana. Mitch from the Techie Bureau has come up trumps with the last known whereabouts of his phone as Avondale Lane, which ties in neatly with what they've found out about Penny Devlin's last known address. God only knows what we'll find when we get there.'

'Want me to alert the emergency services?'

'All taken care of. Now, what's the quickest way, Pad, as you live round here. Right or left?'

Flynn's phone pinged through a message, another one. It had been ringing or pinging constantly since he'd slid into the passenger seat and buckled himself in.

'It's Mitch, again,' he said, preferring to look at his mobile instead of watching Lorrie trying to negotiate the treacherous weather conditions.

He caught her glancing across only to swear under her breath as she narrowly avoided skidding into a tree, the tyres on the vehicle struggling to get a grip on the black ice lurking under the snow.

'Jesus Christ, that's another life lost.' Flynn's knuckles whitened under the strain of holding onto his seatbelt with an iron-tight grip. 'And I don't have that many more left to lose.'

'Don't worry about it,' Paddy said, leaning forward between the seats. 'We're alive, aren't we? What does he have to say?'

'Who?'

'Mitch, of course.'

'Oh, right. William took some photos which, luckily for us, the server picked up and dumped onto the cloud. Look. No, not you, Lorrie,' he added sharply when she went to glance in his direction again. 'You continue concentrating on what you're doing, and I'll describe them for you. There are a couple of red brick houses, quite posh and what looks like the top of some kind of tall, spiky tree thingy. It must be huge as it's taller than the house.'

'Some spiky tree thingy!' Lorrie replied on a laugh.

'You know what I mean.' Flynn barely registered her words, his fingers spread to expand the photo to get a closer view of the top right-hand corner of the building. 'There's something in the window. Look. No! Not you, Lorrie! Paddy. It appears to be a cat. An orange cat.'

'Per.'

Shortly after, Lorrie pulled over on to the side of the North Circular Road, her hands on the wheel. 'What now, Paddy? I don't think it's safe to take the car any further.'

'Well, we obviously wait for backup, don't we?' Flynn said, shifting in his seat to stare at his boss. 'That's what they're always telling us.'

'I'm afraid this is a do as I say not as I do situation, Flynn. Will's life may depend on it.'

FORTY-EIGHT

William was going by touch as, with no glimmer of light, it was one of the remaining senses left to him. There were other clues for him to draw on, other senses that made him certain he was in a cellar. The smell of damp. That earthly odour redolent of graveyards on a wet day. He blinked, his hand following the roughly hewn wall, the bricks snagging against his fingertips. The thought of graveyards seemed apt somehow, he didn't quite know why, not when he was certain he'd heard the sound of a breath.

He held his own, his feet motionless, his ears tuned to the silence. Yes, there it was again, a barely audible shallow rasp and, after a long pause – too long – another one. Alone but not alone. Friend or foe? Certainly, a stranger. He started to move again, but at a much slower pace, his feet sliding over the ground, inch by inch, his head a foggy mess, his mind trying to rationalise where he was and what was happening to him, but it was useless. The last memory he had was sitting in the library in the warmth, the sound of happy children only a whisper away. He'd give anything to be back there, to have another chance at making the right decision when Quigg had left him sitting in the car.

She was slumped in a chair, the chair he'd just stumbled against. He guessed it was a woman, but it might as well have been a man, a man with a ponytail that had brushed over his hand. An unresponsive person despite his urgent tone.

'Hello. Are you awake?'

His training hadn't prepared him for what to do, so instead he followed his instinct. 'Come on, William, what would you do if the positions were reversed? Bearing in mind that, despite the ponytail, you're pretty sure it's a woman.'

'I'm going to give you a little shake. There's nothing to be worried about,' he said, the lie slipping out as he followed the line of her ponytail down to her shoulder, his fingers curling around her collarbone in the gentlest of touches. No response. He continued to speak, his voice low and soft, barely a whisper. The last thing he wanted was a hysterical woman accusing him of touching her up.

His hand shifted as he followed the line of her upper arm, her bony elbow, the way her forearm was pulled taut behind her back, the feel of the cable tight against her skin. No chance of freedom. No opportunity to fight back. A prisoner like him. Finely boned wrists, clammy and cold, so dreadfully cold.

With the screen shard from his phone held between his thumb and his index finger and whispered words on his breath, he repeated the laborious task of slicing through the thick plastic cable tie. Perhaps it was Penny. Perhaps not.

'I'll have you free in a few more seconds.'

No response.

'One more cut. There. All done. Let's get you off the chair, eh. God, you're freezing.'

William knew he was talking to himself but that didn't stop him from his relentless chatter while he slipped off his coat and wrapped it around her before settling her on the floor, her head cushioned by his fleecy-lined hood. There was nothing else he could do for her after he'd rubbed her hands between his. There was nothing else he could do for himself without the luxury of a torch to light the way. Popping a piece of gum in his mouth he made a promise there and then to always carry a couple of essentials in his pockets on the off chance he ever found himself in a similar position. A torch for one and some kind of a blade. Maybe even a whistle. The kitchen sink, if he had room, his mind sharpening with every second that passed.

He knew he was rambling, his thoughts flitting from topic to topic like a bee in a rose garden, but he couldn't help himself.

'There must be a light, a light switch,' he mumbled, finding the wall with his hand and continuing his relentless journey around the edge of the cellar.

'Ouch. Fuck a duck.'

The bench was the next piece of furniture he rammed against; his steps not so slow now he had someone's life other than his own to worry about. William didn't think about himself. Why would he? A strapping lad at the peak of his physical fitness despite the chunk out the back of his head. The nausea was a thing of the past, the wooziness now only a blurring around the edges of his brain.

He knew it was a bench, the shape and feel of the wood similar to the one his grandfather used to have in his workshop. What he wasn't expecting was a foot. No. Two feet under his fingers, the shins as cold as the marble statues that lined the inside of the Royal Dublin Society in Ballsbridge. This one was definitely a man, he thought, removing his hand as if he'd been stung.

'Hello. Hello there. Are you alive? I'm here to help if I can.' William felt stupid at the words. He couldn't help himself let alone anyone else. Was the man breathing? Was there a pulse? All basic questions made far more difficult when having to work through a black wall as thick as molasses, the air heavy with the sound of his heart thumping in his ears and fear oozing out of every pore. He placed the man's hand back onto the slab of wood, unsure of what he'd felt, if anything. The sessions he'd had on first aid had faded to a useless conglomeration of unrelated facts as soon as he'd walked out of the lecture theatre. How to save a life. How to assist with a birth. How to stop a haemorrhage. He wished he'd listened harder and taken more notes. Taken any notes.

The bench was long and wide, six foot or more and full of all sorts of things that might help him but nothing to help his companions. No water. No source of heat. No light.

He carried on his journey, his fingers finally touching the one thing he was looking for: the banister. The start of a step.

The startling noise of a key rattling in the lock. The screech of the handle turning. The glare from the overhead light. The sight of the chamber of horrors in a flashing blink before he scurried back to his corner and dropped to the floor, the intense images still skuttling around his head.

Bell jars with what looked like greyish brown organs sunk to the bottom. Racks of tools and a shelf of liquid-filled bottles. The blueish tinge to the man's skin, a colour that screamed death to William's inexperienced mind. A vivid scar splitting his side in two, the sutures black and thick; doing the job with no thoughts to the scarring they'd leave. It probably wouldn't matter.

The memory of the woman wrapped in his coat caused him to shrink back against the wall, his hands clawed together in an imitation of being tied, the sliver of glass from his phone pressing into his palm, the effort of the last few minutes finally catching up with him.

FORTY-NINE

The house was easy to find, the tip of the monkey puzzle tree standing tall and proud as a beacon, though they'd have found it without, the blood trail from William's head wound the type of calling card he could never have envisioned.

'We're going in, Alana.' Paddy's hand clutched his phone feeling worried about what he was leading Flynn and Lorrie into. The only thing that had the power to counteract his concern was the wail of a siren in the distance.

The kitchen was a mess of overturned table and chairs, and broken crockery littering the floor, which Paddy sidestepped with the air of a ballerina on pointe, Lorrie and Flynn taking an even more cautious approach.

'Lorrie, I want you to wait outside for the rest of the team.' He noted her mutinous expression with a sigh but didn't have either the time or the inclination to deal with her concerns. He'd speak to her later if he had to but, as far as he was concerned she'd more than managed to assert herself during the treacherous drive over. Her gender didn't come into it. 'Flynn, you have a quick recce upstairs while I check out the rest of the rooms down here.'

There were two rooms aside from the kitchen that branched off the hall, the second of which was locked and with no sign of a key – but it wasn't the locked room he was interested in. It was the smell coming from the open doorway of what appeared to be the lounge.

The man sitting bolt upright on the sofa, as if he had a rod stuffed up his arse, was someone who might have been Aidan Crossey in a previous life. It was difficult to tell, as Paddy had only seen him clothed and the body in front of him was as naked as the day he'd been born. Naked of every memory, every feeling, every desire.

The gaping hole where his penis should have been, stuffed with what appeared to be cotton wool caused Paddy's cheeks to fade. The cuts criss-crossing his torso where he'd been sewn back together using black twine. The puckered lips where Danny had again wielded a needle to join the man's lips together. The empty eye sockets. The circular mark around his head, reminiscent of the trick he often played on his sister. The scooping out of the inside of her boiled egg before reassembling the shell. It wasn't a joke he'd be practising again anytime soon.

Paddy backed away, his brow lowered in a frown as he tried to make sense of the scene. Crossey had clearly died in agony, the shit running from his bottom and the scream from his soul as Danny had performed his acts of cruelty; the size and shape of his undertakings in no way compensation for the destruction of the boy he'd been, but instead the mark of the man he'd become. The detective in him was horrified but those feelings of horror were tempered by a far bigger loss. The ruination of the little boy that had once been Danny Devlin.

'You're not going to believe what he's done upstairs.' Flynn hurried into the room only to stop abruptly.

'You look as if you've seen a ghost,' he said, eyeing his pasty skin tone in alarm, unaware that his face was a similar shade of white.

'More than one! Two ghosts and a very dead cat.'

'A very dead cat,' Paddy repeated. 'Damn it. I just knew that picture of the cat was significant. What's the betting he's called Per?' He lifted his hand to stop him from replying, the sound of a noise coming from down the hall filling the air. 'Effing hell. I hope Lorrie's okay?' his voice was now a whisper.

Flynn nodded. 'I spotted her from the upstairs window heading for the gate. There's definitely a helicopter up there, although God knows if it's going to be able to land in this wind.'

Paddy stared at the open doorway, his mouth compressed to prevent the curse of all curses explode at the foolishness of choosing a room with no hiding place for two shit-scared detectives.

FIFTY

Danny ambled into the lounge, his mind on the marbles in his hand instead of the man in the chair. He couldn't wait to drag him up the stairs and settle him between Mary and Sheamus.

It had been a very long time since he'd been able to think of them as his grandparents, blood or otherwise. There'd always been something in the back of their eyes and the edge of their smiles on the odd occasions they'd been forced to visit, his dad standing well back as their daughter Katherine fulfilled her duties. He remembered the laughter on the way home from that last visit, the silly remarks about Sheamus's comb-over and Mary's cooking. His da's vow that the next time Katherine could go on her own, only there wasn't a next time. Within a fortnight Danny was standing by his father's grave, watching his coffin being lowered into the cold ground.

At that moment, Danny had recalled his da's words, 'Not the worms for me, son. If you forget everything else, remember this. Katherine and me want to float up to the stars and the heavens beyond. Forever together with the sun on our backs and warmth in our hearts.'

He'd remembered it all but couldn't do a thing about it.

They'd seen to that. Katherine had got a place in the family plot, while they'd farmed off his da to the cheapest of graves possible on the edge of the graveyard, out of sight of his da's beloved sun.

Danny squeezed the glass marbles, his knuckles whitening under the effort.

He hadn't enjoyed mutilating Crossey's body in the same way he had his grandparents'. It had been something he'd been compelled to do, his face averted from the pain rippling across Crossey's face and body in a tidal wave of emotion. The real joy had come from plunging his hands deep into first his grandfather's chest and then his grandmother's, their pupils dilating as the reality kicked in, the reality of unintended consequences. They'd sent him away, in the hope that they'd never have to see him again, the progeny of the man who'd been behind the wheel when their daughter had died. He'd come back. Not a boy. Not even a man any more. A monster with only one thing on his mind. Retribution. He'd made them pay for every slight and snide comment, but mostly he'd made them pay for the way they'd treated his da and his sister. He didn't matter, Crossey had put paid to that.

He'd almost been surprised when he'd slit Sheamus's chest open in one deep, clean cut and the still-beating heart inside. Death had come swiftly in the end, his fists tight against the thickened muscle until the throbbing had stopped, the light fading from behind his shocked gaze. There'd been no such swiftness with Crossey. Organs removed one by one, the smell of burnt, then rotting flesh filling the air much to the old man's horror. If he could have prolonged his life for twice, three times as long he would have, instead of the paltry few days he'd lasted.

Even now he wondered if he'd been too lenient on Aiden Crossey, the man that had ruined his life of everything that he'd hoped to be. A brother to Penny. Even a husband, and father to his own children, all cast adrift by the evil of one man.

He didn't know what made him lift his head from the marbles, a flicker at the edge of his vision, a noise that Crossey wouldn't be making again this side of the Pearly Gates. He blinked, then blinked again, confused at the sight of the two strangers ahead. One second he was wrapped in the past and the next...

'Danny Devlin, you're under arrest for the murder of Aidan Crossey and for the suspected murder of two, as yet, unnamed individuals. You are not obliged to say anything unless you wish to do so, but anything you say may be taken down in writing and may be given in evidence.'

'No!'

One word but with all the feeling from the last fourteen years wrapped round the letters. It was too soon. He had so much more to do before this.

Danny swung on his feet and launched back through the door, the marbles forgotten, the air suddenly filled with the sound of them bouncing on the wooden floor before rolling to a stop. Then silence for a second before pandemonium.

'After him!'

FIFTY-ONE

Danny hurtled into the cellar and down the stairs, slamming and bolting the door behind him. He'd only been away a few minutes, and yet long enough for everything to have changed.

With his heart pounding from his efforts, he stopped a second to catch his breath, his attention on the first of the tall glass jars and the organs it held. Twin hearts from his grandparents, preserved for eternity and the inspiration for his shift from roadkill to Jasper and then on to murdering his relatives.

'Open up, Danny. There's nowhere to hide.'

His time was limited. So much to do. What first? His eyes scanned the room, landing on one thing then another before hovering over Fergal.

Poor Fergal. By the grey of his flesh, he wouldn't last the day. The truth was, he didn't hate his former roommate. He didn't have space left inside his dustbowl of an existence to feel such a strong emotion as hate. Fergal had been weak but then who's to say Danny wouldn't have done the same thing if their situations had been reversed? That didn't change anything. It didn't change a thing. Fergal had been in a position to help but, instead, he'd chosen to hide under the covers, silent party to the grunts and groans only a handspan away. No, if their positions had been reversed, Danny would have tried to do something, anything, and the reason why his former friend was now hanging onto life by the weakest of threads.

The sound of hammering filled the space. Thump. Thump. Thump. The racket vibrating through his head and addling his mind. There were shouts and screams too. An eruption of noise that roared and swelled like the tide on a windy day, but Danny ignored it. He ignored it all just like he'd ignored the preachers and do-gooders, the social workers and charity workers. The ones that wanted to tell him how to live his life when he knew better than anyone there was no living to be had in the shell-like structure the McSweeneys and Crosseys of this world had left. He'd surrender but not until he'd done what he'd set out to do.

With a thrust of his jaw, he left Fergal and turned to his sister instead.

Penny was the one that had the ability to still pull at the last of his heartstrings. The perfect sister and the person he'd grown to love until that capacity had been stolen from him. He'd come to her rescue in the same way no one had rescued him. The social worker who'd placed him with the Crosseys. Even the Crosseys themselves, who surely must have known the kind of man their son had become. The animals knew. The way the dogs had growled every time he visited which, for a middle-aged man with his own business, was suspiciously frequent. Danny had spent twelve whole months in that isolated Cavan farm until he'd found the opportunity to run. Christmas Eve in fact, when the whole of them were away at midnight Mass, and he'd had a streaming cold that he'd satellited into flu. His mind blanked out the rest because, of course, the life of a runaway living on the streets of Dublin with no friends apart from a sister he was too ashamed to see, had no happy ending.

He took a second to stare down at her unconscious form, stretched out on the floor, his thoughts trying to catch up to the present, but it was too late for that, too late to alter the past or change the future, too late for any of it as the final strands that bound him together snapped asunder, the sound of breaking wood splintering the air washing over his brain. Ignored and irrelevant. The one thought left was that he didn't want to see her suffer despite her amateurish attempts to stop him. There was something he could do about that, the one last thing he could do for her.

His hands were filthy, stained red and brown, so he took a moment to wipe them against the side of his trousers before kneeling by her side and positioning them around her neck.

'Stop right there.'

FIFTY-TWO

'You can't make me.'

Paddy knew he was right, that it might take too long to save Penny. One jerk and her slender neck would snap, and there was nothing any of them could do to stop that. Flynn was straining to get past, to clamber down the stairs, and Paddy didn't know whether to let him go or to stop him. It was the first time he could remember that he'd felt torn between two polar opposite decisions. If Alana hadn't copied him into Irene's profile, he'd have had no hesitation in racing down the stairs but that was irrelevant. In her opinion Danny Devlin was clinically insane and therefore unpredictable in how he'd react.

The report from Irene was still buzzing around his head. There was something, an important detail his mind was circling. If only he could land on what it was. There was only one way in, a narrow staircase and members of the Armed Support Unit only moments behind them. Involving the ASU was standard procedure for such a high-risk situation but their methods differed to Alana and Paddy's preferred softly softly approach. Paddy needed to talk the man down before they arrived on the scene if lives were to be saved.

Danny hadn't moved, his head and hands intent on what he was doing to the exclusion of the gardai presence. Paddy swallowed hard, the noise of saliva forcing down his neck loud in the deathly quiet room. There was Penny to think of but also Flynn and William. It had taken a tenth of a second to read the situation. William collapsed in a heap against the wall. Was he even breathing?

This was about damage limitation. The prevention of any more harm. There was nothing he could do to change what had already happened.

With that thought prominent, he tightened his hand around Flynn's arm to stop him from racing to the rescue. The situation called for a gentle pirouette as opposed to an all guns blazing approach.

'What are you doing? I need to...'

'Go outside and wait for the ASU. They'll need someone to show them exactly where we are. Detective. That's an order,' he hissed between his teeth before adding in a much louder voice for the benefit of the man just visible over the banister. 'I'm coming down.'

FIFTY-THREE

Danny knew it was over, or nearly over but that didn't mean he had to go quietly. That wasn't his way, not after a life on the streets to initiate him to all the ways possible to harm someone. The boy who'd hugged thoughts of his sister close as a means to get by was long gone, the cord severed, the frayed ends of their relationship cut by the sledgehammer of her betrayal. There was nothing left to relate to, no thought, action or deed powerful enough to claw back the last brittle strands of his sanity. There was only madness. Beautiful, irrational madness. A readymade excuse for all his actions. He knew how it worked. A commuted sentence in a padded cell. Wasn't his whole life a prison sentence. If he was lucky he wouldn't notice the difference. If he was lucky, he wouldn't get to see it.

His fingers flexed and released, Penny crumpling by his feet like a rag doll. He didn't kick her or push her away. He'd have had to have some feeling, some emotion running through his body for that final act of betrayal. She was nothing, meant nothing. Whatever thoughts he had left were for the man slithering towards him, his hands raised in supplication, fancy words on his lips.

Danny felt invincible, adrenaline and anger roaring through his veins as he raced across the cellar floor and pushed the man with all his might, his head banging against the wall, his phone skidding across the room.

There was a second of complete silence, only one.

'Hello. Hello. HELLO! Paddy?'

Danny glanced between the man and the phone before turning back to his sister. It was time to put an end to all of this but not before he had his last say.

'He's dead. They're all dead.'

She looked so peaceful lying there, her hair coming adrift in a cloud of brown, her milky white skin smoothed of all the worry lines, her chest still rising and falling...

He picked her up, gentle, reverent, his hands circling her neck. The voice intruded again but in a tone he couldn't ignore.

'They're not all dead, Danny. You're still here.'

'You don't have to worry about me.'

'And what about your sister? I'm worried about both of you.' Her voice was soft now, melodious, soporific. Traitorous.

'Half-sister.'

FIFTY-FOUR

'She's also KC's mother or had you forgotten that, Danny?' Alana replied, aware of the complete absence of noise from the cellar, her mind rampaging through all the scenarios but with two clear winners. Paddy and William were either dead, or incapacitated, both of which meant it was down to her. There was no prize, no feeling of power in being in charge. There was only a sense of blistering sadness before her training kicked the piteous thought to hell and back.

She'd managed to snag Danny's attention, now it was time to capitalise on that. Irene had been insistent that the girl was key but there were two girls to consider, she remembered, drawing sudden inspiration from the doctor's report.

'That beautiful little girl, your niece, deserves her mother or are you going to condemn her to a life similar to yours?'

Alana was adding words as she thought of them; talking someone down on their mobile wasn't the kind of situation any amount of hostage training could ever have prepared her for. 'Crossey was a monster of the worst sort, Danny. Surely you don't want history to repeat itself for KC? Shunted from foster home to foster home with always the threat of a Crossey figure in the background.'

'She'll be all right.' But his voice was less sure, wavering.

'You don't know that and neither do I.'

'You'll make sure that history doesn't repeat itself though.'

'We can't be everywhere, Danny. Yes, I agree we'll try but people fall through the net. You fell through the net.'

'You did nothing,' he spat. 'Absolutely nothing. Even his parents. They must have known what he was like. Poor Jack and Chris knew but at least they had the guts to—'

'To do what? What about Jack and Chris, Danny? What can you tell us?' she interrupted. 'We've been trying to find them.'

Danny laughed, the ugliest sound imaginable. 'You'll need a big boat for that along with a set of deep-sea divers. I would have joined them if it hadn't been for Penny and look how that's turned out. Betraying me the first chance she got.'

'She wasn't betraying you, Danny. She was trying to get you the help you need. Come on, mate. You've done what you set out to do with your grandparents and Crossey. Give it up as a good job and let your sister go free? The courts will take into account what you went through at Crossey's hands, but there'll be no such leniency if you murder your... sister.'

Silence again claimed the space. Alana thought that it was over, that she'd done enough to pierce his thick shell with the truth but with no view apart from the roof of the cellar from where the phone had landed there was no way of knowing.

'Paddy? William? Flynn? Lorrie?'

'Shush, woman. Stop shouting, for feck's sake.'

'Paddy? Thank God. What's happening?'

'Hold on a mo and you can see for yourself.' There was a sound of stumbling then a curse before the image of the roof switched to Danny, his head in his hands, his body wracked with a series of spasms, Penny lying still and unmoving at his feet.

The tension in the room eased as breaths were expelled in a series of deep sighs, the pumping adrenaline tailing off to a thin trickle. Alana couldn't quite believe she'd done enough to avert another death. Penny would live; and Danny would find the help he needed under a controlled environment, as dictated by the Irish legal system.

Danny lurching to his feel, puppet-like, wasn't in the script and took her completely unawares. Unstable for a second, he scanned the room. The first indication that something additional might be about to happen.

'Go, Pad. Don't worry about me!'

'I'm not!' Alana's screen went dark but she could still hear, she could still feel. She was still in the room with them even though she was miles away.

Alana heard the sound of glass breaking quickly followed by short gasps as if someone was struggling to breathe. A bottle shattering on the floor? One of those large brown bottles she'd seen on the shelf above the workbench spilling their contents, or something else?

'Shit. He's swallowed formaldehyde.'

FIFTY-FIVE

CHRISTMAS EVE, 10.00 A.M.

Alana had many unhappy memories of Clonabee Hospital. Sitting by her mother's side as they turned off her life support machine was something a child of seventeen should never have been allowed to witness. Her hand slipped to her stomach, flat and unblemished. The loss of her child, which was comparable with losing the use of her legs, the loss of part of her.

There were happy memories too though, she thought, managing to pin a smile for the benefit of the approaching nurse, a questioning look stamped on her cherry red mouth. Happy memories to obliterate the bad.

Penny Devlin was on a drip, two drips. One in each of her skeletally thin arms. The first was pumping in antibiotics to fight the pneumonia that had settled in the base of her lungs, the second was to keep her hydrated. She was still on the critical list but with mutterings about moving her out of the high dependency unit when a bed became available on female medical. There was also talk of KC coming to visit as soon as Penny had been moved. There would be a spate of police interviews for her to undertake now she was awake, but they could wait. It didn't take a genius to realise that Penny and KC were as much victims in all of this, in the same way Cunningham was.

Alana released her brakes, starting to leave only to pause, a small squeak of sound coming from the bed stopping her.

'KC?'

'KC's fine, Penny. You just worry about getting yourself well.'

'See her?'

Alana squeezed her fingers briefly. 'You will, as soon as you're a little better. We wouldn't want to scare her with drips and things now, would we? She's staying in Glendalough with a lovely family but, as soon as you're well enough, I'll arrange with her social worker to come and visit.' Alana hoped she wasn't making promises she couldn't keep now the courts had been alerted to the situation over at The Lodge. But it would have felt wrong not to give Penny the hope she needed.

Penny slipped her eyes closed only to open them, her gaze meeting Alana's head on. 'My brother?'

'I'm afraid he didn't make it.' There was more she could say, things she hoped that Penny would never have to find out about, certainly not until she was strong enough to face up to the reality of having had a serial killer for a brother.

Fergal Cunningham was in the same unit but not the same bay. With one kidney removed under less-than-ideal circumstances, he was fighting sepsis with everything in the hospital's pharmacy, or so it seemed to Alana. Injections for this, intravenous infusions for that and daily dressings to the weeping wound to his flank. The doctor was sitting bang in the middle of the fence as to whether Fergal would make it or not. They needed him in surgery but there would have to be at least a 50/50 chance of recovery before they'd even consider it.

Alana stayed at his bedside, her mobile silent on her lap while she waited to speak to his wife. It took her two hours to realise that Marian wouldn't be coming, two hours of silence apart from the whirring of the machines and the beeping when his oxygen saturations fell below a certain level, something which happened far more frequently than it probably should.

'I'll be back, Fergal or, if not me, then one of our other officers,' she promised, engaging her wheelchair and heading out of the unit.

It was three p.m. on Christmas Eve. Officially she was off until the twenty-seventh, but Alana still had one more ward to visit.

Male medical was busy, all the beds full and with trolleys lining the corridor. The nurses had done their best to bring the spirit of Christmas into the ward with a bit of tinsel here and a bauble or two there, but there was no cheer to be had. Any patient well enough had been discharged home, leaving the beds full of those not going anywhere over the next few days, all apart from Alfred Gaunt. Dr Gaunt was on a completely different trajectory.

Alana entered the ward, the directions from the nurse running through her mind – last bed on the left next to the fire extinguisher; the one with the closed curtains, which to her mind was the worst of signs.

The curtains were cream floral with a sliver of a gap where the two parts failed to meet, a gap Alana took full advantage of.

Alfred was propped up in the centre of the bed, his breathing laboured, nasal cannula piercing his nostrils. Small. Wizened but with a beautiful smile, a smile not for her but for the two men flanking either side of his bed, his blue-veined hands resting in each of theirs. Alana didn't wait to see any more. Forgiveness, one of the most difficult of emotions, needed no witness or scribe. It asked for nothing except acceptance and an open mind. It wasn't up to her to hamper its progress. She'd felt guilty, disloyal, ungrateful even when she'd drafted a quick email to his sons. A shot in the dark with no guarantee of anything. Alfred's smile wiped away those feelings in an instant.

She had one last patient to visit on the ward, even though he probably wouldn't want to see her.

William had been given a side room. Alana didn't know whether that was something to do with his father or his injury and it certainly wasn't her place to ask. He was propped up against a bank of pillows, his eyes closed against the white glare from the overhead lighting, his head bandaged.

'All right, William?' Alana hadn't brought flowers, chocolates, or grapes. Instead, she placed a stack of newspapers on his bed table. The complete range of Irish and English from the *Financial Times* to *The Sun* and *Star*.

'Getting there.' He nodded in the direction of the pile of reading matter. 'What?'

'You're a hero, William.' She stabbed the front of the *Irish Times* and where his face emblazoned the cover.

'But I did nothing!'

'You were injured while serving the public, which is more than enough for that lot. Don't let it go to your head, though. As soon as your sick note is up it's back to the grind, I'm afraid. There's an interesting case just come in that I'd like you to—'

'I'm still on the team despite going off on my own like that?' he interrupted, sitting forward, his hands gripping the edge of the sheet.

'I think you've learned your lesson, eh and, remember, without your intervention it's likely KC would be facing a life without her mum.'

Before she left the ward, Alana stopped and turned, her gaze surveying the scene for a second time. The small Christmas tree by the station surrounded by what appeared to be an avAlanache of cards while the nurses whisked past, too busy to notice anything other than the next job on their list.

She continued to the entrance. There was still one more

task to fulfil before she could head home, this one with no hope of a happy ending.

'Are you one hundred per cent sure you're fit, Paddy? We've given Flynn the week off and I really think you should be off too, even if it's only until after Christmas. I know what the paramedics said about your lung damage being minimal but what about that knock to your head? How do you feel, really?'

'I'm fine. It was nothing.'

'Then what are you doing here on Christmas Eve? Surely there's a party or something?'

'Nope.'

'I don't believe that for one minute and, if that is the case, then it's up to you to rectify it,' Alana said, shrugging out of her coat and placing it in front of the radiator, taking a moment to warm her chilled hands on the top while she watched him from out the corner of her eye.

Paddy was his own worst enemy. Unhappy with his lot and yet reluctant to change the status quo. It was Christmas. A time for goodwill to all and, with the memory of Alfred Gaunt still fresh in her mind, she decided to do something she had always promised herself she wouldn't: interfere in the private lives of her colleagues. They were all lucky enough to be alive, young enough and healthy enough to stand up to the fumes from the formaldehyde. The same drug that had stripped through Danny's oesophagus and stomach, leaving a bloody mass of tissue in its wake. The only solace was that Penny hadn't witnessed his screaming agony of a death, blood and bubbles splintering out of his mouth, his body writhing in pain, his knees pulled to his stomach, his fingers clawing at his neck in an effort to speed his demise. It was a scene she hadn't witnessed, hearing the noises over her phone had been enough to form the pictures in her mind, the sight of Danny's tortured body on Rusty's slab, shifting those images from supposition to fact.

'I don't know what you mean.'

'Yes, you do. As SIO I have many roles, but the provision of relationship guidance isn't one of them, thank God. Suffice it to say that you like Irene and I'm pretty sure she likes you, so I'd like to help,' she said, holding out her hand.

'What's that for?' He looked suspicious and well he might.

'Your phone. If you're not going to message her then I will.'

'No. Just no.' He rammed his hand through his hair in frustration, undoing what had been a perfectively serviceable hair style, if a tad conservative for her tastes.

'Yes. Just yes, Paddy,' Alana mimicked, copying his accent perfectly. 'Remember that Irene is more than a match for both of you, so play nicely.' She smiled, a wicked glint appearing. 'One final thing. I don't want the firstborn named after me, or the second for that matter. Maybe the third...'

Her knock was sharp, his reply sharper.

'Enter.'

'Ah, you're still here, sir. Good.' Alana pushed the door closed behind her with a snap before swivelling on her wheels and heading for the desk, ignoring the look of surprise on his face. She engaged her brakes and shifted her hands to her lap and where her mobile was resting, a slow, relaxed smile forming.

'Yes, well, I thought you'd be off home by now. It is Christmas after all.'

Her expression changed to crestfallen in an instant. 'I was sure you'd want a report of what happened at Danny Devlin's.'

'You thought wrong, Mack. I'll expect your written report as soon as, but a diatribe on how wonderful you think you are? No.'

'You're saying you want me to stay up half the night losing what little beauty sleep I need while you party into the evening and beyond,' she said, her gaze swerving away from his only to flick back to his face and the look of relief quickly masked. Now he was guarded. Ill at ease. Worried even but then he had every reason to be. Alana started to move her chair backwards.

'I also thought you'd like to know that I've found the department leak. I'll add that to the end of my report, shall I? Or would you prefer it on a separate document?' she said conversationally, almost reaching the door. 'And to save time I probably should copy in the chief superintendent, don't you think? It will be a nice Christmas present for her in addition to cutting out the middleman.'

Ox's ruddy complexion blanched white, the map-like scattering of broken veins now in stark relief against his skin.

'I see I've got your attention, sir.' The *sir* was said with an insolent twang, because the man starting to squirm in his chair didn't deserve even a grain of the respect that she'd been forced to give him over the last two years. 'It was the morning headlines that did it. The names of Danny Devlin, Jack Mauger and Chris Conlan glaring out at me in bold Helvetica script. You see, I know my team and there's no way it would ever have been one of them. William was, of course, an unknown entity but he'd already left the room when we'd reached that part of the briefing. You, however, spent precious moments recording the names, which I thought peculiar at the time. Afterwards it made complete sense,' she said, checking her phone briefly before continuing. 'So, how much were you being paid, sir?'

'Stop right there, Detective.'

Alana leant forward in her seat, her expression saying more than all the words in the dictionary her disgust for the man in front of her. 'No, not any more. I've had to put up with your misogynist shitshow for far too long to turn back now,' she said, heaving a sigh to dampen down her temper, which was starting to lead her astray. The fear was that she'd end up saying or doing something that she'd regret. 'And just so you know, I've already spoken to Billy Slattery. When he realised the bird was out of the cage, he started tweeting like a songbird. You're history, Ox.'

'You little bitch. After all I've done for you, and a cripple, too.'

He launched out of his chair and headed for her, his face now explosive red, the veins on his neck bulging along with his eyes.

Alana wasn't worried, not when she'd arrived at his office and not now. Preparation was everything in her line of work, something that William had learned to his cost.

She raised her mobile in the air. 'I took the precaution of phoning the chief superintendent and popping her on loud-speaker before knocking. I do believe she'd like a word, sir.'

FIFTY-SIX

CHRISTMAS DAY, 5.30 A.M.

Christmas Day started at 5.30 with Goose demanding his breakfast. By the time Alana had sorted him out it was six, and she was in two minds as to whether to go back to bed or stay up despite the lack of anything festive in her apartment.

There were no presents under the tree. There was no tree. She'd been meaning all week to get her act together, but the case had taken over every waking moment and a few of her sleeping ones, too.

There were gifts. It wasn't as if she was a humbug, far from it. Gift tags still unwritten. Gifts unwrapped, undelivered, including one special gift of a cuddly goose, which she was planning to deliver tomorrow in person if the snow abated.

Her friends knew her by now, which didn't in anyway mitigate her feelings of failure. Guilt wasn't an emotion she intended to subscribe to, but it was there all the same, arriving like an unwelcome guest – unwanted and unbidden.

There were also gifts for her, brightly wrapped trifles that she'd look forward to opening when the sun had dropped from its perch. Something to look forward to when there was nothing exciting in the fridge apart from the kiddie leftovers from KC's visit and no shops to call on.

With tea and toast made, she decided to slob out on the sofa with the TV and check her phone. There were messages to draft: Christmas greetings to each of her team and messages to reply to, the one from Paddy holding a special significance.

Thank you for the nudge. She said yes.

Alana laughed. She didn't know what the question had been but, knowing how cautious Paddy was, it hadn't been asked down on bended knee.

'God almighty. A loved-up detective on the team. I only have myself to blame,' she mumbled, flicking to the next message with a sudden frown.

Wishing you a very Happy Christmas, Love Colm.

There was no reply she could give that wouldn't encourage, and she wasn't in the mood for a row on today of all days. Ignoring the message was also wrong but it would take longer than she had to pen a suitably nebulous reply. And anyway, there was nothing happy about her current thoughts, which seemed to be stuck in recent events.

What if? was an important question in policing circles, but one that frequently got overlooked when compared with motive and opportunity. Alana would like nothing more than to see a huge downturn in the number of crimes; however, that wouldn't happen until they got to grips with the under-lying root causes. Some causes, such as poverty and poor education were clearer than others. It was the less tangible ones that they had to crack. If they could understand the point at which a criminal mind forged, then perhaps they could look to step in and prevent it happening. The nature versus nurture debate was the reddest of herrings because it was too late by the time the crime had been committed. They had to break the cycle and to do that they had to understand the criminal mind.

Danny Devlin was a classic example of Alana's What If? Theory. What if Danny's parents hadn't died, the first in a chain of events that had put him into the hands of the real monster in all of this. Of course, they couldn't have prevented either his fathers' or his stepmothers' death, but they could have monitored what had happened to him afterwards.

Last night Alana had stood in Rusty's pathology suite and viewed the atrocities that Danny had inflicted on Crossey's body. The ripped-out finger and toenails, the beds blackened, the skin torn. His missing tongue, which they had yet to find. The missing eyeballs. All the organs removed, including the sexual ones. Devlin's last act in a litany of revenge. In days gone by they'd have displayed Crossey's body on a gibbet in the central square as a deterrent. Evil had met evil head on. There were no winners. Afterwards she'd asked to see Danny's body. Statue-like in death. The sins of the past wiped away. There'd be a funeral when Penny was well enough to arrange, a funeral she'd attend.

The doorbell pealed, causing Goose to lift his head from his paws before dropping it back, his eyes slipping closed under the weight of the can of Whiskas he'd had earlier.

Alana had all the mod cons including a video intercom system. What she didn't have was a clue as to how Billy Slattery had obtained her home address in addition to her phone number. Perhaps she should take him down to the station and grill him about where he was getting his information from. There were flowers too, the largest bunch, which must have cost the earth at this time of year and the only reason she let him in.

'I wanted to thank you in person for saving William. His mother and I are—'

She stopped his pre-prepared speech with a little wave of her hand. 'Just doing my job.'

'No, more than your job and after I refused to tell you who—'

Alana stopped him again, her voice now a soft murmur, a grin breaking. 'I know who it was, Mr Slattery, and I'm delighted to tell you that your source has dried up.'

'Has it now?' He grinned back. 'I can't say I'm disappointed. An unsavoury individual.'

He followed her into the lounge his face expressionless as he examined the room. The overflowing bookshelves. The pile of knitting on the edge of the sofa. The remains of her breakfast on the coffee table. 'This is... homely.'

A word for the room that could easily have been swapped for messy. Alana didn't care, shifting her knitting so that he had space to sit.

'How's William?'

'Back at his mother's being spoilt rotten, probably much to his chagrin.'

She looked up at that. 'You've seen him then?'

'Briefly in the hospital when he arrived in ED. Thanks for that, by the way. You needn't have told me which hospital they were taking him to. Not after I refused to—'

'Water under the bridge,' she said, running her fingers down Goose's back who'd jumped up to say hello. 'Well, if that's all.'

'Not quite.' There was a moment's silence where he looked increasingly awkward, his attention shifting around the room before darting a glance in her direction. 'I've had a look at the accounts over the last few days and the extra sales we've had as a direct result of the information we received. The forty-thousand euro will be a nice tidy sum to help Penny and KC get back on their feet.'

Alana's jaw dropped in astonishment, all of her preconceived ideas about Slattery and journalists in general flying out the window. She didn't know what Penny intended to do about The Lodge but money now, instead of having to wait for any sale to be agreed, was exactly what she and KC needed.

'There's no need to look so surprised,' he said, his awkwardness shifting to annoyance, a myriad of frown lines punctuating his forehead. 'While I have a living to make and employees to pay that shouldn't be at the expense of doing what's right.'

'I wasn't,' she replied, when clearly she was. A change of subject was needed and quickly or he'd start to accuse her of all sorts of biases. 'I think that's a wonderful idea and very generous of you. Thank you for popping in to let me know about William, but I'm sure you need to get on. It is Christmas Day after all.'

He cleared his throat. 'If you're not up to anything I was wondering if you'd like to spend it with me? I have a turkey the size of an ostrich and enough sprouts to set up a stall.'

The ring of her intercom was a welcome relief from having to think up an answer.

'Will you excuse me a moment? Like Paddy's Market around here this morning,' she whispered under her breath, letting out a sigh of relief at the sight of Rusty hovering on the doorstep.

'Come on through.' She wheeled backwards to make room for him in the suddenly overfilled lounge.

'Rusty, I'm not sure if you know Billy Slattery. This is Dr Rusty Mulholland.' She watched them shake hands, an awkward silence ensuing.

'Thank you again for the flowers and the update about William, Billy,' she said, to fill the void.

'Yes. Well, I must be on my way. Wishing you both a Happy Christmas.'

Alana maintained her small smile. 'And to you.'

'You do realise he thought we were a couple,' Rusty said, removing his gloves, his broad wedding band clear to see.

'Nah. Really. No. You're imagining things.'

'And you were happy for him to think that too, Alana. He'll find out at some point. Then where will we be?'

'I'll cross that bridge when I come to it and not a moment before.' She had a sudden thought. 'You're not angry, are you?'

'As long as you don't make a habit of it.' He chuckled.

'What?'

'I'm imagining what Gaby's going to say when you tell her.'

'Me. What?' Alana repeated, horrified. 'She doesn't need to know surely that he was here let alone...?'

'Of course, she does. No secrets makes for the perfect relationship, I find. Come on, grab your coat. It's her that's sent me around to rescue you from a fate worse than death, apparently.'

'A fate worse than... Sorry?' The conversation was rattling along far too quickly for her to grasp even half of what he was getting at.

'The day spent with Billy Slattery.' He chuckled again. 'It looks like it's going to be an interesting year.'

'Ah shut up. I'll get my coat.'

She could still hear his laugh as she headed for the bedroom, in two minds as to whether to go with him. It was Gaby's turkey with all the trimmings or fish fingers. The turkey won.

A LETTER FROM THE AUTHOR

Dear Reader,

I hope you enjoyed *The Puppet Maker*, the first in my Detective Alana Mack series.

If you'd like to join other readers in being the first to know about all future books I write just click the link below. I'd be delighted if you choose to sign up.

www.stormpublishing.co/jenny-obrien

If you enjoyed *The Puppet Maker* and could spare a few moments to leave a review that would be hugely appreciated. Even a short review can make all the difference in encouraging a reader to discover my books for the first time. Thank you so much!

Writing about someone with a disability is a huge responsibility and one I take seriously. Luckily, I've been able to draw on my thirty years' experience of working as a nurse on a specialist neuro rehabilitation unit to present what I hope is a realistic picture of the daily challenges faced by wheelchair users.

I was lucky to attend an amazing event where industry professionals, designers and entrepreneurs get to meet the people they are helping. I was manning a stand when I spotted a young woman zoom past. She caught my attention, even though my glimpse was only fleeting. Eyes forward, never looking left, nor right, a determined tilt to her chin, her blonde hair bundled into a long ponytail, a baseball cap pulled low over her head. It was she that inspired the creation of Alana Mack.

Clonabee is a fictional town that you won't find on any map or travel brochure. It is slotted between two of my favourite beaches on Dublin's coastline, which bring a wealth of happy memories every time I think of them.

Thank you for reading.

Jenny.

ACKNOWLEDGMENTS

As a reader I used to always skip this page. As a writer I tend to read it first.

Book dedications are tricky especially the more books I write. I seem to be running out of willing volunteers. However, this one was easy. When a writer chooses to use their husband's name as their main character, bearing in mind that Alana Mack is a woman... Thank you, Alan!

Alana Mack is part of a new series, one that comes with a new agent and a new publishing house. Many thanks to Nicola Barr, from The Bent Agency, and Claire Bord, Oliver Rhodes, Alexandra Holmes, Melissa Boyce-Hurd, Anna McKerrow, Elke Desanghere, Janette Currie, Shirley Khan and Henry Steadman, and their colleagues from Storm Publishing. I think you've all done an amazing job in helping me produce *The Puppet Maker*, which is very different from the thirty thousand words I started out with. I love it all from the cover, the edits, well not so much the bum-on-seat part of the edits, to the final proof copy so thank you. It's a much better book than my scratchy scrawl of a first effort.

Most writers have a muse. Someone they turn to with their miserable first drafts and someone to run word count races against – even though I never win. For me it's fellow writer, Valerie Keogh. Writing would be a very lonely place without our daily chats, so thank you.

My books always have some sort of a medical twist, which isn't surprising given my forty years as a nurse. Research is important though and I don't know it all so thanks to Dr Richard Shepherd, the author of *The Seven Ages of Death*, for helping me out with some important facts about the human liver.

Naming Goose took ages, until I finally remembered my friend, Linda Christin's adorable, sleek white cat. Thank you, Linda.

I have a small group of fans who have been with me since the beginning in a 'they found me way', rather than the other way round. In no particular order thanks to Beverley, Michele, Maureen, Diane, Elaine, Susan, Lesley, Tracy, Amanda, Sarah, Sharon, Pauline, Jo, Daniela, Carol, Madeleine, Tracey, Terri, Maggie, Lynda, Hayley and Donna. You all rock!

Rogene Javier, thank you for letting me use your name. I hope you like your character? The same goes for Kari Clayton-Jones, one of my CHOG friends.

Finally, as always, thanks must go to my three children, even though they're all adults now. Putting up with a mother who always has her head in the clouds trying to work out how to murder people must be difficult. Buns for tea!

Printed in Great Britain
by Amazon

36826771R00169